THE INHERITORS OF MOONLYGHT TOWER

J. C. Briggs

THE INHERITORS OF MOONLYGHT TOWER

Published by Sapere Books.

24 Trafalgar Road, Ilkley, LS29 8HH,
United Kingdom

saperebooks.com

Copyright © J. C. Briggs, 2024
J. C. Briggs has asserted her right to be identified as the author of this work.
All rights reserved.

No part of this publication may be reproduced, stored in any retrieval system, or transmitted, in any form, or by any means, electronic, mechanical, photocopying, recording, or otherwise, without the prior written permission of the publishers.
This book is a work of fiction. Names, characters, businesses, organisations, places and events, other than those clearly in the public domain, are either the product of the author's imagination, or are used fictitiously.
Any resemblances to actual persons, living or dead, events or locales are purely coincidental.

ISBN: 978-0-85495-563-3

PROLOGUE

1936

The mirror, like everything else in the room, was a shabby thing. An ugly brown wooden frame, and the glass tarnished with greenish spots; the reflection it gave was greenish, too, as though the person looking into it was underwater, everything behind them shadowy and slightly wavering. But that could have been the reflections seen through tears.

The mirror was good enough for someone who simply wanted to adjust a hat or a scarf, or to tuck a stray hair behind an ear, someone who was not interested in seeing herself, except to check that she didn't look odd or noticeable. The shadowy furniture in the room was acceptable for someone who thought it sufficient to be able to sit down at a table or by the fire. Some books on a set of shelves in an alcove, a sideboard pushed up against the wall. Some cutlery in the drawer — two knives with discoloured bone handles, two forks, two large spoons, three teaspoons, one silver, the others not, a couple of large plates, two small ones, two cups and saucers, a soup tureen with a cracked lid and a cruet set with nothing in the glass jars. One of everything would have been enough. There were never any visitors to the rented rooms on the top floor of the narrow, terraced house.

Along with the living room was another room that had been partitioned in two. It contained a single bed, an upright chair, and a chest of drawers on top of which were two glass candlesticks on a glass tray and a photograph in a well-polished, if rather dented, silver frame — a photograph of a young man in a military uniform with a confident tilt to his chin and a half-smile at his mouth. He looked young and hopeful. He was a stranger in the photograph she had bought from a market stall because he reminded her of a boy she had known a long time ago whose photograph was lost. The bottom drawer of the chest was deep and wide enough to hold two grey skirts and two grey sweaters — the woman looking in the mirror was wearing the third grey skirt and sweater. On the back of the bedroom door hung a brown raincoat, an overall, and a headscarf. The other side of the partitioned room made up the scullery, in which there was a sink, a draining board, and a gas ring with two burners. There was another chest of drawers on top of which was a kettle, a teapot, two aluminium pans, and a bread crock. The shared bathroom was on the floor below.

The woman was still looking at the reflection in the mirror, at a pair of eyes she hardly knew — eyes that were filmed with tears, which she wiped away. She hardly knew the face, either, for it was not her habit to look for more than a moment. Only this evening she had looked. She had wanted to see if there were any trace of the girl she had been, the girl whose name she had seen in the paper. Yesterday's paper, which a fellow passenger had left on the tram and which she had taken thoughtlessly. She could not remember him at all, just a man in a shabby raincoat and a flat cap, who smelt of stale tobacco and damp, and of poverty and hopelessness. She could smell him now, as if he had crept home with her and loitered at the door. A man with a bad cough, who had left the paper open at the situations vacant page, where he had marked the advertisement for a warehouseman. A man whose face she could not remember, but a man who had left her with something that had the power to cleave her in two.

The newspaper was still on the sofa. She could have thrown it on the fire, but she knew that she could not have forgotten what she had read. Words cannot be unread, just as words spoken cannot be unsaid. Lies cannot be untold, and deeds cannot be undone. And memories will come unbidden, however hard you try to bury them. It was the face of her mother, she realised now, as she looked in the mirror at a face fallen in, seeing the loss of teeth, the thin lips, the faintly waxen sheen. A face etched with suffering and hardship. Prison did that to a woman.

Moonlight shone through the skylight, silvering the tarnished glass, and making a ghost of the reflection there. She looked at the newspaper and went to sit down. She opened it at the page of obituaries.

She thought of the mirror and memory, and Moonlyght, the place she had not been able to forget.

PART ONE: 1916

1

Jessie Sedgwick understood the words. They were simple enough, but she didn't understand why they were being spoken by her mother. She was to leave Swarthgill Farm the next day. Her mother's cousin, Ada Cobb, had offered her a place in service at Moonlyght, the country house where she was cook and housekeeper. Jessie was to be a kitchen maid under Ada's supervision.

She stared at her mother, unable to speak. Her mother didn't look back at her. She simply carried on peeling potatoes.

'But why?' Jessie managed at last.

'It's an opportunity. There's nowt here for thee.'

'There's the school — I'm to train. Mrs Roberts says —'

'It's no good, Jessie. What if Josh don't come back an' somethin' happens to me, what then?'

Jessie couldn't answer that. As for her brother, Josh, she knew it was possible that he'd be killed, but she had pushed that thought as far back as she could, into the shadowy corners where dreadful things hid, things you dared not think about. She looked at her mother again, at the thin figure turned away to the range. Ma looked old. She wasn't much more than forty, but she looked worn out. There was something haggard in her face. Something yellow about her skin. Jessie had noticed how her mother would sometimes hold her hand to her side and how she would seem to struggle for breath, but when she asked, Ma would only say that she was tired, and it was the worry about Josh.

For the first time in her seventeen years, Jessie thought that her mother might die. People died, she knew that. Grandad

Albert had died when she was ten. He had been in his fifties, but he had seemed an old man to her. She hadn't felt much about his death because she'd been frightened of him. He had been an angry man, ready with his curses and his fists. He had hit her once when she had fallen and dropped a basket of eggs. He hit Pa, too, but Pa hit back. And Pa had laughed and said it served the old bugger right when Grandad Albert had been found dead in the lane. At the Red Lion down in the village, the landlord had said that Grandad Albert had been roaring drunk that night and picking quarrels all over the place. The inquest had concluded that he'd died of suffocation when he'd vomited after falling. His nose was broken and his face bruised, but no one at the pub admitted to having punched him, which was more than likely. They'd all have been drunk.

Ma hadn't said anything. She hadn't gone to the funeral, and there'd been no wake at the farm. No one mentioned him again, and Pa and Josh worked the farm until the war came and Josh joined up. Pa was enraged. Farming was a reserved occupation. Josh had no need to go, but Josh said he wasn't having any of the lads calling him a coward and folk giving him the white feather. 'An' what'll you do if the Germans land in Morecambe Bay?' That question had floored Pa for a minute or two. Josh had heard about the threat of invasion at a recruitment meeting in Kendal, where he heard the call for men of pluck, grit, and endurance. The lads from school were going and so was he. They were needed to fight the Germans.

'You can't stop me,' Josh had said, and he'd gone the next day. Letters came and Ma put them in her apron pocket. She read them to Jessie late at night when they hid in Jessie's bedroom because Pa was out at the Red Lion, and they didn't know what he'd do when he came back. Ma wedged a chair under the door handle. Jessie never said Josh's name to Pa.

Then Ted Gorman came. He said he was too old to go fightin' any Huns — not his business, and anyway, there was his gammy leg. Ted Gorman had a limp — sometimes — but he was strong enough in the arm and chest. He got on with Pa all right. Two of a kind, Ma said. Jessie didn't know what she meant. She only knew that she was frightened of Ted Gorman, who had a habit of coming up behind her when she was feeding the pig or the hens, or in the barn mucking out the horse. Sometimes he'd touch her on the back of the neck and when she turned, she'd see his big brown face and hard eyes, and smell his breath as he lurched at her, whispering her name, sounding the 's' through his broken teeth, his tongue darting out of his mouth and licking his lips. She dared not tell Pa. She was frightened of him, too. Of his rages. Rages that erupted even when he wasn't drunk.

Jessie stood looking at Ma's thin shoulders and bent back, and felt a terrible sick emptiness. What if Ma died and Josh never came back? She'd be alone with them. Pa might not let her go to school. She was a pupil-teacher and she wanted to get on, to earn her own living, but Pa would keep her drudging on the farm and in the house. What would Ted Gorman do to her then? But to leave Ma now, to give up all her hopes and dreams — to give up her future…

Ma turned round and looked at her trembling lips and tear-filled eyes. 'No use cryin', Jessie, tha knows it's for the best. He'll have thee married to Ted Gorman, an' I can't do a thing to stop it. I haven't the —' Ma sat down wearily — 'I haven't the strength to worry about thee an' our Josh. Do it for me, Jessie, my lass. I'll know tha'll be safe when…'

'When what?'

'I've to go to hospital for an operation. It'll take me a while to get right again, an' tha'll not manage here on thy own.'

'But I'll come back — I'm not going forever. I'm not.'

'There's nowt more to say. Go an' fetch me some water from the pump.'

Jessie didn't move. 'Ma, please — tell me I'll come back, and go back to the school? Mrs Roberts'll let me, I know she will. She says I can be a proper teacher.'

'When I'm up an' about again, I'll send. Now get on before they come in for their tea.'

Jessie went with an old carpet bag containing a homemade dress, two nightdresses and undergarments, her Bible, her few books, a hairbrush and comb. Ma had given her a purse containing ten shillings and told her to look after it. It was everything she had. She left on the milk cart, listening to the rattling churns, on the day when Pa and Ted Gorman were at market. She looked back to see Ma standing in the yard, holding up her arm to wave her away. She settled her bag on her knee and in that moment, just as the cart was rounding the bend, she looked again. Ma was gone, and there was an empty space in the yard where she had been.

2

On the way to Moonlyght, Jessie stared at the passing landscape — the high moors now dark purple and bronze as the heather began to change colour, the still yellow gorse and broom, the sheep grazing high up, and the barns in every field. She watched the waterfall that rushed down the crag where she and Josh had once hidden in a cave; there had been shining white spears descending from the roof and rising from the ground. Josh had told her they were stalactites and stalagmites formed by the constant dripping of water. They looked like the icicles that hung from the farmhouse roof in winter. They were dragon's teeth, Josh had said, dragons frozen in time, dragons which would come to life when a very hot summer came, a summer which would make the world burst into flames. She knew later, of course, much later, that a hot summer had come, and the dragon had indeed roared to life.

She had believed in magic back then, in that cool crystal cave in which Josh's lamp had lit up the marble columns and the stone threaded with silver and gold. Josh knew things. He took books from the parlour where Grandad Albert had used to sit on a Sunday. She didn't know if Grandad had ever read any of the books because no one was allowed to disturb him. Pa and Ma never read anything. Sometimes Josh would sneak a book into the barn, and he'd read to Jessie about flowers and trees, and from the book about geology which she didn't really understand. In the spring and the summer, when they could get away, Josh would show her the fossils and stones and the flowers, the yellow cowslip, the Star-of-Bethlehem in the hedgerows and the sweet-smelling honeysuckle, the purple violet hiding in the woods, and the white stars Josh told her was enchanter's nightshade. Josh, the enchanter, was gone, and with him light and warmth and laughter.

She missed him. As much as Ma missed him, she thought, but in a different way. He was her friend and protector. He was safety. He'd come back for her and Ma, he had told her, and they'd be free to go where they wanted, but in the meantime, he had to go. He was twenty. It was a man's duty to fight for his country. The country had called for help. A man had no choice. And he'd see something of the world. He'd write, of course, and they said — whoever they were — that it would soon be over. 'Jess, don't cry. It'll not be long, and I'll save some money, then we can do as we please. You've got to carry on at the school — you'll be a teacher and I'll be able to do something. We'll get away from here. It's our chance. You've got to be brave, Jess.'

But Josh had been gone a year. He had come back twice on leave, but not to the farm. Jessie and her mother had hitched a lift on a milk cart to meet him when he'd come from the training camp — he'd been his usual cheerful self, telling them about life under canvas in Wensleydale. It was early summer, and Josh had looked brown and well. In November 1915 his battalion, the Lonsdales, had sailed for France. The second visit was on a cold and wet April morning in 1916. Jessie and Ma took the milk cart to Gressthwaite before Josh went back to France. She'd asked about France and Josh had laughed. But not in the old way. There was a harshness to it, as if he didn't mean it. France was cold, mud and broken trees, trenches and noise, bully beef and hard biscuits. His voice changed then when he talked about the Lonsdales, who were great pals. They looked out for each other. There was Jim and Archie and Will and Myles. It was all right in its way. They weren't to worry about him. But Jessie hadn't been sure. Josh was different. His hazel eyes seemed darker, as if the light had gone out of them, and when he laughed it didn't reach them. It was as if he had a secret that he couldn't tell.

When she and Ma had gone with him to the station and she had hugged him, he hadn't felt the same. His easy strength had been comforting when he had lifted her from a stile or put her on the horse's back, but now he seemed stiff and unyielding in the unfamiliar uniform. And he didn't call her Jess, as he always had. He hadn't said her name at all, a stranger suddenly. She had lost him, and she didn't know how.

The cart rumbled past the little school. Jessie had liked it there. She'd enjoyed learning to read and write on the slates given out at the beginning of the lesson; then there were lead pencils for the juniors and real paper and ink when she went into the senior class until she was fourteen. Ma had persuaded Pa that she should stay on and earn her shilling as a pupil-teacher, and Mrs Roberts in the senior class had told her she was clever enough to become a certified teacher on a salary after her five years' apprenticeship.

She remembered the pot-bellied stove in the winter classroom and the smell of scorched wool from the jumpers and socks that were hung there to dry for the little ones in her care, who walked with their big brothers and sisters from the outlying farms, as she had walked with Josh through great snowdrifts and mud. And Josh in the playground with Will Beswick — Will who had gone to war, too, with Jim Gresty, Myles Woodhouse of Birkrigg, and Archie Handley from Sedgecroft Farm in Thorndale. Josh had taken her there once. She remembered the firelight and the buzz of talk and the click of the knitting needles.

Sedgecroft Farm was a home where folk laughed and chatted, where someone played a fiddle and a girl with long golden hair sang. She thought of Will, whose father had the bicycle shop in Gressthwaite. Will Beswick, who had taught her to ride a bike; he had given her a toffee apple at the bonfire held at Sedgecroft Farm and held her hand in the dark. She had loved him almost as much as she loved Josh. They had gone together. And they hadn't yet come back.

Mud, trenches, broken trees. *No flowers*, she thought. *No flowers in France.*

The sick emptiness of the previous day shuddered through Jessie as she got off the milk cart and stood for a few moments on the pavement in front of the railway station. Ma was sick. Ma might die and Josh might not come back. She was lost. At any other time, she would have been tempted by the market stalls. Not today. What could she buy? What could she take to the place where she was going? What use would a new ribbon be to a kitchen maid who knew no one and who had nowhere else to go?

The carter, who had not spoken during the ride, now looked at her curiously as she stood seemingly staring into the distance. She looked very young, he thought, but that was the way of things. Lasses had to go into service and make the best of it. She'd be best off away from Swarthgill. Bert Sedgwick were a bad lot. Talk were that he'd done away with his own pa an' that he beat his wife. Esther Sedgwick looked like a sick woman, he had thought when she brought the girl out to his cart. She didn't look as if she were long for this world. An' that nice lad, Josh, at the front. Poor lass, though. She looked right lost.

He fumbled in his pocket and found a threepenny bit, which he held out to her. 'Get thee a cup o' tea an' a bun, lass.'

When she smiled up at him, he thought, surprised, *She'll be a beauty, that one.*

Jessie caught the train from Gressthwaite and got off at a place called Crossgill Head. The ferryman was waiting for any railway passengers. He took Jessie across the ford in the river in a rowing boat and pointed the way up the lane which would take her past Blades Wood, into the hamlet of Mossgarth.

'Moonlyght,' he had said. 'Mile an' a half up the hill. After about a mile, tha'll see the gate to Fiddler's Hill Farm on the left and then a bit beyond tha'll see the gates to Moonlyght. Expected, are thee?'

Jessie nodded. 'Mrs Cobb knows I'm coming today.'

'Oh, aye, dost know 'er?'

'She's my Ma's cousin. I'm to be a kitchen maid at the house.'

He looked at her, frowning a little as if he thought her words somehow odd. ''Appen she needs more 'elp, now. There's only — well, it's quiet up there these days an' not the visitors there used to be. Not since — ah, well, tha'll find out for thyself. I'm Joe Widdop — if tha wants me to take thee back any day. Cowpot Cottage by the river. Just knock, or if I'm on t'other side, give us a shout.'

She heard the plash of the oars as the ferryman turned his boat away. She was surprised by his words. Last evening she'd persuaded Ma to tell her something about Moonlyght. She was amazed to hear that Ma had worked there. Ma had reassured her that there'd be plenty of people to make friends with. She'd probably share a bedroom with another maid, and she'd be that busy the time would fly by. Always guests and parties.

Plenty of food to eat. Hard work, yes, but Jessie'd manage that. She'd worked hard on the farm.

Now she wondered why the ferryman had offered to take her back when she'd only just arrived. Was there something wrong with the place? He said it was quiet up there, though Ma had told her there'd be lots of visitors. It had been dark in the bedroom, so she hadn't seen Ma's face when she was whispering to her. She'd been making it sound better than it was, perhaps. And Mrs Cobb? Ma hadn't much to say about her — she was all right. Not much of a talker. She'd be strict, no doubt, and Jessie'd have to take her orders. That's what servants did. In the dark, Jessie had asked again about when she could come back, and Ma hadn't answered. In the silence, Jessie heard her laboured breathing and felt her stiffen, but she couldn't see her expression when eventually Ma had said, 'Don't mither me. I'll send — in a few weeks. Be said.' That meant there were to be no more questions.

Jessie looked up at the trees on either side of the path. This was Blades Wood, then. It looked forbidding and impenetrable in the gathering dusk. She counted the crows flying in to roost. What was that rhyme they used to chant? "Five is sickness; six is death." She thought there were five. *Oh, Ma, get well, please. Let me come home.* She heard the hoot of an owl. She'd heard owls many times before, when she'd stood in the farmyard at dusk. She wasn't afraid of the white face in the twilight or the whirr of wings as the owl flew near, nor of any of the night-time animal sounds of home — the vixen that screamed in the woods, the rats that scuttled in the barn. It was Pa and Ted Gorman she'd been afraid of, but there was something about the unfamiliarity of these woods and the darkening path before her that made her feel afraid. She suddenly felt terribly alone.

That path would take her to Moonlyght and to a life she couldn't imagine, a life she didn't want.

There was no choice. Jessie picked up her bag and set off along the lane. Lights were coming on in the cluster of houses that must be Mossgarth. A dog barked somewhere. An unseen voice called out, and there was laughter nearby and the sound of running feet. Children, she thought, called home for their tea. She and Josh had often had to run, skidding in the mud in the yard when they heard Ma calling or, worse, Pa shouting that there'd be a leathering if they didn't come at once.

Then she was walking up the hill and the lights became fewer, and the high hedges gave way to dry stone walls broken by five-barred gates through which she could see tracks going up to farms. Over a low stone wall, she saw the faint glimmer of a lamp in a farmhouse window. A wooden board told her that it was Fiddler's Hill Farm. It looked very far away. She thought of a warm kitchen, firelight, and Josh. Behind her she heard the sound of wheels and turned to see a horse and cart turn into a lane. The shapes of cows could be seen in the next field; she could hear their snorting breath. The hills far beyond were dark now. The lane ahead was empty and disappeared into the unknown distance. Maybe back home, where Ma would be washing up or sitting by the range, warming her feet.

Ma seemed as impossibly distant as the hills in this empty road. On the right, Jessie saw trees.

That would be where the house was, somewhere in the dark. And then she came upon the great stone pillars, wound about by ivy and topped by round balls of green verdigris. A rough drive led up to the house, all rutted and stony, with darkening woods on either side. She couldn't imagine the carriages of well-dressed folk that Ma had described coming up here. Then more trees on each side and Moonlyght was there.

Jessie couldn't tell if it were a house or a castle, for there was a tower on one side with battlements at the top. Some were crumbling, and the narrow windows were empty of glass. Ivy had crept up to twine itself through the old stonework and through the pointed window frames. The grey house with its forbidding battlements loomed above her, its stone-framed windows dark and the huge oak door in its battlemented porch firmly closed. The place was silent. In the autumn twilight no birds sang, and Jessie wondered if Ma had made a mistake. Perhaps the house was empty. There was no Mrs Cobb to meet her.

She looked up. There was smoke curling from a chimney, and she could see a light in one of the upstairs windows. She dared not knock at the front door. It looked too forbidding with its great iron studs and hinges. Carved into the great stone lintel was the image of a knight, with helmet and plumes and three crescent moons beneath him and the date 1640.

The drive curved to the right, away from the house and the tower. The back door would be round there. Jessie found herself in a big yard where there was an open door, and she was startled to hear the sound of raised voices. A woman's voice shouted, 'You'll not be welcome back, Ethel Widdop! Make no mistake about that!'

A girl came rushing out, carrying a bag, a girl with a flushed and angry face and wild red hair who ran out of the yard, calling back over her shoulder, 'Says you!' She vanished through a gate and into the trees.

A woman appeared at the door and looked after the girl. Then she saw Jessie.

'You'll be Jessie Sedgwick. You'd best come in.'

Jessie took in the tall, stout figure of the woman she supposed must be Mrs Cobb, whose face still bore signs of the anger she had directed at Ethel Widdop. A severe face with thin, unsmiling lips, a long nose and very dark eyes, which looked her up and down critically as if Jessie Sedgwick were not what she had expected at all.

3

If Ada Cobb had not expected the pretty Jessie Sedgwick, who had appeared in the yard on that first evening, then the old house called Moonlyght was not what Jessie Sedgwick had expected.

There were few servants now. The housemaids, the bootboy, the groom and the gardeners were all gone. Lady Emmeline de Moine's maid was the elderly nurse who had once ruled the nursery. Now maid and nurse to her mistress, she kept to the top floor below the attics, and Mrs Cobb ruled below. The dining room, the library, and the drawing room were shut up, but Mrs Cobb went in once a week to dust and to bring out the silver for Jessie to polish — a monotonous task. There were heavy knives, forks, and spoons with the de Moine monogram engraved on the handles, which made the job fiddly and tedious. Most of the bedrooms were shut up, but Nurse, as they called her, kept Mr Alexander's room ready for his return — Jessie learned that Mr Alexander was Lady Emmeline's son, away at the war. *Like Josh*, she had thought. She didn't say, knowing instinctively that Mrs Cobb's terse information required no response. Mrs Cobb had her own bedroom and small sitting room on the first floor, where Jessie had a little room tucked into a corner at the end of the corridor, a room accessed by the back stairs up which Jessie climbed with her heavy coal scuttles and dusters.

The grand oak door which Jessie had seen when she had arrived was opened only when Doctor Kennedy came once a month to see Lady Emmeline. Mrs Cobb always answered the door, but Jessie's job the day before he arrived was to sweep out the hall and the main stairs, to flick her feather duster over the suit of armour, and to polish the oak chest and the massive chairs that were placed by the great hearth and carved overmantel with its swags of stone garlands. Here was another shield of the de Moine family carved into the stone. Like the one above the front door, it featured the knight and the three crescent moons, and words she didn't understand: *Lux in Tenebris Lucet*. *Latin*, she thought. There were Latin words in the flower book Josh had given her for her birthday once. She'd have liked to have learnt Latin. Too late now.

The fireplace contained a couple of huge logs, but the fire was never lit. The hall seemed vast to Jessie, full of shadows and strange green light from the stained-glass window, in which more knights stood at arms and the moons shone greenly during the day, and there was the suit of armour, gleaming dully, standing guard at the bottom of the stairs. She'd felt a shudder of terror the first time she'd seen it. In the dimness it had looked for a moment as if someone was there. Afterwards, she always expected the vizor to pop up and reveal a face inside. She came into the hall through one of the three doors situated behind what Mrs Cobb had told her was the screens passage. The first door led out from the kitchen, the second from the cellars, and the third from what had been known in the olden days, according to Mrs Cobb, as the buttery. That door was locked now.

Jessie wasn't the kitchen maid, just the maid of all work at the beck and call of Ada Cobb, who was not cruel, just indifferent. She showed no approval of Jessie's willingness and competence. She asked nothing about Ma and Pa; she just gave her orders, then left Jessie to clear up the supper things in the kitchen and make her lonely way to bed. She was always too tired to read at the end of the day, but never too tired to check that her purse with her precious ten shillings was still safely hidden in the pocket of her second dress that was folded up in a drawer. She often thought about Joe Widdop, the ferryman who'd said he would take her across the river. She thought about Ma and when she would send. That ten shillings meant she could go home. Nothing had been said to Jessie about wages, but she knew her earnings, paid on Whit Saturday and Martinmas Day, were to be sent directly to Pa.

Ethel Widdop didn't come back. Mrs Cobb never mentioned her, and Jessie knew better than to ask, but she often wondered if she would see her again. When she emptied the potato peelings and kitchen scraps into the midden in the yard, or scattered grain for the few hens, she looked at the gate that led into the trees and thought about Ethel and why she had gone. This was Hag Wood, according to Mrs Cobb. Even the name made her shiver. She was not to go wanderin', Mrs Cobb had ordered. An' she was not to be talkin' to anyone. What went on at Moonlyght was de Moine business an' Jessie wasn't to forget it.

Who would I talk to, Jessie thought to herself, *if I am never to go out?*

Few people came to the house. Aside from the doctor, only the postman and the laundry man appeared — the latter once a week from Kirkby Lonsdale, the nearest market town. Jessie was thankful she didn't have to wash the heavy linen sheets that she brought down from the bedrooms and packed away in the linen cupboard when they came back. She and Mrs Cobb made the beds, though Nurse stripped and made up Lady Emmeline's bed. Sometimes a delivery of oil and candles or coal came from Kirkby Lonsdale, and a man came to service the range. Mrs Cobb dealt with all that and with the nearby tenant farmer of Fiddler's Hill, Mr Simon Turner, who brought a chicken, extra eggs, butter, milk and vegetables, and chopped the wood for them. Jessie kept to the kitchen when the farmer came. Mrs Cobb talked to him briefly, but he was a taciturn man with a long, miserable face and simply got on with his chopping.

Mrs Cobb made the bread and cooked all the food. Lady Emmeline hardly ate anything — soup or an egg, toast, perhaps, and Mrs Cobb and Jessie ate whatever Nurse ordered, and the roast chicken or ham that wasn't wanted upstairs. Stout Ada Cobb ate plenty and Jessie didn't starve. Ada Cobb knew the value of a girl strong and healthy enough to do the heavy work.

One of her jobs was to take up the coal scuttles to the bedrooms, to light the fires and to rake out the ashes. The curtains of Lady Emmeline's room were always closed and in the half darkness, Jessie could never see anything of the woman in the bed, and Nurse was always careful to stand by her patient. In any case, she had strict instructions from Mrs Cobb to be in and out as quickly as possible and to make no noise. Nurse did not look at her when she came into the room. She was just a figure by the bed, though Jessie was aware of the crackle of an apron and the dark dress she wore, and something hostile about her. It was in her breathing, Jessie thought. It sounded impatient. She always felt Nurse's eyes on her, and she tried to be careful, but she couldn't help the scraping of the shovel as she collected the ashes and once, when a fire iron had clanged against the coal scuttle, she had heard the woman in the bed moan.

When she looked back at those first few weeks, Jessie thought she had been too numb with exhaustion to question what was happening, and too afraid to ask anything of Mrs Cobb. It was as if she had been struck dumb, held motionless in an endless grey dream. And when something happened and she had woken from her dream, Jessie Sedgwick could not escape from Moonlyght and the dark tower which haunted her dreams.

4

At the end of the first month, when autumn was turning into winter and when the leaves were falling fast, and crows cackled at the tops of the bare branches, Jessie went through the gate. Mrs Cobb was in her own room, where she always retired after lunch, leaving Jessie to wash up and prepare whatever might be wanted upstairs by way of tea or a light supper. Jessie had felt her heart leap when Mrs Cobb had brought in the letters. Perhaps, she had thought, there might be something, but Mrs Cobb said nothing. She had looked thoughtful, and Jessie had seen her examine the envelopes before she put them in her apron pocket and sat down for a cup of tea.

Her work done, Jessie stood at the back door and watched the restless clouds and the treetops waving in the wind in the wood beyond. Nothing else moved. She gazed up at the broken battlements of the tower and thought of the stories she had read at school, of princesses locked in towers waiting for a knight to rescue them. There was a poem she'd loved about the Lady of Shalott, who escaped from her prison only to die of the curse upon her. Perhaps she was cursed to stay here. No knight would come in the shape of Josh in his uniform. How would he know where she was? But surely, Ma would have written to tell him that Jessie had left the farm?

She'd been waiting, she supposed, believing that a message would come to tell her to come home. That was always her last thought and prayer before she fell asleep. "In a few weeks," Ma had said, but only because Jessie had insisted. She remembered Ma's haggard face and that laboured breathing. In that moment, she knew Ma would never send because Ma knew she was dying.

The thought sent her flying across the yard, through the gate and into the woods, where, huddled by a tree, she howled as all the held-in anguish poured out of her in a stream of tears. When the storm was spent, she sat with her head on her knees, unable to move.

'You all right?' a voice asked, and Jessie felt a hand on her shoulder. Looking up, she saw the face of the girl who had fled the evening she had arrived. Ethel Widdop had a sharp, pretty face with a smudge of dirt across her nose, and two curious eyes of an almost golden colour, full of glinting life.

'New kitchen maid, aren't you? Jessie? Cobface sent you packin', 'as she?'

Jessie wiped her eyes on her apron and looked at the red-haired girl staring down at her. 'No, I just wanted —'

Ethel squatted down beside her. 'Bit much, is it, on your own with 'er? She's an old cow. She didn't like me, I can tell you. I only went back for me things an' me wages. Wouldn't 'ave got 'em otherwise.'

'Did she sack you?'

'Aye. Said I wasn't fit for — oh, well, it don't matter. No one else there 'cept Cobb an' the lady?'

'And Nurse.'

'Oh, aye, tartar that one. No visitors?'

'Only the doctor.'

'Can't you go 'ome?' Ethel's golden eyes sparked defiantly. 'I mean, it ain't a prison, Jessie. You got family?'

'Yes, but —' Jessie's eyes filled with tears again. How could she explain?

'Sent away, were you?' It wasn't really a question. Everyone knew that girls were expendable in poor families.

'My ma — she said she'd send for me, and I was waiting for a letter. There were letters today and when there was nothing for me, I just… I'll have to get back. Mrs Cobb'll be —'

'She won't be down yet, if I know her. She'll be 'avin' her sherry on the quiet. You've a minute or two. Where are you from?'

'Up Gressthwaite way — a farm out on the hills.'

'Tidy step, but you can get the train. Pa said he brought you across the river.'

'Yes, but it's not that — Ma's sick. I think she might…' Jessie trailed off, unable to say the words.

'I see, an' you've no one else at 'ome?'

'Pa, he's — well, he'll not want me back, an' my brother's a soldier in France somewhere.'

'Bit of a pickle, that, but mebbe you should ask Cobb if you can go an' find out about your ma. I mean, mebbe you could write to her — you can write, can't you?' Jessie nodded. 'I'll take the letter if you don't want Cobb to see it.'

'You'd do that?'

'Course, anythin' for a pal. Your ma might tell you to come 'ome if you explain. Come on, lass, you'd best keep Cobface sweet. Meet me at the same time tomorrow in the tower.'

'Oh, I don't —' Jessie didn't like the tower, but she had to go in because there was a huge heap of coal from which she had to fill her scuttles. She always left the door open and was in and out as quickly as she could be. It was a creepy place in which the wind always muttered around the narrow windows as if someone was whispering secrets, and she always imagined someone watching from the unknown regions above. On one occasion she thought she had seen a figure on the stairs, where she never dared look afterwards. She couldn't bear the thought of waiting in there.

'It's safer. No one'll see us there. I come through Hag Wood to a little broken door round the back — off its hinges, but you can squeeze through. Cobb won't see me.'

She hauled Jessie up and showed her where she would find the tell-tale crushed ferns where Ethel had trodden to get to the back door of the tower.

'Them letters you mentioned. Know who they were from?'

'Mrs Cobb didn't say.'

'She wouldn't. Mr Alexander comin', mebbe — on leave, p'raps, or that Miss Caroline.'

'Who's she?'

'Tell you tomorrow. You make your mind up — write to your ma. Tell 'er you don't like the place. It ain't no place for you. Cobb'll work you to death an' that mad woman won't do a thing about it. Nor will Nurse. It's a rotten place. Now run. An' don't say you seen me.'

Mrs Cobb was waiting. She looked Jessie up and down and saw the tear-stained face, but she only said, 'I had a letter from your pa.'

Jessie sat down. She heard the rustling of paper and when she looked up, Mrs Cobb had the letter in her hand. Her face hadn't changed, but Jessie knew.

'Your ma's gone. I'm sorry. She was a good woman.'

Jessie didn't move. She sat looking down at her reddened hands and the leaves on her dress until she heard the scrape of the chair on the flags, the footsteps, and then the closing of the door. She looked at the letter on the table where Mrs Cobb had left it.

It was very short. Esther was dead. There was no need for Jessie to come. Her ma was buried already.

Jessie crumpled up the letter and threw it on the fire. She watched the paper curl and turn brown at its edges. She watched until the words crumbled to ash and were gone. Not that the truth could vanish. Ma was dead, but she had known that, she thought, before she'd seen the letters in Mrs Cobb's hands. She thought of the five crows she had seen flying into Blades Wood — there must have been six. Not that it mattered. She thought of the empty space in the yard where Ma had been. She had known then.

Mrs Cobb said no more. When she came back to the kitchen, it was as if nothing had happened. Mrs Cobb prepared a tray for Lady Emmeline and Nurse and took it up. Jessie was instructed to put some potatoes on to boil and when they were ready, they sat down to some ham and potatoes which Jessie couldn't eat. Mrs Cobb didn't comment, but when she stood up to leave the kitchen, she said, 'By the way, Mr Alexander is coming home on leave an' Miss Caroline's coming home from the school in London, so there'll be a deal to do tomorrow. You'd best get to bed when you've washed up.'

Jessie washed up, damped down the kitchen fire, and went up to her room. But she couldn't sleep for thinking about Ma, hardly able to believe that she would never see her again, that Ma was dead and buried already, and that Pa didn't want her. No need for her to come, he'd written. She stared at the moon looking in through the window. Moonlight. Moonlyght. What had Ethel said? *It's a rotten place.* She didn't have to stay. But she couldn't go home, and it was no use writing to Pa.

She sat up then. Did Josh know about Ma? Maybe Mrs Handley would have written to her son Archie, who'd perhaps know where Josh was.

Millie Handley's kind, round face came to her, and that night at Sedgecroft Farm, the laughter and the singing. Mrs Handley wouldn't turn her away, and she was bound to know about Ma. That's what she'd do. She'd meet Ethel Widdop, tower or no tower, and she'd tell her that she would go across the river and take the train, and she'd walk to Swarthgill and up the moor to Sedgecroft. Maybe she could write to Josh through Archie and Josh could tell her what to do. And if she couldn't stay at Sedgecroft, she'd find work somewhere, and she had her ten shillings. You could do a lot with that. Find lodgings, anyway.

It was a plan, and that gave her comfort. The thought of Ethel and her father Joe, the ferryman, gave her comfort. He had looked kind, too. She wasn't alone.

Jessie slept at last. In her dream she walked up the lane to Swarthgill Farm, but the house was a ruin, its windows broken, the front door hanging off its hinges, and there was no sound at all. There were no sheep in the fields and the stable door was open, but when she went into the house, the rooms were the same, except there were dust and cobwebs everywhere. Cups and plates on the table, knives and forks, as if the table had been set but no one had come to eat, as if the people had simply gone and no one had set foot in the house for years. She stood looking at the range where Ma had used to sit, but there was no fire now. The old black kettle was on the cold range, the teapot ready on the pine cupboard. Then she heard footsteps upstairs. Someone was moving and she heard the sound of sobbing. Ma was upstairs. Ma needed her.

Jessie woke suddenly. The moon had gone and in the dark silence she didn't know where she was or if she was dreaming, or if the footsteps and the sound of weeping were real. The empty kitchen at home was still vivid for a moment or two and then it was gone, and she felt the slippery satin of her counterpane. She was at Moonlyght. She sat still, aware of the strangeness of this house to which she did not belong, a house that creaked at night, a house that whispered when the wind blew down the chimneys and through windows that didn't quite close, and that tower where shadows moved on the stair, a house of strangers who did not welcome her. Mrs Cobb, about whom she knew no more than she had on the day she'd arrived. Nurse, who never spoke to her. And the woman in the bed whose face she had never seen. Ethel had said "that mad woman" — did she mean Lady Emmeline? And Ethel's pa had said she would find out for herself.

Well, she hadn't found out anything except that it wasn't where she wanted to be. Tomorrow then. She'd meet Ethel Widdop, find out when the train stopped at Crossgill, and go to Sedgecroft.

She lay down again, huddling under the counterpane for warmth and closing her eyes. The sound came again. Footsteps on the floor above. She sat up. She wasn't dreaming. She strained to listen, feeling her heart beat too fast. Then she was sure. Someone was crying, the same someone who was walking about in the room above. Not Lady Emmeline's room. Jessie went to open her door and in the darkness of the corridor, she heard Mrs Cobb's door open. She'd heard it, too. Jessie dared not move or call out. She heard footsteps walk to the end of the corridor and then the stairs creak as someone went up.

Silence again. Jessie closed her door and climbed back into bed. Above her there was the creak of a door opening. More footsteps, heavier this time, and then the sound of two pairs of feet crossing the room above. A door closing. And, clear as anything, the sound of weeping. As if someone's heart was breaking.

5

'I've taken up the coals an' I've lit the fire, Jessie. Lady Emmeline's not so good. No need for you to disturb them up there, an' we'd best get on — you can give the hall an' stairs a good sweepin', an' I'll see to the drawin' room an' dinin' room. Then you can help me make up the beds.'

'When are they coming?'

'Miss Caroline arrives this afternoon — the London train at Oxenholme station. She'll want tea. Mr Alexander tomorrow — don't know where he's coming from an' he didn't say a time. There'll be breakfasts to do an' dinner tomorrow night. Miss Caroline can have her supper in her room tonight. Farmer'll bring a chicken and veg tomorrow morning.'

Jessie took her broom and dusters to the hall. She knew it was pointless asking about the previous night's disturbance. Mrs Cobb wouldn't tell her, nor did she tell her who Miss Caroline was. As she swept and dusted, Jessie wondered if she would have a chance to meet Ethel. Maybe she could dash to the tower and leave her a note to say she would come to Cowpot Cottage. It would have to be at night, after Mrs Cobb had gone to bed, but how would she find her way in the dark? Dawn then — just as it was getting light.

Mrs Cobb came from the dining room. 'Beds,' she said, indicating that Jessie should accompany her up the main staircase.

'Miss Caroline's room's on this floor, so we'll do that first.'

Jessie followed Mrs Cobb along the corridor, carrying the clean sheets from the linen cupboard next to Mrs Cobb's room. Miss Caroline's room was pretty with a blue carpet and blue-flowered curtains at the windows which matched the blue velvet of the chaise longue at the end of the bed, with a carved mahogany frame which ended in curls and flowers. There was a table with a triple mirror and silver and glass pots, a huge mahogany wardrobe, and a neat little desk on which there were silver-topped inkwells and a blotter. If Jessie envied anything, it was that: she imagined sitting there and lifting one of those silver lids to dip in her pen.

'Who is Miss Caroline?' Jessie dared to ask as they tucked in the crisp sheets and unfolded the pillowcases.

'She's not a de Moine. Daughter of some cousin of the General's. Left an orphan, an' Lady Emmeline took her in. The boys were at school — boarding school, see, an' Miss Caroline was only six, so she was like a daughter for her. Twenty now, so she's leavin' the school — what they call a finishing school in London. For young ladies, it is — they learn French an' fancy cooking. What for, I don't know. She was supposed to come at Christmas, but I daresay she'll do as she pleases. What happens next is up to Lady Emmeline. Not that she's fit to — well, never mind that. Time we went up to Mr Alexander's room.'

There was no sound from Lady Emmeline's room and they continued down a long corridor to the end, where there were two doors next to each other and one opposite. Jessie thought that the room facing the back of the house was the one above hers — where she'd heard the footsteps. But Mrs Cobb opened the door to the other room, in which there was a similar bed to the one in Miss Caroline's room, a large desk with a silver inkwell and pens and photographs in silver frames. There were books stacked on the desk and on the shelves next to it. The carpet and curtains were green and the wardrobe large and forbidding. It was a man's room, Jessie thought, noting the cricket bat and tennis racquet leaning by the desk. There was another door in the room which led, Mrs Cobb told her, to the room Mr Charles used when he stayed. They'd best make that bed, too. He'd be coming sometime, Mr Alexander said. Jessie didn't ask who Mr Charles was.

As they went out of the room, Mrs Cobb pointed to the opposite door. 'Don't be goin' in there. It's Mr Jonathan's — as was, I should say. He died. An accident. Terrible time, it was. No one goes in there now, 'cept Mr Alexander sometimes. Just as Mr Jonathan left it. It should be locked, but —' Mrs Cobb made a tutting sound and turned away. 'An' don't you be askin' questions of anybody. It's not to be mentioned, and you know as much as you need about that business.'

A dead man's room, Jessie thought, from where she had heard footsteps and weeping. Her heart jumped for a moment, but she knew it had been a real someone. Mrs Cobb had gone upstairs, and those heavier footsteps must have been hers, but she knew better than to mention that. Mrs Cobb's mouth had closed like a trap after her last statement.

However, when they went downstairs for lunch, Mrs Cobb said, 'I suppose you ought to know somethin' about the family so you'll not need to ask any more questions.'

Two questions, Jessie thought. She'd only asked two, but she kept quiet and ate her bread and cheese.

'Lady Emmeline's a widow. The General — that was her husband — died of a heart attack five years since, so there was no more parties and dances like in the time your ma was here — though that were more than twenty years back. I was just a maid an' there was a different housekeeper. Mr Jonathan's accident was in 1914 — home from the war an' fell to his death. Terrible business, it was. Finished Lady Emmeline, it did. Her favourite son. Mr Alexander wasn't the same, neither, but Lady Emmeline ... well, you can see that she's not a well woman.'

Mrs Cobb stood up to signal that that was the end of the conversation. 'Now, I've things to do upstairs. I'll be down by half past three, so you can wash up an' get some eggs on the boil for Miss Caroline's tea. She'll like a sandwich, I daresay, an' there's fruitcake. You can give that silver teapot a polish an' wash that good tea set I brought in. An' be careful. That china's fragile. Set a tray for two. I'll take it in an' sit with her for a bit.'

'What time will she come?'

''Bout half past four, I reckon. Mr Wiggins'll bring her from the station by the main road and through Old Park.'

The directions meant nothing to Jessie. She only thought about the half hour she would have to meet Ethel and be back in the kitchen when Mrs Cobb came down.

She worked on, boiling the eggs, polishing the silver, washing the crockery, setting out the tray, and cutting thin slices of bread for the sandwiches and cutting up the fruitcake. She heard the clock strike three and took a bucket of vegetable peelings. An excuse if Mrs Cobb was waiting when she came back.

She slipped through the trees and into Hag Wood, found Ethel's pathway, and picked her way through the nettles to find the little door that Ethel had told her about.

She was relieved to find that Ethel was waiting. Jessie told her that there was no point in writing. Ma was dead, but she had a plan. She'd go to a farm called Sedgecroft to find out about her brother, Josh. 'But I can't ask Mrs Cobb to let me go now. There's visitors coming, Mr Alexander and Miss Caroline. Mrs Cobb says there's a lot to do. She'll be watching me.'

Ethel thought about that. 'No need to rush, now your ma's gone — I mean, you'd best think about it. Sure them folk at Sedgecroft'll take you?'

'I don't know. I think so — for a while, maybe. I'll have to try.'

'Worth writing to 'em?'

'Yes, that's a good idea. I can ask about Josh and whether there's any work there for me, or on another farm — just till Josh gets back.'

'Did Mrs Cobb say owt about Mr Alexander comin'?'

'She said he was coming on leave, but she didn't know when.'

'Oh, right. Did she mention Mr Charles?'

'She mentioned his room. Who is he?'

'Cousin of Mr Alexander — sort of looked after 'im after Mr Jonathan died.'

'Mrs Cobb said it was an accident.'

'Fell from up there —' Ethel pointed high up the tower to where Jessie could see what looked like a ledge jutting out, topped by an arch. She had never dared look before. It looked as though it might fall down at any moment. Her eye took in the way the ledge continued round the wall, where a floor must once have been. She could see right up to the grey clouds. It was a sickening drop to the stony ground on which they stood. She imagined for a moment the young man swooping down like a great bird and the thud of the body hitting the stones. What an eerie place the tower was, so full of shadows and creeper winding its way up the walls and the worn stairs which rose to the ledge. There was rough stone under her feet and patches of nettle in the corners and the smell of damp and coal dust. It was intensely cold, too. She could feel the muttering wind sneaking in through the narrow, empty windows.

'No one knows what 'e were doin' up there,' Ethel continued. 'Takin' a look at the land before 'e went back to the fightin', my pa said, but some folk said 'e jumped cos 'e didn't want to go back to the war. Their ma never got over it. Took to 'er bed. Blamed Mr Alexander. Said 'e should 'ave stopped Mr Jonathan goin' up them stairs. That's why this place is a wreck. Mr Charles went to school with Mr Alexander an' now they've both gone to fight.'

Jessie thought of Josh gone to fight. And the young man who had killed himself rather than go back. Was it so terrible? She couldn't speak.

Ethel was quiet for a few moments, too, until she said, 'I thought mebbe — p'raps you'll get a chance to ask if Mr Charles is comin'. Miss Caroline might know — got 'er sights on Mr Alexander, she 'as. The heir, see — she's got nowt. 'E's too good for 'er. 'E's a nice way with 'im, Mr Alexander, kind, you know. 'E don't look down on servants, but she's a piece of work. Full of airs an' graces an' she ain't even a de Moine. She ain't nobody, far as I can tell. Don't you trust 'er — she'll not do you any favours an' she'll 'ave you waitin' on 'er. Don't I know 'er tricks. Still, won't be for long. Meet me in three days, eh? I got things I need to do. I'll take your letter for them farming people.'

'Three days — I don't know if —'

'I'll be 'ere, Jessie. I'll see it's posted, an' if you don't 'ear anythin', we'll think again. There'll be a way, trust me.'

'I will. Thanks ever so, Ethel. I'd best get back.'

'Thursday then. An' don't forget to ask about Mr Charles — I've a message for 'im, but don't mention that. It's about — someone — I can't say who, but 'e'll want to know. Don't forget your bucket.'

Jessie left her and was meekly standing by the range waiting for the kettle to boil when Mrs Cobb came in.

'Carrier's trap has come from the station an' Miss Caroline's here. You'd best come through. I shall want help with her luggage.'

6

'This is Jessie, Miss Caroline, the new kitchen maid — her mother was a cousin of mine. She'll help with the luggage.'

Jessie bobbed a curtsey. She didn't know if that was the right thing, but the tall young woman who looked her over briefly seemed to Jessie's inexperienced eyes the kind of person to whom anyone might curtsey. She hardly dared look up, but she was aware of a scent in the air, of flowers and something she couldn't identify, but which she never forgot. Years later, she only had to see or hear the name "Caroline" and that perfume came to her, sweet and musky at the same time, a scent which confused you, a deceiving scent which suggested innocence and knowingness at the same time. That was Caroline Mason, but Jessie didn't know her then. When she looked up as the carrier came in with the trunk, her only thought was that Miss Caroline looked like a princess.

Miss Caroline was taking off her hat to reveal hair the colour of chestnuts and just as shiny, parted in the centre and piled loosely on the crown. She held out the hat to Jessie, who was only too conscious of her red hands as she took it. She had no idea what she was supposed to do with it, as Mrs Cobb was busy directing the carrier to take the trunk upstairs. She waited, feeling foolish and clumsy in her thick grey woollen dress and apron.

Caroline looked at her appraisingly and smiled. Jessie thought she was lovely. 'Fetch the other things from the trap, will you please, Jessie, and you can bring them upstairs and help me unpack.'

Jessie watched her go upstairs, noting her smart coat with its velvet collar and cuffs, the long, narrow skirt, and the neat, highly polished lace-up boots. Jessie only had Mrs Roberts from the school to compare with Caroline. She had always thought Mrs Roberts the kind of woman she would like to be. She had seemed so talented — a needlewoman who made her own dresses, which always seemed so neat and fresh. She'd admired Mrs Roberts's hats with their cotton or velvet flowers, which she made herself, too. Looking now at the neatly elegant dark green hat with its softly curling feather and feeling the silky smoothness of the velvet, Jessie knew that Caroline Mason had not made this one, just as she knew that Mrs Roberts's dresses were nothing compared to that close-fitting coat that had just swept up the stairs. Whatever 'finished' meant, Miss Caroline looked perfect.

The door was open as Jessie came to the landing. She heard Mrs Cobb's voice.

'She's a kitchen maid, Miss Caroline. She's not meant to be a lady's maid. You'll have to ask Lady Emmeline if we can get someone for you.'

'So Ethel's gone. A pity, she was quite good at doing my hair. Too pert a tongue at times, though. What happened?'

Jessie stood still, waiting for the reply. She shouldn't eavesdrop, but she wanted to know about Ethel.

'I had to get rid of her. Pert tongue is about right. Too cheeky by half — gettin' above herself. Only takin' it upon herself to wait on Mr Charles —'

'Charles was here? When?'

'September — just for a day or two. Said he was goin' on some trainin' course — guns or some such. Stayed a couple of days an' I didn't like the way Ethel was pushin' herself forward, makin' eyes at Mr Charles —'

There was a silence in which Jessie heard the click of suitcase locks being opened, and then she heard Miss Caroline again. 'At Charles? I don't think he'd be taken in by a common girl like Ethel Widdop. He has far too much taste.'

'I'm not sayin' he would, but she was trouble, that one. I saw her hangin' about for him. Never where she should be. I told her off, but after Mr Charles went, of course she didn't like havin' to get back to scrubbin' the floors, an' when my cousin — that's Jessie's ma — asked me to take the girl, I told Ethel she could go. Came back for her wages an' I told her not to come here again. Bad lot, that one.'

'Is Charles coming?'

'Mr Alexander didn't say.'

'Jessie looks all right. She doesn't seem very forward. Surely you can spare her for an hour or two to do my hair and clothes? Please, Mrs Cobb, it won't be for long. When Lady Emmeline is feeling a bit better, I'll ask about another maid. I'll tell her you need more help. In fact, I'll mention it to Nurse in a while.'

'We'll try it, but don't be givin' her ideas.'

Jessie retreated to the top of the stairs, where she made a noise putting down the luggage on the landing, and then she walked along to the door.

Mrs Cobb instructed Jessie to unpack the trunk while she and Miss Caroline went down for tea. Jessie was surprised when Caroline turned round at the door, smiled again, and mouthed a thank-you. Perhaps she wouldn't be so bad after all, despite what Ethel had said. Anyway, it would make a change from scrubbing, even if she had to wait on Miss Caroline. That made her think of what she'd just heard. Ethel pushing herself forward and never where she should be. These thoughts made her wonder what Ethel was doing in the woods, why she had asked about Charles and what message she had for him. Everything seemed complicated suddenly, as if the pieces of her life at Moonlyght had shifted to make a different pattern like the bits of glass in the kaleidoscope she and Josh had played with as children. Ethel had said not to trust Miss Caroline, but could she trust Ethel? Ethel, who had been sacked and who seemed so insistent on Jessie asking about Charles. Ethel had her secrets, it seemed.

She would write to Mrs Handley, she decided, as she hung up two fine wool dresses. There was a third dress with a skirt made of tiers of flounces in a pale mauve colour. It would be for the evening, she guessed. There were three woollen skirts, four blouses in finely embroidered white cotton and one pink one with a gleam on its textured surface, which Caroline told her later was called Crepe de Chine — silk from China. She unfolded three lovely white petticoats, three camisoles and matching drawers, and three nightdresses, all trimmed with lace, though one of the camisoles was torn at the breast. She wondered if it would be her job to mend it. Perhaps Miss Caroline was careless about her clothes. She thought about that smile and that secret message of thank-you. Maybe she wouldn't mind waiting on Caroline Mason.

But she'd still write her letter. She wanted to get a message to Josh. It wouldn't matter if she was at Sedgecroft Farm or here at Moonlyght because he'd know where she was. He'd come and then Mrs Cobb, Caroline Mason, and Ethel Widdop wouldn't matter, because she and Josh would have each other and a future — somewhere. Josh had said so.

7

Ethel didn't come. Jessie waited impatiently, her eyes on the little broken door at the back of the tower through which she had squeezed. Watching shadows, she started at every sound, the wind murmuring its secrets through the cracks, little stones rattling down the stairs, the creaking of the rotten door. She had heard the hall clock strike the half hour. Caroline and Mrs Cobb were in their rooms. Jessie was supposed to be preparing the tea tray, but she had taken her bucket and her letter and dashed across the yard. In and out of the tower in five minutes, she had thought. That's all it would take to give Ethel the letter and tell her that neither Alexander nor Charles had come. Alexander had sent a telegram to say that his leave had been cancelled.

Caroline had been disappointed. She had told Jessie so when Jessie was doing her hair. Caroline had got her own way, and now Jessie had to rise earlier in order to make up the fires and set the breakfast trays so that she had time then to help Caroline. She'd mended the torn camisole. Caroline couldn't remember how she'd torn it. Jessie didn't mind attending to Miss Caroline. Her visits to her room made a change from Mrs Cobb's dour company. Caroline was bored to death already and talked freely — about herself, of course. She had so looked forward to Alexander's coming and had hoped Charles would come because he was such good fun, she explained to Jessie. There was a car in the stables — Charles could drive, and she thought they might have gone out — to Kendal, maybe, or to one of the great houses where there'd be people — *people*, she'd said, emphatically. Oh, she knew there was a war on, but still people must want visitors for tea or something. What was the point of trying out her new Crepe de Chine blouse or a new hairstyle if there was no one to see it? Caroline did not expect an answer.

Caroline was very forthcoming, too, about the de Moine family. Jessie didn't have to ask questions. Sometimes Jessie thought that Caroline was really talking to herself. Caroline had wanted to see Lady Emmeline about a maid. Nurse was a dragon at the gate. She'd said Lady Emmeline wasn't well enough to be bothered about maids. Caroline could see her providing she didn't mither, nor was she to mention anything about Alexander cancelling his leave. Lady Emmeline needn't hear anything about the war. Lady Emmeline never wanted to know anything about Alexander, Caroline told Jessie. She still blamed him for Jonathan's death, which wasn't fair. Jonathan was always getting Alexander into hot water. If they got into a scrape with their father, Alexander always took the blame. Jonathan's death was an accident. Poor Jonathan, of course, but poor Alexander, too. He was a nice fellow, but he was inclined to be — well, too much on his own. Mooning about the tower. And dear Charles, who'd always looked out for Alexander. Charles would inherit Moonlyght if anything happened to Alexander. Lady Emmeline preferred Charles, anyway.

Jessie looked up at the ledge from which Jonathan had fallen and thought how she had always thought eyes were watching. There was something about the place, something suffocating, despite the cold, and that wind at her neck as though someone was breathing on her. Her breath caught in her throat. A young man had died here — it was a terrifying thought. And his mother lay in bed because he was dead. Jessie had heard her voice the morning after Caroline's arrival, when she had crept in to lay the fire. Nurse wasn't there. She could hear water running in the bathroom beyond and she hesitated, not knowing whether to complete her task or come back later. She froze when she heard the voice ask, 'Jonathan? Jonathan, is that you?' And then there was the sound of weeping. Jessie had fled. It was the sound of someone in dreadful pain. It was the sound of grief. Jessie knew how that felt and almost wept herself as she ran along the corridor to take refuge on the back stairs. She had stood for a minute or two to compose herself before going back up to find Nurse at her post.

The memory made her think of Ma and Josh, and the ache of loss swept over her. Oh, why didn't Ethel come? Through the tower's open roof, she could see the sky darkening. She dared not wait in the dark, and Mrs Cobb would wonder where she was. What to do? Leave the letter where Ethel could find it? But what if Ethel never came? Ask Miss Caroline? Surely, she'd know. She'd tell her she was only writing to find out about Josh.

Jessie felt better when the letter was eventually sent. It took more than a week before Jessie felt confident enough to ask Caroline, who gave her paper, an envelope, and a stamp. She risked another couple of visits to the tower, but there was no sign of Ethel. She hoped Ethel might leave her a note, but she never found anything. In the meantime, she carried on with her kitchen work and looked forward to the times when she was allowed to go up and help Caroline with her clothes or her hair. She found that she was good with the pins, the curling tongs and the ribbons, copying the styles from the newspapers and magazines that Caroline showed her, and Caroline seemed pleased with the results.

There was a wooden post box in the hall, where Caroline put Jessie's letter with one of her own to a school friend, whom she was hoping might invite her for the Christmas holidays. It wasn't going to be any fun at Moonlyght without Charles and Alexander. Perhaps Mrs Cobb would let Jessie come with her as her maid. Jessie didn't answer. *Pigs might fly*, she thought. She hadn't time to speak, anyway, for Caroline was wondering next if Charles or Alexander might get leave and that would be…

She burbled on while Jessie pondered the word "leave". What if Mrs Handley wrote back to say that Josh was coming on leave? Maybe he'd come, or maybe if Caroline went away, she could go to meet Josh at Sedgecroft —

'What are you smiling at?' Caroline's voice interrupted her thoughts. 'You weren't listening to me, were you?'

'Sorry, Miss Caroline. I was wondering if my brother might get leave at Christmas.'

'Oh, yes, your brother. Where is he?'

'I don't know. That's why I wrote to Mrs Handley. I explained, if you remember.'

'Yes, yes, you did. Were you thinking he might come here?'

'I don't know. I thought I might be able to —'

'Go to see him? I don't see why not. Mrs Cobb ought to give you a day off. I could talk to her, if you like? If I tell her I'm going away, she might let you go, though it would be nice if you could come with me … but then if Charles or Alexander come — oh, Jessie, this war! Nothing's ever certain. I thought that when I left that wretched school, things would be so — oh, I don't know — straightforward. I'd have to decide between Alexander and Charles. Charles is very fond of me, you know, and I do like him, but Alexander was meant for me, and he is the heir and I like him, too, of course. But now, what if they can't come and we're stuck here — and not a Christmas party in sight?'

'Will you ask Mrs Cobb about me, though?'

'I could — I will when you get a reply from — what's her name?'

'Mrs Handley — at Sedgecroft Farm.'

'Oh, yes. Now, let's try my hair again. Look at this one in the magazine. We can practise that one. It would be good for a party — or I could wear it like that when Charles or Alexander come. You use the tongs to make the curls and then pin them in swirls at the back, and use this ribbon over the top. Brush it out first, though.'

Brushing the thick, heavy hair with the silver-backed brush was soothing in its way, and Caroline stopped talking while she gazed at herself in the mirror. She was very pretty, Jessie thought, looking at the creamy skin and wide mouth. Lovely teeth, Miss Caroline had. Did Charles or Alexander love her? Caroline seemed more fond of Charles. Jessie noticed how a flush came to her cheeks when she talked about him. Did she love him? Will Beswick flashed into her mind, and she felt the heat in her own face.

Jessie couldn't imagine what Will might feel about her. It was only when she caught sight of herself in Caroline's mirror that she fully took in what she had become. Her hair was hidden under her cap, which was too big for her — it must have been Ethel's. Her grey apron was of coarse linen and her grey woollen dress was shapeless and darned in places. Suddenly she saw what a faded thing she seemed beside the glowing Caroline. Will Beswick wouldn't know her.

8

Caroline flung the Crepe de Chine blouse on the bed.

'Oh, what's the use? It'll be out of fashion by the time I get to wear it. And that wretched Alice hasn't replied to my letter. Two weeks and nothing.'

Jessie hadn't heard from Mrs Handley at Sedgecroft either, but she didn't say so. She just picked up the blouse and said, 'You look lovely in it, though. That pink is your colour. I'm sure you'll get to wear it, and everyone will admire you in it. And there's your mauve silk with all the flounces.'

'I don't want to look like a schoolgirl. I want something — dramatic, something modern. Like this —' Caroline picked up the newspaper that was on her dressing table. 'See that lovely dress in the picture? It has a silver collar, apparently. And look at the length — to the calf, and chiffon sleeves. But when would I wear such a thing? No one has any dances here. Oh, life is such a bore.' The newspaper was tossed onto the floor.

It was like dealing with one of the children at the school, Jessie thought, always having to say something to distract her, to make promises about tomorrow or the next day to coax her out of the sulks. Not that she minded. She enjoyed watching Caroline dress up and admire herself in the mirror, but the sulky mouth didn't lift this time.

'Shall I wash your hair? I could beat an egg with water to give it a lovely shine, or we could use vinegar.'

'Oh, the smell.'

'We'd rinse it off with rosewater or your toilet water. Just think, your hair, your wrists, behind your ears — all with that lovely scent. Shall I put the tongs in the fire?'

'Oh, I don't know — I'm not sure that curls suit me, and the tongs get so hot. You oughtn't leave them so long.'

'I could plait your hair and make a crown on your head?'

'Maybe...' Caroline was examining the blouse. 'Everything is so dull. No one ever comes — not even to tea, never mind supper.' Then she looked up, smiling again. 'I know what. Let me dress you up. It'll be fun. We can pretend you're going to a party.'

Jessie was horrified at the thought. She wasn't a doll. 'I can't. Mrs Cobb will be wanting me soon.'

'Pah — it won't take long. Come on, Jessie, take off that hideous cap first. Let's see your hair.'

In a moment the cap was off, and Jessie was pushed down onto the stool before the mirror and Caroline was wielding the brush. Jessie had washed her hair in the bath a couple of days ago, so she wasn't ashamed that it was too dirty for Caroline to handle. She'd almost forgotten what it was like to see her hair down. She bundled it up under the cap or tied it with a bit of string at night. But now it fell below her shoulders in a pale mass.

'Your hair's really lovely, Jessie. I like blonde hair. Men like it, they say. I wonder if I should dye mine?'

'Oh, no, Miss, yours is a lovely colour, and so shiny.'

Caroline looked in the mirror. 'You're right. I don't suppose blonde would suit me. It would be awful if the dye made it fall out or something. Now, let's concentrate on you. Just try the blouse — off with that apron. You can button the blouse over your dress.'

It was easier — and quicker — to do as she was told. Caroline sat her down again and tied up her hair with a pink ribbon, making a curly knot on the crown of her head.

'Bite your lips. It makes them redder, and here —' Caroline leaned over and pinched Jessie's cheeks — 'it's what the girls do at school. See, it brings out the colour of your eyes — such dark blue. Unusual, I think. Do men prefer blue to brown, though?'

'I don't know, Miss, but your eyes are lovely. Like brown velvet.'

'Oh, you do say sweet things, Jessie.' Caroline opened her eyes very wide as she gazed in the mirror. 'Now look at yourself. See what I've done.'

Jessie couldn't help smiling at her own reflection — the girl in the mirror was no longer a drudging kitchen maid. Her lips looked fuller, and her cheeks were glowing. And, it was true, the colour of her eyes was somehow bluer. She saw the old Jessie. The Jessie who had worn a broad ribbon to tie back her hair. The Jessie who had been top of the class. The Jessie who had wanted to be a schoolmistress and learn Latin.

'Oh, you do look pretty, Jessie. That pink is really your —'

The door opened to reveal a red-faced Mrs Cobb, breathing heavily as if she had rushed up the stairs. Jessie stood up, horrified, conscious of the pink blouse and the ribbon in her hair.

But Mrs Cobb didn't look at her. It was Caroline she wanted. 'You're wanted. Mr Alexander — a policeman. Mr Charles is—'

Mrs Cobb hurried off. Caroline's face was ashen as she turned to Jessie. 'Oh, God, not Charles. Come with me — come!'

Caroline was down the stairs in seconds, and Jessie arrived at the bottom of the steps in time to see her fling herself at one of the two young men in military uniform. 'Charles,' she cried, 'I thought — Mrs Cobb said a policeman —'

'Steady, steady,' the young man said, holding her off. 'Nothing wrong with us. But there is bad news —'

'If we could go somewhere — the lady'll want to sit down,' the accompanying policeman said.

'Oh, Constable Birks, yes, perhaps the drawin' room. Jessie, get that kettle —' Mrs Cobb looked at her as if for the first time. 'Gracious, what on earth are you wearin'?'

Jessie felt the blood rush to her cheeks as everyone turned to look at her. What a fool she felt wearing the blouse over her dress and the curls on top of her head.

'Who's this?' the man Caroline had addressed as Charles asked.

'The new kitchen maid,' replied Mrs Cobb. 'Though what she's doin' dressed up like a dog's dinner, I don't know.'

'I was trying it on her to see what it looked like,' Caroline snapped, 'but it hardly matters just now. What is going on?'

'Come into the drawing room, Caroline. Mrs Cobb, can we have tea, and is there a fire?'

'Jessie'll light it.'

Charles seemed to be in command. The other young man in uniform didn't say anything. 'No, I will. You two get the tea and bring it quickly.'

Jessie didn't dare speak, but she obeyed when Mrs Cobb said, 'Take that thing off and get that ribbon out. You look a sight. I don't know what Miss Caroline was thinkin', and you lettin' her dress you up. I knew no good would come of it. Get on with that tray. I'm gettin' back to the drawin' room. I want to know what's goin' on with that policeman.'

Jessie was glad to be alone. She had to wait for the kettle, which gave her time to take out the ribbon and stuff it in her pocket, then gather up her hair quickly and tie it back with a bit of sting from the drawer. She dared not go upstairs for her apron and cap, but she straightened her dress, put on a clean apron, and took in the tray. As she entered, Caroline was sitting on the sofa with the young man who must be Alexander. Mrs Cobb was perched on a chair by a table, while Charles was standing by the fireplace. The policeman was looking at him.

'Don't get upset, Caroline, nor you, Mrs Cobb. You'll have to know and it's best you know now. Ethel Widdop has been found dead in Hag Wood. Alexander and I found her. We were on our way here from the station. That's all we know. We went for Constable Birks at Crossgill. He wants to ask Mrs Cobb about Ethel — if she's seen her about at all.'

Jessie froze in the doorway, gripping the tray. She could hardly take it in. Ethel was dead. She waited for Mrs Cobb to speak, terrified that the policeman might ask her if she'd seen Ethel. She couldn't say that she had met her in the tower over a week ago. She couldn't say that she had planned to run away with Ethel's help. Or that Ethel had said she had a message for Charles. No one would believe her — two kitchen maids making up stories about a gentleman like Charles. And one of them had been sacked for being cheeky.

'Bring in the tea, Jessie,' Charles said. 'We all need some. Mrs Cobb will pour.'

Jessie put down the tray and waited to hand round the cups. She felt her face flaming again, and in the silence the cups seemed to rattle too loudly in the saucers. The noise of the constable's slurping was awful. She dared not look at anyone, but she had to look up when she handed a cup to Charles. He smiled at her and thanked her. Alexander took his cup and she saw how his hand shook, but he didn't look at her.

'Now, Mrs Cobb,' Birks began when he had put down his cup on a side table where there was no mat. Jessie saw Mrs Cobb frown. 'Tell me about Ethel Widdop. When did you last see her?'

'The day Jessie came. Middle of September — the fifteenth, it was. Ethel came for wages owed an' I told her not to come back.'

'Sacked her, did you?'

'I did. A week before. She wanted to leave. Had somethin' lined up, she told me. And I wasn't sorry, I can tell you. Far too cheeky, Ethel Widdop, and she didn't want to do her work.'

'Did she say what she had lined up?'

'Not as such. Some nonsense, I expect. I wouldn't be surprised if there was a man in it somewhere. Too forward by half. Anyway, it wasn't my business. I'd Jessie coming, so Ethel Widdop could go to the —'

Charles interrupted. 'Mrs Cobb, the poor girl's dead. We mustn't blacken her reputation.'

Birks addressed Mrs Cobb again. 'You think she was walking out with some fellow?'

'Just a feelin' — she was always lookin' at herself in mirrors, fiddlin' with her hair, an' she changed her dress when she went out — supposedly for a walk to her pa's. Joe Widdop, the ferryman, lives at Cowpot Cottage.'

They seemed to have forgotten Jessie was present. She pressed herself into the doorframe, as if that might make her invisible. She felt sick at the thought of Mrs Cobb drawing attention to her, scolding her for hanging about doing nothing. Then the constable would ask if she knew anything about

Ethel. Her face would surely give her away. She'd never been any good at lying. Yet she couldn't go out in case that made the constable look at her. She thought about the kindly ferryman and wondered if Charles or Alexander had told him of his daughter's death. Ethel hadn't told her about a sweetheart, and then there was that message for Mr Charles. She hardly dared breathe and she felt her face flame again when she looked up to see Charles's eyes on her.

Birks turned his attention to Miss Caroline. Jessie was surprised to hear her tell him that she had thought Ethel was quite happy to act as her personal maid. 'She was coming along nicely.'

'And she didn't mention a sweetheart to you?'

'No, constable. She was a servant — I don't encourage that sort of confidence. Why, is it important?' Caroline put her hand to her mouth. 'Oh, you think someone — oh, how horrible — I rather liked her —' She looked at Charles. 'What did you see, Charles?'

'Nothing, Caroline, only that Ethel was lying there. Alexander and I know a dead body when we see —'

A queer sort of cracking noise and what sounded like a stifled sob caused Jessie to swivel her head to the sofa. Alexander was staring down at the crushed teacup in his hand, his shoulders heaving. There was blood dripping onto the carpet.

'Alexander, what is it?' Caroline asked.

Charles was quick off the mark. 'Constable, I think that's enough. You are aware, no doubt, that Lieutenant de Moine has just come from the Front — what we saw — well — and this… I'll answer any questions, but let the others leave.'

Constable Birks looked appalled at the weeping Alexander. 'Of course, sir. I'm sorry to have caused such distress.'

'Mrs Cobb, please take Mr Alexander upstairs, and — er — Jessie, is it?' Jessie nodded. 'Take Miss Caroline to her room.'

Mrs Cobb took Alexander by the arm and led him to the door. Jessie stepped to one side and as she looked at him, he looked back at her. His eyes had no light in them, as if holding a secret that couldn't be shared.

9

The inquest brought in a verdict of "Murder by Person or Persons Unknown". Ethel Widdop had been hit with a heavy stone, so the evidence said. The police had concluded that the victim had fallen or been pushed, and her assailant had brought down the stone several times to kill her. The medical evidence suggested that she had been dead for a few hours when she was found, though it was not possible to be exact about these things. A post-mortem also revealed that she had been pregnant at the time of her death. Mrs Cobb gave her evidence that she believed Ethel to have been involved with a young man. When she had left Moonlyght, Ethel had told Mrs Cobb that she had something else "lined up", but the housekeeper was unable to say more than that. She told the court that Ethel had been sacked because she was not doing her work properly. She thought Ethel was dissatisfied with her lowly position.

Lieutenant Charles Bennett gave evidence of finding the body as he and his cousin, Second Lieutenant Alexander de Moine, were returning to Moonlyght for a few days' leave from the Western Front. Lieutenant Bennett knew Miss Widdop only as a servant in his cousin's house. He could not say anything about her personal life. He regretted that Lieutenant de Moine was unable to attend the inquest. His health had suffered during the recent intense period of action at the Front — and an old leg injury had flared up. A shrapnel wound — he was sure the coroner would understand that. His doctor had ordered bed rest for a week. The coroner expressed his hope that Second Lieutenant de Moine would soon be fighting fit. Lieutenant Bennett assured the court that his cousin wanted only to return to duty. A written statement from Lieutenant de Moine was read to the court, which repeated the evidence of the finding of the body with Lieutenant Bennett and explaining that his absence from home meant that he had no knowledge of the deceased other than that he had recognised her as a servant of the household at Moonlyght.

Miss Caroline Mason, ward of Lady Emmeline de Moine, told the court that during the summer holidays Miss Widdop had sometimes helped her with her clothes and hair. She did think that Miss Widdop was unhappy with her main role as kitchen maid; however, she could say nothing about the maid's personal life. She had been surprised to learn that Ethel Widdop had been dismissed, but, of course, she trusted Mrs Cobb's judgement — they all did.

The coroner adverted to Lady Emmeline's invalid status, which precluded her giving any evidence. She was looked after by her devoted nurse who had nothing to do with the employment or dismissal of servants, which matters were left to the housekeeper, Mrs Cobb, whom the coroner thanked for her evidence.

It was clear, he concluded, that the young woman had been conducting a liaison with an unknown person. That she was expecting a child confirmed this, but there was no evidence of who this might be. The deceased's father could give no information on that matter. He had admitted that his daughter could be headstrong, and he knew that she had not liked working as a kitchen maid at Moonlyght. He was sorry that she had been dismissed, but she had always been a good daughter to him, a widower. She had said she was looking for work — there was a shell factory in Carlisle. Ethel had thought to try there.

The coroner made no mention of this in his summing up. He expressed his sorrow that the unfortunate young woman had been so foolish as to enter into an illicit relationship which had led to her untimely death. However, he was sure that the police would continue with their enquiries, which he believed would take them to friends and acquaintances of Miss Widdop in the hamlet of Mossgarth and the village of Crossgill and its railway station, where there was a number of men employed. Though, he concluded, it would be a difficult task, given that it was a busy line with passengers travelling north to join the Carlisle line, and goods trains bringing men from the Ingleton collieries and limestone quarries.

All this Jessie pieced together from what Caroline told her and what she read in the local newspaper which Mrs Cobb, called away to minister to Alexander, had inadvertently left on the kitchen table. There had been no need for Jessie to attend the inquest. Charles had assured her of that. He had waylaid her as she was coming out of Caroline's room. She had left her lying on her bed, looking pale and shocked. 'It's too ghastly for words — poor Alexander, and poor Charles, too, finding her like that.' Not a word about poor Ethel.

'Don't look so anxious, Jessie. You've nothing to worry about,' Charles said, looking at her so intently that the tell-tale flush rose at her neck. 'I explained to Birks that you arrived after Ethel was dismissed. It'll be an ordeal for all of us, but it's nothing to do with you, or any of us, for that matter. It's best forgotten.' He must have seen some doubt in her face, for he added, 'Of course it's very sad — tragic, really. I'm sure the police will do their best, but we can't do anything more for her. And Alexander has enough to deal with without worrying about Ethel. Promise me you'll put it out of your mind?'

Jessie had managed a faint, 'Yes, sir.' Afterwards, she had felt puzzled. Charles was very kind, but he didn't seem to care much about Ethel. It was over as far as he was concerned. And he had no idea that she had known Ethel, did he? She thought of him looking at her as she was pressed against the door. He'd looked as if he was weighing her up. And he'd asked her to promise to forget. Why would he do that? She was only the kitchen maid.

She could understand his concern regarding Alexander. They must have seen terrible things, worse than Ethel lying dead in the wood.

But she couldn't forget Ethel. When she had read the account of the inquest, her first reaction had been one of horror — the thought of Ethel being beaten about the head made her feel sick. It sounded so violent, as if the killer had hated her. This had been followed by shock. Ethel had been expecting a baby. She hadn't mentioned a sweetheart, but there had been that message for Charles. Jessie couldn't help but think of Mrs Cobb's words about Ethel being forward and making eyes at Charles, but Ethel had said the message for Charles was about someone else and that she'd things she needed to do before she could come back to meet Jessie. Maybe she was meeting her sweetheart. Maybe it was someone Charles knew. That might be it: Charles didn't want to say because that person might be the one who had killed Ethel.

No one really cared about Ethel. From what Jessie had read, even the coroner had been more sympathetic about Alexander, the brave injured soldier, and the invalid Lady Emmeline de Moine, than he had about Ethel. And Charles had looked so tall and handsome in his uniform as he and Caroline had left for the inquest. He seemed to shine, from the toes of his boots to the top button of his jacket. It was called a service dress uniform, Caroline had told her — they didn't fight in those clothes. No wonder the coroner had been impressed. And they were gentry, of course, and Ethel only a servant who had got herself into trouble.

Caroline told her a bit about the inquest, but she, too, seemed to want to put it away. Jessie was puzzled by Caroline's contradictory opinions about Ethel. She had said she was surprised that Ethel had been dismissed, but had said something quite different to Mrs Cobb. No one seemed to tell the truth. It didn't seem fair on Ethel, but, Jessie reflected guiltily, she hadn't told the truth either.

'I know it's awful,' Caroline said, seeing Jessie's stricken face, 'but when you read about the war in the paper, you can't help thinking that her suffering isn't as terrible as it is for the soldiers out on the Somme. I read a few months ago that there were more than fifty thousand casualties on one day. I mean, poor Ethel, but — well, she sort of got herself into a mess, didn't she?'

Jessie couldn't answer. She was no longer thinking of Ethel. *Fifty thousand soldiers.* Where was Josh?

10

'It's too late now. We've given our evidence. We didn't know anything. You didn't know — when I — oh, stop this — the girl's dead. For God's sake, Alexander, pull yourself together. Put it out of your mind. We've other things to contend with in a few days.'

The connecting door was open and when Jessie went into Charles's room to clear out the ashes, she could hear him. The same words he had used to her. Alexander was out of bed after the inquest, but he barely spoke, even though Charles and Caroline had tried to cheer him up with music and cards in the evenings. Caroline had worn the Crepe de Chine blouse for dinner, which Jessie had helped to serve, but Alexander barely looked at her and only moved his food around his plate.

Charles had represented the de Moine family at the funeral. Naturally, women did not go, certainly not a kitchen maid who had not known Ethel. It turned out that the de Moine estate owned Cowpot Cottage — and most of Mossgarth hamlet, too. After his daughter's burial, Joe Widdop was seen no more.

Alexander was speaking now. Jessie remained where she was, not daring to pick up her shovel. Besides, she was curious.

'She was alive … those golden eyes full of light. And then she was dead in that wood. Her eyes —'

Charles was becoming impatient. 'Stop it, I tell you. She was a bloody servant, Alexander, golden eyes or not. We can't do anything about it. It's over — it has to be. And we've seen worse — a lot worse.'

'You weren't there on that day in July — you didn't see — a hundred of us lost. The colonel, the Kendal lads: Atkinson, Baines, Seddon, Nash — Nash just eighteen years old, and Gibson missing. And the rest. You weren't on the Leipzig Salient raid when Barnes was killed —'

'I was at Aveluy, Ovillers, Pozieres — it was slaughter... For God's sake, I'm not getting into this. It's not a bloody competition. I couldn't help being in England on that day.'

'I was fighting for them, and the people here in Mossgarth, our people on our land. Decent people like Joe Widdop — where's he gone? Into the dark. A broken man. And it's my —'

'Widdop chose to go. He chose to take the money — what else was there to do?'

'He lost his daughter. Ethel was one of us and now she's dead. It's all pointless, useless. We're wrecked. Everything's wrecked. This place says it all — the tower's a ruin, the woods are rotting. That woman in her bed up there. She won't do anything about the house — it's nearly a ruin, too. "Jonathan," she said when I went up. She didn't even look at me. It's still my fault — it was my fault.'

'It was an accident, for God's sake — the inquest said so.'

'Was it? How do I know any more? She believes I killed him. Perhaps I did. I saw him, his dead eyes looking up at the moon. Was that the last thing he saw? Did he think of Moonlyght — the legacy of courage and gallantry, and did he know that he was a —'

'Stop it! It's rubbish. She's half mad — and you will be too if you don't stop torturing yourself.'

'She'd rather the place fell down than my inheriting. She won't believe it. She couldn't stand it if I came back. When are we to go, Charles? I'd rather be in that wreck then this one.'

'We can be away to London tomorrow — if you're fit.'

'I don't care if I'm not.'

'Then I'll start packing and you do the same. Anything to get away from here. Shift yourself, and we'll take Caroline for a walk.'

Jessie tip-toed to the other door, where she fetched her coal scuttle from outside and came back in to see that Charles was back in his own room, the connecting door closed.

'The ashes, sir.'

'Oh, yes, carry on.'

Jessie darted to the fireplace where she'd left her shovel and bucket. She hoped he hadn't seen it and realised she had already been in the room. She set about clearing the grate, feeling his eyes upon her, hearing him strike a match to light his cigarette.

She almost dropped her shovel when he asked, 'Are you happy here, Jessie?'

She had no idea what to say. How could she be happy? Ma was dead, home was gone, and for all she knew Josh might have been one of the fifty thousand killed on one day. She couldn't say any of those things. 'I'm all right, sir.'

'It's just, well, you sometimes look very sad. I know that you are related to Mrs Cobb, but where is your family?'

Jessie carried on sweeping the hearth. 'Near a place called Gressthwaite — a farm, Swarthgill.'

'And how do you come to be here at Moonlyght?'

'My mother was ill — she wanted me settled.'

'No sweetheart back at the farm?'

That wretched blush. He'd think she had someone. But she didn't — only Will Beswick, and that hadn't been real. Just holding hands. She kept her head down.

There was a smile in his voice. 'Someone called Josh? Caroline tells me you're spoken for.'

Caroline couldn't even remember that Josh was her brother. That's how much she cared. She felt the tears well up and then Charles's hand on her arm, helping her to her feet.

'I'm sorry, Jessie. I didn't mean to upset you. Is your sweetheart at the Front?'

'Josh is my brother. I don't know where he is…' And the tears spilled over. She found herself sobbing and Charles's arm about her. He was the first person to have touched her or offered any comfort since Josh had gone away. Her last embrace of Josh hadn't counted — he hadn't responded, and Ma had only patted her on the back when she'd left home.

Charles held out his handkerchief.

'Excuse me, sir, I just wish I knew.'

'Isn't there any way you can find out? Your father?'

'He — they quarrelled. Pa didn't want Josh to join up, but Josh went anyway. Pa won't want — he won't read any letters. Josh only wrote to Ma.'

'Which regiment?'

'The Lonsdales.' She saw recognition in his eyes and was aware of the idiocy of her next words even as she blurted them out. 'Do you know him?'

He smiled. 'No, but I might be able to —'

They heard movement in the next room and then Alexander's voice called out, 'Charles, come in here, will you?'

Charles put a finger to his lips and whispered, 'Later — meet me, just inside the wood — when Mrs Cobb is resting. I'll have a think.'

He went through to Alexander's room and closed the door. Jessie started to lay the fire. Of course he knew the regiment. It was local. Josh had joined the Lonsdales in Kendal with the other lads. Her heart lifted. Charles would find out and she could write to Josh, and he would write to her.

And the man who had killed Ethel — maybe he was a soldier and that was why Ethel had wanted to send a message to Charles. Maybe he was in Charles's regiment.

11

The tower was the only place Jessie could think of to hide. She was afraid of it, but she dared not go into the house. Her legs trembled and her heart beat too fast. She couldn't face Mrs Cobb like this, nor Caroline for that matter.

Charles had been waiting as he had said, just inside the cover of the first trees. She nearly missed him as she stepped into the shadows, but he reached out and pulled her into the shade of the tree under which he stood. He didn't let her go at first and she felt his strong arm steadying her. She wanted to pull away — it didn't seem right, but she didn't want to offend him.

'Alexander knows your brother — he didn't make the connection, but then so much has happened. The 11th Battalion Border Regiment is Alexander's regiment; Josh serves with his pals in the same C Company of the Lonsdale Battalion, under a Captain Bridges. Alexander is a second lieutenant.'

'Josh is alive?'

'I'm sure he is — the battalion is behind the lines just now, in reserve, before the next big push. That's why we've to go back tomorrow, but Alexander'll take a letter and make sure your brother gets it and knows where you are. You can send him something if you like —'

Jessie stared at him. What could she send except her love? 'I don't — I didn't know — can I do that?'

'Oh, yes, all men get parcels from home —'

'Not Josh — nothing —'

'Never mind, now. You can put it right later. You can knit something, or send a cake, Bovril, Oxo cubes —' he smiled at her astonished look — 'they improve the taste of soup no end, or tobacco — a book, maybe. Is he a reader, your Josh?'

Her heart sang. She had the flower book with all the pretty illustrations that Josh had given her, bought with his own money. He'd know she still loved him if she sent that.

'Could I send a book — would Mr Alexander take it tomorrow?'

'I'm sure he could, if you bring it to me early tomorrow morning.'

'Oh, thank you, sir, thank you. Can I go now? Mrs Cobb will wonder where I've been if I'm late.'

'You've a few minutes yet. I want to ask you something — about Ethel.'

'But I didn't — I don't —'

'I think you did know her, pretty Jessie — your face gave you away. There's something worrying you, Jessie, I can tell.'

'It's nothing, sir, only — I couldn't tell —' She looked up. He wasn't angry. He looked sorry for her. Reassured, she continued, 'I know I should have said, but I was too scared of—'

'Mrs Cobb, I know. But you needn't be scared of me. I'll bet you're worrying for nothing. I'm not going to tell on you.'

'Ethel was going to help me leave. Ma died, you see, and I wanted to know where Josh was.'

'I am sorry, Jessie. And you were going to go away all on your own?'

'Yes, I didn't mind, but then Miss Caroline came, and Ethel said she had a message for you.'

'For me? I hardly knew her. Are you sure?'

'I don't know what she meant. She said it was about someone else.'

'Who?'

'She didn't say, sir, but I've been thinking about it. If her sweetheart was a soldier and she wanted to get a message to him about — you know —'

'Ah, the baby — she wanted to tell whoever he was about it and thought I might know him if he was a local man.'

'Mr Alexander knows Josh, so maybe…'

'You're sure she didn't mention a name?'

'I'd have remembered, sir. I know I was a coward, but I didn't think anyone would believe me and to mention your name — I couldn't have done that.'

'No, indeed, it would have complicated matters. It is a pity, though. I can't very well take it further without a name. Poor Ethel. If only she had told you. Well, there it must rest, and you have no need to worry. It'll be just between us. It's possible that the police may find out something. We'll have to hope for that.'

'Thank you, sir. You've put my mind at rest.'

'Ah, words, words, words. A goodbye kiss for a soldier is in order, I think, from a lovely girl.'

Jessie was shivering now, aware of the damp walls and the cold stone floor of the tower. That kiss — she thought he had meant a kiss on the cheek, but Charles had held her and taken off her cap so that her hair spilled down. He had turned her head and found her lips, and it had gone on too long. He had held her very close, and she dared not break free. For a few moments, she had liked his strong arms about her. She had liked his murmured compliments and the way he stroked her hair. It was only the crack of a twig along the path that had released her. He had thought someone was coming and he pushed her away. 'Quick now, back to the house.' She had run.

What must he think of her? That she was like Ethel? Jessie, the farm girl, knew very well what Ethel and her lover had done. Jessie had heard what went on in the big bed at home. And she had known what Ted Gorman wanted. But Charles was a gentleman. He wouldn't … but did he think she would? Had she seemed forward? And he'd pushed her away. The kitchen maid. No one must see him with a servant.

She stood, feeling the prickle of tears. She did not know how she would face him, but she had to take the book for Josh. Maybe she could give it to Alexander, but then he was in such a state, and Charles might be angry. Suppose he had meant nothing but kindness? He would think her ungrateful.

Just as she made up her mind to go back to the house, a noise made her jump. Someone was coming into the tower. She shrank back into the shadows, feeling for the little door. She could sneak out the back way. Her hands felt empty air. She stood, frozen into indecision. She heard footsteps on the stones and the scrape of a boot and then another heavy tread. Someone was going up the stairs to the ledge. Something fluttered about her feet, followed by an angry squawk. One of the hens had got in.

'Who's there?' It was Alexander's voice. A frightened voice.

Jessie stood still, not daring to breathe. Perhaps he would carry on up the stairs and she could escape. But why was he going up there to that dangerous ledge? She thought of that young man who'd plummeted to his death and Alexander describing his dead eyes looking at the moon. She thought of the broken teacup in Alexander's hand. She was filled with terror, but she made up her mind and stepped forward, her boot crunching the loose stones on the floor.

'Jonathan?'

The terror in his voice frightened her. 'No, sir, it's Jessie, sir. I was just after one of the hens.' She looked up and saw Alexander crouching on the worn staircase and staring upward, as if there were something above him, something which frightened him. 'Sorry, sir, I didn't mean to startle you.'

'Ethel?'

She willed her voice to be calm. 'No, sir, Jessie — the new kitchen maid.'

He stood up, still staring at the ledge above. 'Ethel's not here?'

'No, sir, just me. I'm going back to the house now to make the tea, if you would like a cup? It's very cold in here.'

'The beaches are frozen, they say — the sea is frozen at Boulogne. The grave is warmer than France. Jonathan's all right in there. He cannot come out of his grave. He didn't want — did you know Jonathan?'

'I'm new, sir.'

'Ethel had golden eyes — where is she now?'

She dared not say that Ethel was dead. She didn't know what he would do, but she did know that he ought not to be on those stairs; he ought not to climb up to the ledge from where Jonathan had fallen. 'Mrs Cobb will be waiting for me. I daren't be late, sir. I have to get the tea and you'll be wanting yours —'

'The sun was shining. The wire wasn't cut … keep the line. They kept it. Walking to… Better for Jonathan. He couldn't have… And no one knew — the wire…'

'Mr Charles and Miss Caroline will be waiting, sir.'

'Ethel and Jonathan are waiting in the dark — they're waiting for me. It won't be long.' He went up onto the next step.

'Won't you come now, sir? It's a bit dark for being on those stairs — you might slip, sir. Hot tea, sir, will be just the job.'

'Yes, that's what we have — the orderlies bring it — and the rum, of course. Bucks us up, that does. Over the top, see —'

She heard his boot scrape on the step as if he were about to move again. Jessie felt desperate. 'Please come down, sir. I don't want you to fall.'

Something in her voice stopped him and she saw the pale oval of his face looking down at her now. 'Tea, yes, of course. You'd better get off. I'll just —'

To her relief, he came down, and she saw that he was smiling. A nice smile, which changed his face. It was like Josh's face before, but Mr Alexander's eyes were still in shadow and his dark hair flopped over his forehead as if he hadn't combed it. 'You're very kind, Jessie, thank you. Yes, I'll come for that tea.'

He opened the door for her and as she went across the yard, she heard laughter. Caroline and Charles, coming in at the gate. She ran before they could see her.

Mrs Cobb was waiting, her face set. 'Where've you been, girl?'

'A hen was in the tower —'

'Oh, never mind, get that tray set. I've made some sandwiches and there are crumpets. Mr Charles has a fancy for them. Some tea cake, too. I'll make the tea. Miss Caroline'll want you upstairs, I daresay. I'll take in the tray in ten minutes. Go on, now, quick!'

Caroline was half-undressed when Jessie entered her room. There were leaves in her hair and mud on her skirt. Her face was flushed and her eyes glittering.

'Whatever…?' Jessie began.

'Slipped in the mud.' Caroline turned away, but not before Jessie saw that her flush deepened. 'Charles was very good about it; he picked me up, and only laughed a bit. I could have cried, though. I'm still blushing at the thought.'

'I'll brush the mud off and do your hair.'

'I'd better change this skirt. Oh, and there's a button off my blouse.'

Caroline chattered on while Jessie removed the leaves from her hair and pinned it up again. She seemed almost feverish.

'Right. How do I look?'

'Lovely, Miss, as always.'

'You're a darling, Jessie.'

12

Writing to a stranger. That's what it felt like. Josh seemed so far away. Where was the boy who had taught her so many things, protected her, made her laugh? Jessie tried to conjure him, but there was only the stranger in his unfamiliar uniform with the pained eyes of Mr Alexander. It was as if Josh had turned into Mr Alexander, or the other way round, as if they were the same person.

Supper in the dining room had been no different from the other evenings; the fire lit, the candles glowing, their reflections in the deep, gleaming mahogany of the table, the silver shining, and Caroline talking to Charles while Alexander sat silent, hardly touching his food. Charles had thanked her and smiled when she served his soup, but in a distant way, as if the kiss under the tree had not happened at all. She was glad to get away from them and up to her own room.

She took up her pencil again. What could she tell Josh? She didn't even know if he knew about Ma. She'd have to write something about that, but she couldn't tell him that she was lonely and unhappy when he was facing such terrible danger. Charles did not seem to be so affected by the war. No shadows in his eyes, like Alexander. He had said that the wire wasn't cut. What wire, she wondered?

In the newspaper Mrs Cobb had left on the kitchen table, she'd seen the words "Roll of Honour" and a list of names — twenty, perhaps, all killed or missing, and three grainy photographs of three young men. One was twenty, the same age as Josh when he had joined up. Just a boy. She thought about those faces now, so young, so serious, and yet ordinary

— like the faces she used to see in Gressthwaite. The farmer's lad, the one that used to sell veg at the market, the one who used to wink at her, and the shepherd lad who drove his sheep up the street and whistled to his dog, and the boy who worked at the draper's — he wore specs and had very small, white hands. He wore a neat grey shop coat. Surely, he couldn't be out there. He might be dead.

No, she could only tell Josh that she was working hard. The work wasn't too bad. She found the writing easier when she had got over the news of Ma's death and had told Josh about Pa's letter which meant she couldn't go home.

She told him about Moonlyght, and Lady Emmeline and Nurse whom she rarely saw, and Mrs Cobb, Ma's cousin, who was all right, and Miss Caroline whose clothes and hair she looked after. She was almost a lady's maid…

How to end? She put down the pencil. Her writing looked so childish in pencil. After washing up the supper dishes, she had slipped into the library, where she had seen envelopes and paper. She dared not take any ink, and she hadn't a pen anyway. She'd had to write to Mrs Handley in pencil. Why hadn't she replied? No one had noticed her going into the library. She could hear music and high-pitched laughter from the drawing room — Caroline was enjoying herself at least.

She thought about what to write — that she missed him and hoped that he was all right. She hoped that he would like to look at the flower pictures in their book, and she would send parcels now that she knew where to send them…

In the meantime, dearest Josh, this comes with all my love and best wishes. I hope you keep safe and have some time to look at the pictures, and think of your sister.
    Jess

She wrapped the book in used brown paper from the kitchen drawer and wrote Josh's name in large capital letters so Alexander wouldn't forget. But how to get it to him? She couldn't go to his room. Oh, Lord, what to do? It would have to be at breakfast. Charles would be there, but it wouldn't matter. She wouldn't be alone with him.

Jessie snuffed out her candle and watched the moon. The moon must know where Josh was. It must be shining down on him now. 'Look after him,' she whispered. 'Watch him with that great silver eye.' Foolish, she knew, but it was a prayer and that was all she had to offer. But the moon looked cold and so far away. How could it care about her or all the young men out there? She thought of the moon looking down on a battlefield, then sailing on like a ship in a picture she'd seen, leaving behind a wreck of lost souls. Perhaps Josh was watching the moon sailing away, too, from behind the lines. Charles had said he was sure that Josh was alive. But they were waiting for the next big push... Her heart seemed to miss a beat at that thought. Josh was all she had.

She pulled the covers almost over her head and turned over to try to sleep, and then from above she heard the footsteps again, a heavier tread this time. A man's tread. It wasn't Lady Emmeline. It was Alexander then, pacing back and forth across his dead brother's room.

13

Jessie was taking her parcel to the dining room. Alexander was in the hall, looking up at the knights at arms in the window and the three moons gleaming greenly in the morning light.

'Knights of old, eh, Jessie? With their helmets and their plumes and their motto. The light that shines in darkness. The moon, see. Not content with one, though. Good God, if only they knew — no light — I'm sorry, Jessie. I'm sorry about yesterday.'

He looked as tired as she felt. She seemed to have listened all night to those steps, back and forth, back and forth. She must have fallen asleep for an hour or two, but she woke as usual. It was still dark, of course, but Jessie always woke before she heard the faint chime of the hall clock telling her it was six.

'That's all right, sir. Mr Charles said you could take a letter to my brother — he's in C Company, sir.'

'Josh Sedgwick, yes,' said Alexander, looking at the name on the parcel. 'Good man. He and I — alive when... Yes, of course — a book, is it?'

'About flowers, sir, I thought Josh would like —'

'The English countryside — yes, yes, I'm sure he would. Home, yes, good. Flowers —' that lost look again — 'the flowers of the forest all wasting away in Authuille Wood ... lost forever —' He looked at her again. 'There are violets hiding in the woods in spring. Pick some for me. Remember me then —'

They heard voices. Charles and Caroline at the top of the stairs.

'Goodbye, sir — and good luck,' said Jessie.

He nodded. 'I'll make sure your brother gets his book.'

Jessie vanished into the screens passage, where she stopped to listen.

'Breakfast, Alexander — you must eat something before you go,' Caroline said.

'All right, maybe I'll have some toast.'

Jessie went back to the kitchen to wait. She'd give them twenty minutes or so and they'd go back into the hall and collect the luggage. Mr Wiggins's trap was coming at nine to take them to the station, where they'd catch the train to London. She heard the hall clock strike the hour and went to wait in the screens passage.

Caroline was talking. 'A cake from Mrs Cobb, socks from Nurse for both of you — a bit knobbly in parts, but warm. Proper oiled wool, she says, from Kendal, and cigarettes from me. Oh, what's in that parcel, Alexander?'

'It's for Jessie's brother — she handed it to me before you came downstairs. He's in my company.'

'Oh — it looks like a book. What a funny thing to send — I mean, you'd think she'd send something more practical.'

'I shouldn't think she could afford cigarettes, Caroline,' Charles said. 'She didn't know she could send anything.'

'How do you know that?'

'Because I asked her. The book is probably all she has to send. All the lads like things from home. You ought to take her shopping so that she can get cigarettes or chocolate or something. And you can give her my best wishes.'

'And mine,' Alexander said. 'Josh Sedgwick is one of my lads.'

From the dining room window, Jessie watched them go. Caroline hugged them both. Alexander stood stiffly in her arms like Josh, she thought. He climbed into the trap. Charles kissed Caroline on both cheeks and shook Mrs Cobb's hand, and then they were rolling away, both women waving until the trap was out of sight. Charles waved, too, but Alexander looked straight ahead.

Caroline found Jessie in the dining room. 'They sent their best wishes,' she said. 'I didn't know you'd spoken to Charles.'

'When I was clearing the ashes, he asked about my family. I told him Josh was in the Lonsdale Regiment, so he asked Mr Alexander, who said he'd take a letter and the book. They are very kind.'

'Yes, they are. I'll miss them — it's been fun, having Charles to walk with. Alexander is a bit down in the dumps, though.'

'I suppose he's seen things — horrible things, and to come home to Ethel's death —'

'Well, they didn't really know her, did they? It's a shame, but — let's not talk about it. I know — Kirkby Lonsdale has good shops. I could take you. You might want to get some things for your brother — cigarettes, chocolate?' Jessie's heart leapt at the thought of her ten shillings. There had been penny bars of chocolate in the grocer's shop in Gressthwaite. She could afford to spend a shilling. She opened her mouth to ask what cigarettes would cost, but Caroline was still rattling on: 'We could take that ferry — oh, that was Ethel's father, wasn't it? I wonder if someone else runs it now. A nuisance if it isn't running. We'd have to order the trap. Why do we have to live in such an out-of-the-way place? It really is inconvenient.'

Of course, they didn't go shopping. The idea went right out of Caroline's head when she received a letter from her friend, Alice Herd, who lived near Manchester. Caroline was invited for Christmas — not that there would be a ball. Parties, she was sure. Alice's father was an important manufacturer with pots of money, Caroline told Jessie. They'd have to look at her clothes. Jessie was good with her needle. Maybe they could make something of that mauve silk. She wasn't sure that all those flounces were quite the thing. Something of Lady Em's, perhaps, could be re-modelled. Lady Emmeline had always had very fine silk. Nurse would let her have something, Caroline was sure.

Jessie sewed a button onto the blouse and cleaned the mud from the skirt. She didn't say anything about them to Caroline — it wasn't her place. Her place was to launder the petticoats, delicate camisoles and silk stockings, not to wonder how they had been torn. She told Caroline how lovely she looked in Lady Em's pale green silk, from which Jessie had removed the bustle and the sleeves. She had also shortened it to ten inches from the ground to make it a copy of an evening dress in a magazine.

And when Jessie had some time to herself, she took up the knitting needles and wool. At least she could send socks, even a scarf to keep Josh warm. Caroline had begged the wool from Nurse on the grounds that she wanted to knit for Charles and Alexander. Perhaps Jessie could knit socks for Charles and Alexander as well as her brother — while Caroline was away in Manchester. There was no mention of Jessie going with Caroline as her lady's maid.

The first snow came near the time of Caroline's departure at the end of the second week in December. Caroline was all of a jitter, supposing that she might be prevented from going, supposing that the train would not be running, supposing that the trap would not come, supposing that Alice might tell her it was impossible to travel. Jessie watched the sky, hoping that Caroline would be able to go. She thought she'd go mad if she had to listen to any more wails of anguish. 'There's a war on,' she wanted to say, but she didn't. The sky cleared after a few days, and the trap came, and Jessie was glad to see the back of her.

14

'Where's Missus?' the taciturn farmer, Simon Turner, asked Jessie, who had come out to take in the eggs and vegetables.

'Mrs Cobb is laid low, I'm afraid. Bad chest.'

'Tha'll have thy work cut out, then.'

'Yes, but I don't mind.'

He looked at her shrewdly. 'Bit o' peace an' quiet, I daresay. Want any wood choppin' or coal bringin' in? Tha'll have a few fires to keep in. If I can do aught, tha's only to ask.'

Jessie was surprised at his kindness. She had always thought his long face rather intimidating, but his blue eyes were looking at her sympathetically. 'I could do with some coal for the range — if it's not too much trouble.'

'Nay, lass. I'll bring it in so tha can fill the buckets by the range, then tha can avoid 'avin' to get the coal from that tower, an' I'll clear a pathway to the gate.'

And he did, telling her again to ask if she needed aught else, and when he had gone, she felt her loneliness assuaged for a while.

Then it was freezing again with a bitter wind from the northeast, and Mrs Cobb sneezed and coughed and looked flushed. Nurse sent down for some beef tea, and her hacking cough followed Jessie down the corridor after she had delivered it. Then the snow came in earnest, in great flurries borne by the wind, blurring the kitchen window, and gathering on the back step.

Mrs Cobb's cough worsened, and Nurse took to her bed, too — both with bad chests. Fortunately, Doctor Kennedy had been on his regular visit to Lady Emmeline and had seen straightaway that Mrs Cobb was struggling to breathe. He'd ordered her to bed when he had gone up to see his regular patient and Nurse. There was medicine in a bottle and Jessie was bidden to supply regular beef tea and stone hot water bottles. Lady Emmeline had to be looked after as well. Nurse was querulous and demanding when she was awake, and ready to doubt that Jessie was competent enough to look after her lady. 'A kitchen girl to see to my lady,' she tutted. 'You'll need to wash her down — oh, I never thought such a thing. You're not to speak of it — just do it — and be gentle. My lady's to stay in bed. Don't you be gettin' her up.' Mrs Cobb was irritable, waving Jessie away, telling her not to bother her, but she took her beef tea quietly enough.

It was a queer time of waiting and watching, waiting for the postman, or watching her patients and the snow which banked up in the yard where she had found a big pile of coal left by Farmer Turner — she blessed him silently. She didn't have to drag the scuttles from the tower. He'd delivered plenty of wood, too.

Only the doctor managed to get through on horseback. The laundry cart didn't come, so Jessie had to steep the heavy sheets in the copper in the shed outside and hang them on the rack which hung from the ceiling, but they wouldn't dry. Thankfully, there were plenty of supplies from the linen cupboard. And the postman didn't come, either, though Jessie had had a letter at the end of November from Josh, who had been very glad to hear from her. The address was just France, 11th Battalion, Border Regiment. Josh was safe and well, he told her, glad of the rest behind the lines, though there was still training and parades. The battalion was waiting for orders to march in a few days.

Jessie enjoyed a few minutes' peace before she had to take toast and tea upstairs. The letter, all creased now, was in her apron pocket. She had read it over and over:

We had a rough time back in July. A lot of our pals were killed or wounded. I don't know if you've heard from Mrs Handley, but Archie's been invalided home — a blighty one, we call it here, which means an injury that gets you home. Poor Archie lost a leg, but he'll be brave about it, I know. It could be a lot worse. I'll miss him, though. If you get a chance, you might go and see him for me.

Will Beswick and I are still all right and look out for each other. Will always shares his parcels with me and now I'll have yours to share with him. It was good of Lieutenant de Moine to bring the parcel. He's a good officer and thinks a lot about the men.

And thanks for the book, Jess. It was a good thought and I appreciated it. It's nice to look at the flowers we used to find. One day we'll do it again, so keep cheerful, and think about me. I'll look forward to your letters and parcels. Will sends his best, too.

Your loving brother,
Josh Sedgwick

A rough time in July. July was the month Alexander had mentioned when Jessie had overhead him speaking to Charles about the day that a hundred men had been lost — and Josh had been there. She thought of Alexander, his blank eyes, his disjointed sentences. *You weren't there.* Alexander had seen terrible things, and so had Josh. He couldn't write about it. There wouldn't be the words, she supposed. She knew about Archie Handley's leg. Mrs Handley had written at last, apologising for the delay. Jessie would understand. Jessie did, appalled by the idea of strong, upright Archie Handley with one leg missing. A farmer's son — how would he manage?

Josh had said it could be a lot worse. She'd rather have Josh back, even injured, than learn that he was dead.

The battalion had been waiting for orders to march. To battle, she had thought, fearing what that meant. She had written back straightaway, and Caroline promised to post it in Manchester. Jessie hoped she would remember. Her head was so full of parties and dresses, but she must have written to Charles and Alexander — she wouldn't have forgotten them.

The kettle's high whistle interrupted her thoughts. Time to visit her patients. Mrs Cobb was all right, really, just miserable and irritable. Jessie was used to that, and she could put up with Nurse's scolding. She didn't need to stay long; she'd just plump up the pillows, stir the fire, and arrange the tray on her knee. Nurse looked like a little old lady sitting in a chair while Jessie changed the bed. She wore an old-fashioned night bonnet with her grey hair dangling in two plaits on her thin shoulders. Jessie knew that she fretted about Lady Emmeline, to whom she was devoted, and she always made sure to report that her lady had taken a little toast or egg. Neither Mrs Cobb nor Nurse would accept her help to use the chamber pots, which were kept in cupboards beside the beds. She only had to leave them where they could manage them and then, of course, she had to empty them down the lavatory in the bathroom. She was used to that as well.

It was Lady Emmeline whom she found most disconcerting. She had to sit by the bed and feed her the beef tea, for Lady Emmeline wouldn't or couldn't feed herself. She didn't ask about Nurse or Mrs Cobb. Jessie had told her who she was, but Lady Emmeline had only nodded wearily and sipped at her tea. Jessie plumped up the pillows for her so that she could sit up a bit and then she helped her lie down. And every morning she had to help her with the chamber pot, and she washed her gently with a flannel. Lady Emmeline didn't seem to notice, and Jessie got over her initial embarrassment. Jessie felt sorry for her. She looked so sad and frail.

She had to make three trips up the stairs with her trays. Mrs Cobb first, to whom she reported the farmer's supply of coal and wood in the yard. She half expected Mrs Cobb to ask her if she had talked to him, but she didn't. She was feeling a bit better, she said. 'I'll be up in a few days. I could fancy some soup later.' Nurse didn't look much better and wanted to know when the doctor was coming.

'Friday,' Jessie said. 'He said he'd look in if the snow's not too bad.'

She went down again for Lady Emmeline's tray and found a nice tray cloth and a linen napkin, which she put in a silver ring. She didn't usually do this, but she thought a prettier tray might tempt Lady Emmeline to eat something.

The china was lovely, she thought, arranging a silver spoon and knife. There was a little pat of butter, too. What else could she add? A glass dish of jam, perhaps. On a whim, she took a couple of sprigs of dried lavender from the jar on the windowsill and placed them inside the napkin in its silver ring.

She helped Lady Emmeline sit up and placed the tray on her knees. Lady Emmeline stared at it as usual, as if she didn't know what it was or what she was supposed to do with it. Jessie sat on the stool and slid the napkin from the ring. The scent of lavender wafted to them.

Lady Emmeline looked at Jessie as if she were seeing her for the first time. 'Lavender,' she said.

'Yes, it's a lovely smell, isn't it?'

'Who are you?'

'Jessie, my lady, the kitchen maid.'

'Where's Nurse?'

'Feeling poorly, my lady. I've taken her some tea.'

'How long?'

'A week, and Mrs Cobb is not well, either.'

'Who is looking after them?'

'I am, my lady. The doctor's seen them and I'm giving them their medicine.'

The faded blue eyes looked puzzled. 'Where's Jonathan?'

'Mr Jonathan is away at present, my lady.'

'Oh, I see. He'll be home soon, I expect. What day is it?'

'It's Wednesday, my lady.'

'Jonathan was born on a Wednesday. Wednesday's child is full of woe. I think he is. He shouldn't go away from home. He was happy here — until —'

'Until, my lady?'

'I can't remember. There was something he had to do. He wore a uniform. Why was that?'

'Could you manage the cup, my lady? I'll hold the saucer.'

Jessie lifted one of Lady Emmeline's hands and placed the cup in it, and saw that Lady Emmeline automatically raised her other hand to cradle the cup. And then she drank.

'More?' Jessie asked. 'And perhaps a little toast and jam?'

'Yes, I think so. And then do I get up? I get up sometimes. I want to check on Jonathan, you see. He has nightmares, you know — the General says — shall I go now?'

'No, my lady, I think it's better to rest until Nurse —'

Lady Emmeline smiled vaguely, and then her face cleared for a moment. 'Oh, yes, she's poorly. Dear old Nurse.'

Jessie felt deeply sorry for her. It seemed dreadful that Lady Emmeline believed that Jonathan was still alive, that she should live like a prisoner in her own room. How different she seemed when she smiled in that puzzled way, as if there was another woman inside that fragile shell who couldn't find a way to get out.

It was another week before Mrs Cobb was fully fit, and she was quite prepared to let Jessie take the stairs with the trays for the other two. It was two weeks before Nurse was able to dismiss Jessie from Lady Emmeline's room with an impatient, 'I hope you haven't been worrying my lady with idle chatter and questions. Lady Emmeline likes it quiet. She'll not want you again, except for the fires.'

But in the time Jessie had spent with her, nearly three weeks, Lady Emmeline had made progress. She ate more and Jessie helped her out of bed to sit in the comfortable armchair by the fire, hoping that Nurse wouldn't come in and scold her for talking and allowing her mistress out of bed. Lady Emmeline talked lucidly to Jessie, mainly about Jonathan, though Jessie never dared mention that he had died. Lady Emmeline said she'd heard him in his bedroom. Why didn't he come to see her?

Jessie reassured her that Mr Jonathan was away at present with his friends. Lady Emmeline had accepted that, but she had no idea of time, and Jessie's heart was wrung with pity when she saw the lustre come back to the faded eyes when Jessie said she was sure that Mr Jonathan would be home soon. She didn't know if she was doing right, but how could she tell her that he would never come back?

She learnt a good deal about Jonathan, how sensitive he was, how he loved poetry and music, what a talent he had for the piano, how he sang like an angel, how he had been frightened of his father, the General, who had never understood him. The General had wanted his son to join the army — the family tradition. 'The army,' Lady Emmeline repeated, her cheeks burning so much that Jessie worried that she had let her talk too much. Her role was to listen, to murmur soothingly, and when the blood fired in the pale face, she would say, 'Time to rest, my lady. You mustn't overdo it.' And she would dab cologne on her temples and help her back to bed. Then she would sit until Lady Emmeline slept.

And during the long evenings while she knitted, she wondered about the lad with the voice of an angel who had fallen from that great height in the tower. He had been due to go back to the Front — Jessie knew that, and when she thought about Alexander and Josh, she wondered what Alexander had seen and if the fall was an accident, or if he had done it on purpose as the gossip had said. Lady Emmeline never mentioned Alexander, but perhaps he knew. Perhaps he felt guilty that he hadn't been able to save his brother. She thought that somehow the deaths of Jonathan and Ethel and the lads at the Front had all become mingled in Alexander's mind. His eyes were so full of shadows and that peculiar blankness sometimes — like his mother's. Lady Emmeline's eyes were blank again when Jessie cleared the ashes and lit the fire. She had found the dried sprigs of lavender in the ashes. Nurse had thrown them away.

PART TWO: 1917

15

Caroline came back in the New Year with a new jewelled bracelet on her wrist and a good many parcels.

'Garnets,' Caroline told Jessie, 'a gift, a Christmas gift.'

'From a gentleman?' asked Jessie.

'That would be telling. So many gifts. Oh, it was wonderful, Jessie, like a dream. Alice's brother on leave, and a friend of his. He's at the War Office in London. Not at the Front, I'm glad to say. What a sell that would be if he was always abroad...'

Jessie looked at the profusion of things on the bed: two new dresses, what looked like a dressing gown, a silk scarf, handkerchiefs, scented soaps, a bottle of perfume, and a pair of white kid gloves.

Not at the Front. Lucky man at the War Office, she thought. The Lonsdales were on the front line. Caroline had remembered to post her letter, and Josh had replied telling her that the weather had been awful, the mud was up to their knees, and it was bitterly cold. There wasn't much to eat, either. They'd come under heavy fire — bombardment, he called it — from the German artillery, but they'd taken some ground. The Germans were a cowardly lot, pretending to surrender and then dropping to the ground so that some of the British men were shot. He and Will Beswick were all right and glad to get back to the billets behind the lines. On Christmas Day they'd had Church Parade and a goodish dinner with plum pudding. And he'd been so glad to get her parcel — the condensed milk was a treat, and the Oxo cubes. Will sent his thanks, too — dead keen on an Oxo cube in hot water was Will. These, and the tin of condensed milk, Jessie had begged from Mrs Cobb, who'd supposed it'd be all right. Josh had written that the battalion would be back in the trenches in January...

Caroline was handing her a parcel. 'I didn't know what to get you, Jessie, but — it's for you, of course —' Jessie looked at the parcel, neatly wrapped in tissue paper and tied with ribbon — 'I didn't expect Mrs Cobb would get you anything. Go on, open it.'

Jessie untied the red ribbon very carefully and unfolded the tissue paper to reveal a lace collar. It was lovely. 'Oh, thank you, Miss Caroline. How kind of you to think of me.'

'I know you can't wear it now, Jessie, but you will wear it someday — when your brother comes home, perhaps.'

Jessie couldn't imagine how a lace collar would fit either of her two dresses. Both looked fit for the ragman now, but it really was kind of Caroline. 'I will,' she said. 'I'll keep it safe until then.'

'I had a letter from Charles. He didn't say much, but he's safe, and being brave, I'm sure. He's a captain now in the Border Regiment.'

'Not the Lonsdales? Where Mr Alexander and my brother are?'

'I don't think so — his letter said — oh, I can't remember. Let me find it.' She unlocked her writing case and rummaged inside. There were several letters, Jessie saw. She wondered if Alexander had written to Caroline. He certainly hadn't written to his mother, or Nurse, or Lady Emmeline.

Caroline unfolded a letter. 'Here we are. Oh, yes, 5th Battalion Border Regiment. I remember now — Charles joined up in Carlisle. His father is a vicar near Keswick. Charles's mother was General de Moine's sister. She died ages ago, so Charles was often here. Rather a favourite of the General's.

You see, Charles always wanted to join the army, but neither Jonathan nor Alexander was keen. He was terribly strict, the General. Always had a soft spot for me, though. He liked a pretty girl, I think. Always treated me like a daughter. I think he'd have liked me to have married Alexander — just a feeling I had, but I don't know, Jessie. It's a pity Charles isn't the General's son. But now I wonder about —'

'Who?' asked Jessie, wondering about the bracelet at which Caroline was gazing, like a cat with cream.

'Oh, Jessie, I'm in a quandary now. Don't say a thing — promise.'

'Who could I say anything to?'

Caroline laughed. 'I know you won't say anything to Mrs Cobb or Nurse. Lady Emmeline doesn't count. She wouldn't know if I married the postman. But — if Charles or Alexander come, promise you won't —'

'Of course not, they wouldn't talk to me about you.'

'Well, it's the chap from the War Office. Utterly charming and good-looking — we danced a lot and went visiting some of Alice's friends in his car. And he gave me this bracelet. Well, Alice gave it to me from him. I mean, it wouldn't do for a single man to be giving an expensive bracelet to a single woman. It's just not done. Garnets symbolise love, you know, so I rather think there's a message in this. Alice had a diamond bracelet for Christmas — they're frightfully rich, of course. But garnets, Jessie — who needs diamonds?'

'And the other things?'

Caroline picked up the red floral dressing gown. 'I bought this. It's a kimono style — the latest thing. Glamorous, don't you think? The scarf and hankies are from Alice's mother, the scent and soap from Alice — she knows what I like, and the dresses were Alice's. She said they suited me better than her.

Hardly worn and a bit on the small side for Alice. She's become rather plump.'

'Does she have a sweetheart?'

'Oh, Jessie, you are old-fashioned. A beau, you mean. Well, Harry Mountjoy — that's the handsome one — was supposed to be very taken with her. I didn't see it myself. He danced with me rather than Alice — it was rather thrilling. There's a suggestion that we're all to meet in London in the spring. Now, that would be even more thrilling. The Mountjoys have a house in London — imagine that. Harry's father is a baronet—'

'What's a baronet?' Jessie asked.

'He's Sir Henry Mountjoy — very grand.'

Jessie was none the wiser. She was more interested in what was happening at the Front. 'Did you hear from Mr Alexander?'

'No, only Charles. Did you hear from your brother? I did post your letter.'

'Yes, thank you. He's safe, too, behind the lines. He says the weather is dreadful. I sent him socks and a scarf. It snowed heavily here.'

'And in Sale — it's near Manchester — but that didn't stop us. They had lovely big fires and a tree all lit up with candles. We went to church on Christmas Eve. Terribly moving. There were prayers for those at the Front. Alice's brother has gone back now. She was rather cut up about it. Christmas dinner was lovely, too — chicken and things, and champagne.'

'Nurse and Mrs Cobb were poorly — bad chests.'

'Oh, glory. Grim for you. Who looked after Lady Emmeline?'

'I did. It wasn't difficult.'

'Did she talk to you?'

'Not much.'

'I'd best go up and see her when we've put away all these lovely things.'

Jessie put away the dresses, the handkerchiefs, and the silk scarf, while Caroline arranged her dressing table. She was singing to herself about someone who was the only girl in the world.

Josh said he had heard a lark singing out there in the sky above the ruined land.

The days and weeks passed. They were ordinary days for Jessie: lugging coal, clearing the grates, making fires, breakfasts, suppers, soup, sweeping and mopping the cold hard floor in the kitchen, her clogs clattering on the cold flagstones, Mr Turner chopping wood. And yet all that time throughout the war, men were dying and families were being torn apart, and you didn't realise the full extent of the tragedy until it affected you or someone close to you.

Like the day that Mrs Cobb told her that Mr Turner's son was dead. Killed in France by a German sniper.

'A shame,' Mrs Cobb had said flatly. 'His only son, an' his wife's dead — a few years ago. Servant here, she was, years back. Mebbe he'll be giving up the farm now — too much, all on his own.'

Jessie's blood had turned to ice at the news. She had never forgotten Mr Turner's kindness on that day of snow.

Letters, too, punctuated those ashen days of January and February. She read Josh's letters over and over until she had them by heart.

Josh had written to tell her that he had been in action in January 1917 and that the battalion had been part of the move forward, gaining some yards of ground. The German trenches were as full of mud and snow as their own, but he and Will were pretty fit. He thanked her for the socks and scarf — much needed and very warm. It was freezing at night, even the water taps were frozen, so he'd keep them on and think of her. They kept their coats on, too, and their boots, even though they were thick with mud. If they took them off, it was almost impossible to get them on again, the leather was so hard. They'd be going into the line again soon and he'd write when he could. Another letter in February told her that the Lonsdales had been in action again and had taken German prisoners, and that C Company had been successful in taking more ground. Josh always sent his love and said he was thinking of her, and passed on Will's best wishes, too.

Caroline had a short letter from Charles in March, who wrote to say that there was a lull in the hostilities on the Western Front where the battlefields were ice-bound. The Germans were withdrawing, and the Allied troops were moving forward, re-building roads and bridges. It was rumoured that the Americans would join the war. They'd be welcome, he said. More men were needed if the Allies were to consolidate their gains. The Lonsdales had been in the thick of it at times, but he had heard that Alexander was all right, and Caroline was to tell Jessie that her brother was safe.

It was kind of Mr Charles to remember her, Jessie had told Caroline, who had agreed that Charles was a darling and wondered if he might get leave if there were a lull in the fighting. Caroline had an invitation to London, but she wasn't sure whether she wanted to stay at Moonlyght and hope for Charles, or go away. It was a dark red silk dress that decided the matter — one of the ones that Alice had given her. Caroline had looked blank when Jessie had told her about Mr Turner's son. 'Oh, the farmer,' she had said. 'What a shame.'

And then she had packed her suitcase, or rather Jessie had wrapped the silk dress in tissue paper and folded it carefully into the case and put the hats in their boxes.

She saw the elegant hand waving goodbye under a bitterly cold late April sky. Gloves of the softest leather and a slender wrist encircled by a bracelet of garnets. Caroline Mason, off to meet her lover. It had snowed on the Western Front, Jessie found out later.

16

Mrs Cobb had gone to answer the bell which was only rung by the doctor, and he had already made his call. It pealed through the empty hall so deeply and loudly that they always heard it in the kitchen.

'Who the devil is that?' Mrs Cobb said, starting to her feet. 'That Miss Caroline, I shouldn't wonder. Like her to arrive without letting us know. You'd better come and see to her luggage.'

But it was Charles who came into the hall. Jessie couldn't help the blush burning her cheeks. However, he didn't look at her.

'I'm sorry, Mrs Cobb. I know you weren't expecting me, but it was necessary, I'm afraid. It's bad news. I can't spare you the shock. Alexander has been killed.'

Jessie gasped as Mrs Cobb said, 'Oh, I'm that sorry, sir. Whatever will we tell Lady Emmeline?'

Charles looked at Jessie. 'Take heart, Jessie, your brother is safe. Alexander was killed in action on April the fifteenth. I'm sorry I couldn't come sooner, and I didn't want to send a telegram, Mrs Cobb — for obvious reasons. I didn't know if Caroline would be here — she wrote to say she was off to London.'

'She's still away, sir, but Lady Emmeline?'

'I'll speak to Nurse — see what she thinks. I doubt if — well, it may not be worth upsetting her. Lady Emmeline might think we're talking about Jonathan. She can't go through that again.'

'You're right, sir. Thank the Lord you could come.'

'I've got special leave to sort things out, but I can't stay long. I've come from Kendal and Mr Manvers, the solicitor.'

'Oh, of course, with Mr Jonathan and Mr Alexander both...'

'I can't talk about that now, but yes, I'll have to take the reins. You needn't worry, Mrs Cobb. Things will be the same until I'm here for good. Your job is to look after things for me and make sure Lady Emmeline is cared for, and —' Charles looked at Jessie and smiled — 'Jessie here will stay with us, I'm sure. Miss Caroline will need you, Jessie.'

'Yes, sir. I'm sorry, sir, about Mr Alexander.'

'Nurse has been ill, sir, and me, but Jessie's coped for us. She's a good girl. I always say so.'

Jessie blushed again. She couldn't remember Mrs Cobb saying anything of the sort, but the housekeeper would want to please Charles if he was going to preside over Moonlyght, even if she had to pretend that she cared anything for the kitchen maid.

'Good, well, I'd better go upstairs and see Nurse. Bring some tea, if you will, Mrs Cobb. I should think Nurse will need it. I know I will.'

Jessie was surprised to find Mrs Cobb quite talkative when they went back to the kitchen. 'There'll be changes, mark me, Jessie Sedgwick, and we'll have to keep this place tip-top for when Mr Charles takes over. Miss Caroline'll have her sights set on him, I'll be bound, when she finds out. She'll not be pleased to have missed him. Anyway, we'll have to keep her sweet — just in case. I'll take up that tea. See what's doin' with Nurse. They'll not tell Lady Emmeline — she couldn't stand it.'

Mrs Cobb bustled away, eager to get upstairs and listen in. Poor Lady Emmeline, Jessie thought, and worse, poor

Alexander. Mrs Cobb hadn't mentioned him. She was too concerned about pleasing her new master.

She could perhaps ask Charles more about what had happened. She wanted to know about Josh, of course. In his last letter at the end of March, Josh had said that they were digging in, which meant that they were digging trenches, though they had been under heavy fire from the Germans. He expected they'd be in action soon. But Charles had said he was safe. She wondered how he knew.

Mrs Cobb came down to tell her that nothing was to be said about Mr Alexander to Lady Emmeline, and that Mr Charles was returning to see the solicitor in Kendal the next day and he would be going back to the Front the day after.

'Poor Mr Alexander,' Jessie ventured.

'I remember them two boys. Nice boys, they was, but sensitive, you know. Not very — I don't know — adventurous, I suppose. Lady Emmeline was too soft with Mr Jonathan. He was frightened to death of the General. Mind, he was a stickler. All about the Army, see, and Mr Jonathan being the heir, like, he was supposed to be all for it. But he wasn't. He did join up, but he wasn't the same when he came back that time — all nervous like. Whatever he was doin' in that tower, we'll never know.'

'What about Mr Alexander?'

'See, Mr Jonathan was the handsome one — fair hair and them blue eyes like his mother's. Tall, too, but Mr Alexander, well, he was dark like the General, not that the General cared much for him. He was lonely, I think, in some ways, Mr Jonathan being with his mother a lot, but they got on, them boys, looked out for each other when the General was on the warpath, and then Mr Charles was here a lot. His ma was the General's sister. I think the General thought Charles was more like what he thought his sons should be. Mr Charles was good at games and he could ride well. Should have been in the cavalry, I daresay. Ah, well, it's funny how things turn out. Here's Mr Charles coppin' the lot. I wonder what the General would have thought of that.'

That was the longest conversation Jessie had had with Mrs Cobb, but it came to a sudden stop, as if Mrs Cobb was conscious that she'd said too much. She stood up. 'Well, we'll see, no doubt. Time we got some supper for Mr Charles. There's that pie and some potatoes. Get them on while I set the table. He'll like it done proper.'

After supper, Jessie washed up. Mrs Cobb told her to get to bed after she'd finished. Charles was having his port in the dining room. Jessie could deal with the cheese and the glass in the morning. But Jessie lingered over the crockery and the cutlery, trying to decide if she would go into the dining room with the excuse of collecting the cheese. She so wanted to know more about Alexander and what kind of action he had been in, and if Josh had been part of it.

She went into the screens passage and waited. There was no sound and that made her frightened. She didn't dare disturb him. In any case, she'd blush, and he'd wonder why. He had that way of looking at her.

She sat in the kitchen by the dying fire, watching the embers, thinking about Josh and longing for him. When would the war be over? Caroline had brought a newspaper from Manchester and Jessie had retrieved it from the wastepaper basket, thinking that there would surely be news of the war. She'd read that the Allies had rejected a peace offer from the Germans. It seemed that the Germans wanted to keep possession of Belgium and the Flanders coast. There had been Belgian refugees in Gressthwaite — Pa had said they were a lot of scroungers an' who was goin' to pay to keep them when honest farmers what was feedin' the country hadn't a shillin' ter spare? No one had answered him, but she had thought how dreadful it must have been for them to find themselves in a strange land. Homeless and penniless, Josh had told her. Now she knew how they felt — uprooted from everything you knew and cut off from those you loved, enduring a loneliness that was sometimes a piercing pain, always a dull ache about the heart. She supposed it was right that the Allies should refuse peace for the sake of those people whose lives had been invaded, but it was very hard to read about the numbers of dead. In the newspaper there had been a story about two brothers, one killed and one missing. How could anyone bear that, not to know what happened to your brother?

Jessie looked again at the pictures of the fashions that Caroline had shown her in the paper. Ladies in fur-trimmed coats. A coat that cost six guineas. And Caroline had pointed out a play that she had seen at the Theatre Royal in Manchester. It was impossible to imagine sitting and laughing in a theatre while men were dying in the trenches, but then she had to think about making soup or boiling potatoes, about preparing a tray for Lady Emmeline, and sometimes she didn't think about the war at all, especially when she was emptying the buckets in the yard or toiling upstairs to do the fires. What an odd business life was, so full of contradictions, so hard to work out what it all meant.

She started from her reverie at the sound of the door opening. Mrs Cobb would be annoyed to find her still here. A voice whispered 'Damnation' as someone stumbled on the step in the dark. It was Charles.

There was nowhere to go, so Jessie stood up and whispered, 'Mr Charles.'

'Jessie? Good Lor', what are you doing in the dark?'

'I was just thinking, sir. It's time I went up.'

'Well, light a candle or somethin' so we can see where we're going.'

Jessie fumbled for the matches and the candlestick. In the flickering light she could see him. He looked a bit dishevelled, his tie loose and his waistcoat unbuttoned, and he wore no jacket. She could smell the drink that he had taken. How could she get past him?

'What were you thinking about?'

'The war, sir, Mr Alexander, and my brother.'

'Your brother's all right, I told you. When I got the news about Alexander from Captain Bridges, I telegraphed back to ask about your Josh.'

'It was very kind of you, sir, to think of me.'

'Oh, I'm always thinkin' of you, little Jessie.'

He came towards her, half-stumbling, his eyes oddly unfocussed, not at all like the Charles she knew, always so smartly turned out, and his last comment frightened her. She was afraid of what he wanted from her. She recalled that kiss under the trees.

'What happened to Mr Alexander, sir?'

'Dunno — the usual. Heavy shelling, I'll bet. Tha's what happens. Savy Wood, the place. Lonsdales took it, but Alexander was killed — devil of a thing, young Jessie, devil of a shock. Like a brother, old Alexander — always been around…'

'Do you want some tea, sir? It might —'

'Sober me up? Oh, I don't want to be sober. You think too much when you're sober — like you, Jessie, you're sober, ain't you, and you've been thinkin'. Does no good — no good at all — any whisky in here?'

'I don't think so, sir.'

'Brandy, then — there must be brandy — Christmas cake, eh? Where's Ma Cobb keep it?'

'I daren't, sir —'

'But I'm your boss now, Jessie. Cobb don't count when the boss says jump. Captain Bennett says "jump" and the lads jump to it. Orders, see, Jessie. Gotter take your orders from the captain.'

He sat down suddenly on one of the wooden chairs. The screech of the legs on the flags sounded horribly loud as he pulled it to the table. Jessie had no idea what to do. He shouldn't have more drink, she knew that, but how could she refuse?

'Good girl, Jessie,' Charles said when she put the bottle in front of him. 'Know whish side your bread's buttered. Do anythin' for a pal.'

Jessie watched him unstop the bottle and raise it to his lips. Now he was sitting down, maybe she could just leave him.

'Asked about your brother, Jessie. Anythin' for a pal, an' we're pals, ain't we?'

'We couldn't be that, sir. I'm just —'

'A poor little kitchen maid —'

Jessie flinched at the mocking edge to his voice. She eyed the door and thought about simply walking out. He looked up as she took a step. His voice changed. 'Sorry, Jessie, didn't mean to — don't know what I mean —' He gulped more brandy and she flinched again at the thump of the bottle on the table. 'You're more'n that to me. Like you a lot, litt'l Jessie. Happens all the time. Your Josh an' Mr Alexander — great friends, they were. Didn't know that, did you?'

'No, sir, Josh said Mr Alexander was a good officer.'

'Oh, he was, the best, but it was too much, see, all of it — knew he'd not come back. In his eyes. Knew it. Not his fault. Not fit — takes a man like that. Shell shock. Tha's what they call it — bloody right — damn 'em all…'

It was grief, she thought, her fear turning to pity. Charles felt the loss of Alexander, and he was drinking to forget, but she shouldn't stay. She shouldn't be hearing this. He'd regret his words in the morning.

'I'll have to go up now, sir.'

'Yes, yes, tha's right.'

He stood up and shambled to the door and opened it. She put away the bottle so that Mrs Cobb wouldn't know, but when she turned round again, he was still there, propped against the door, his arms folded, looking straight at her, and then he stood aside.

It was as she passed him that she felt the strength of his arm round her waist. She smelt the brandy on his breath, but she could do nothing. She couldn't cry out; she couldn't struggle. She simply stood still and then she felt his grip loosen so that she could step back. She thought of Alexander and Josh and what they had all seen.

'You ought to rest, Mr Charles. It's very late, and you've had a long day.'

'You're a good pal, Jessie Sedgwick,' he said as she passed out into the screens passage. She knew he was watching, and she heard him laughing drunkenly, and then what sounded like a sob in the laughter. She didn't look back.

17

Mrs Cobb was up and about early. She came from the dining room to say that Mr Charles wanted an early breakfast and, naturally, Mrs Cobb would be serving her new master. 'He's away to that solicitor and won't be coming back. He's got to go to London, he says. I've to get in touch with the solicitor, if anything... Dear Lord, we've had enough bad news. And the solicitor, Mr Manvers, is to come to see me every month about money an' how the place is runnin'. He don't think Nurse or Lady Emmeline are fit enough to be bothered, so I've to take the reins. Trusts me, he says, an' he's hopin' you'll not be wantin' to leave — I don't know where he'd think you'd be goin' to —' she gave Jessie a sharp look — 'you haven't been saying so to him or Miss Caroline?'

'No, Mrs Cobb, I haven't said anything about leaving.'

'It's a good place you've got here, my girl, and don't you forget it. Now, hand over that plate. These eggs is ready, and the bacon.'

Mrs Cobb bustled away with the tray, leaving Jessie glad not to have had to say that she'd spoken to Charles, and relieved that she wouldn't have to see him before he went. From what Mrs Cobb had said, she thought that Charles wouldn't be back for some time. That was a relief, too. She felt guilty then — what if he never came?

She took her scuttles of coal upstairs and lit the fire in Lady Emmeline's room. Nurse wasn't there and Lady Emmeline was asleep. Jessie looked at the still figure on the bed, thinking that Lady Emmeline looked more fragile than ever. It was a shame. It was almost as if she had come back to life in those few weeks when Jessie had looked after her. What about Nurse? Was she getting too old to tend to her mistress? Her absence was unusual. She didn't think Mrs Cobb would listen if she told her she was worried about Lady Emmeline. "Not your business," she'd say.

In the corridor, she was startled to find Charles standing outside the bedroom. He looked pale, but he gave her a half smile. 'Is she up?'

'No, sir, she's still asleep.'

'I'll leave it then.' He looked straight at her. 'Still friends, little Jessie? I wasn't myself last night. I shouldn't have — and that other time — I was stupid. Forgive and forget, eh?' He held out his hand. 'Shake on it. We might not meet again.' He held her hand, looking at the rough red skin and nails. 'You deserve better. I'm sorry.'

And then he was gone, and Jessie went down to stand on the back stairs. He was such a puzzle to her. The war, she thought. It changed people, brought out the best and the worst, perhaps. Pa had only thought about what he might make out of it — it made him greedy. Ted Gorman lied to get out of it. Caroline admired the man who was safe in London. Josh had wanted to fight for his country — but he too was changed. She knew that. And Alexander — he had changed from minute to minute. Like in the hall — even in mid-sentence. She remembered the violets then. *Remember me then*, Alexander had said. In the spring. As if he knew. A premonition of his own death.

And Charles had said they might not meet again. No wonder he was a puzzle. Imagine knowing that you were probably going to die. Did you tell anyone? Did Josh and Will Beswick talk about it? What loneliness, then, if you couldn't. She thought back to last night in the kitchen. Charles hadn't wanted to be sober because he didn't want to think about Alexander or all the others he had seen die. He hadn't meant to frighten her. She was glad they had shaken hands.

She hurried down the stairs, clanking her buckets. Mrs Cobb was coming into the kitchen with a tray. 'Mr Charles has gone — he said he'd walk through the wood to Old Park then Moredale Farm, and try for a lift there. He knows the farmer there. He didn't eat his bacon and eggs — didn't look so good, I thought. Well, I'll make a pie out of the leavin's. It'll keep.'

How many men would die, Jessie thought to herself, *by the time the egg and bacon pie was eaten?* Mrs Cobb was staring out of the window.

'Looks like rain. I hope Mr Charles gets that lift.'

A few days later, Caroline came back in Mr Wiggins's trap. Charles had been to see her in London, so she knew about Alexander. 'Awfully sad,' she said to Jessie, who was examining the red silk dress, which had a stain down the bodice. 'Charles said he couldn't tell Lady Emmeline, and that was sad, too. He did seem down in the dumps.'

'He seemed very miserable about Mr Alexander.'

'Oh, you talked to him? What about?'

'He told me that my brother is safe. I think Josh must have been in the same action as Mr Alexander.'

'Why, are they in the same regiment?'

'Mr Charles said that Josh was in C Company in the Lonsdales with Mr Alexander — my brother wrote to say that Mr Alexander was a good officer.'

'Well, he would be. I mean, he was brought up to it — public school and all that. I should think all the officers must be heroes. They look so handsome in their uniforms. Such shiny boots.'

Jessie didn't think the boots would stay shiny for long in the mud that Josh had told her about, and she wondered if Caroline thought only the officers could be heroes. Jessie didn't say anything about what Charles had said about shell shock. She only said, 'This stain, Miss, I don't think it'll come out.'

'Oh, dash, that was Charles spilling his whisky. He was drinking rather a lot. I met him for dinner at his hotel. I suppose the drink cheered him up, and we went to a night club called the Mimosa — lots of people dancing to a jazz band, but somehow it wasn't much fun. Charles didn't want to dance. He wasn't the same old Charles. Too much whisky. I thought he might … now that…' Caroline looked in the mirror, as if assessing what might have been wrong with her. 'Do I look the same?'

'Yes, your hair looks very nice.'

'My skin's a bit muddy — Alice said you have to drink plenty of water and not so much alcohol. Her skin is lovely, so it must work. It was Charles's fault, giving me too many cocktails.'

'What's a cocktail?'

'They're lovely — lots of different things in them, like whisky or gin. The ones I had were called Pink Lady — gin and something pink, of course, but they do go to one's head and make one giggle.'

'Did your friend Alice go with you?'

'No — I wanted to see Charles on my own, and as I told Alice's parents he's my cousin, they let me go. You see, they're a bit stuffy. They wouldn't have liked Alice to go to a night club. She was out having dinner with Harry Mountjoy. Now, he's good fun, Jessie. We went to the Shaftesbury Pavilion — it's a picture house. We saw a film called *Sins of Men* — all rather amusing. Dorothy Bernard was the star. What a pity I shan't be called de Moine now — Caroline de Moine sounds romantic, doesn't it? Or Dorothea Mountjoy ... hmm, I like the sound of that. I might change my first name. You can, you know.'

'You still like Mr Mountjoy?'

'Yes, I do, but Alice was always with us, so it was difficult — well, to be alone. But when Alice went to the dentist, Harry and I went out for an afternoon to a — to Richmond for tea. I don't know, though. I mean, Charles is the heir to Moonlyght now, but Harry, he's so very ... and he does like me. He thinks I'm beautiful ... so why didn't Charles?'

Jessie wasn't meant to answer, of course. Caroline was clearly waiting for a proposal from one of her admirers. But Charles was mourning Alexander. Surely he wouldn't be thinking of marriage now. Caroline would have to wait — unless she met someone else. Someone richer, probably, or French, she thought, watching Caroline examine her face in the mirror again.

'Oh, Charles gave me some money. I nearly forgot. He said that as you are my maid for some of the time, he thought you should have two new dresses. He thought you looked very shabby, Jessie, and hadn't I noticed? Well, of course, I hadn't — I've hardly been here, but now I do see what he meant. You do look rather drab. I suppose he's thinking that now he's the heir, things ought to be smartened up.'

Jessie concentrated on the unpacking. *Shabby*, she thought. That's what he thought of her. Well, she was. A poor, shabby kitchen maid in a patched dress and clumsy boots. Tears welled in her eyes as she unfolded the delicate petticoats and knickers and thought of her worn linen shift and darned drawers. But Charles had said that she deserved better — perhaps he meant it.

'So,' Caroline continued, 'we'd better go to Kirkby Lonsdale and buy some material or something — you'll be able to make them, won't you, Jessie? I've no idea where one buys servants' clothes.'

Mrs Cobb looked a bit surprised by Caroline's idea that Jessie ought to have two new dresses, but when Caroline said that Mr Charles approved, she was able to supply the thick grey cotton for one dress and the grey wool for the other, and two new aprons from the linen cupboard. Jessie got out her sewing box.

18

Jessie was glad of her grey wool dress, even though it was a bit too big. She'd relied on guesswork, really, and the pattern of her old dress. Still, the lace collar looked nice for best when she tried it on. *Best*, she thought. When would the day come when she might wear her best? She didn't dare wear the collar. She remembered only too well Mrs Cobb's scorn when she had worn Caroline's blouse, but she looked more like her old self on the Sunday in early June when a visitor came.

Caroline had gone to tea at Singleton Hall, the home of a neighbouring family who had sent a car for her. Mrs Cobb was resting, and Jessie was in the kitchen knitting, listening to the rain hammering on the window and looking up from time to time to watch the leaves swirling in the wind. The bitter cold of April with its snowfalls had given way to a miserably wet early summer. She thought of Josh in the rain and the mud. The battalion had been on the move in May. Josh had sent brief letters, just to say he was all right and not to worry. He and Will were still together…

Someone was coming through the yard gate, a grey figure emerging from the driving rain. Her heart gave a leap. It was a man. For a moment she thought of Alexander — as if he had come back, had risen from the mud.

She watched him come towards the door, his shoulders hunched and head down against the wind and rain. She stood up and waited for the knock, her heart thumping, and when she opened the door, she saw his face and was stunned into speechlessness.

'Jess, it's me. It's me, Josh. Are you going to let me in?'

Jessie threw her arms around his neck. 'Josh, Josh! Oh, Josh, I never thought — oh, come in. Sit by the fire. How…?' She took a step back.

'Leave — I was determined to see you, even if it's only for a few hours. I got off the train at Crossgill, and some fellow told me there was a ferry that sometimes crossed the river, and the ferryman was probably waiting for the train, which he was. I'm going to Sedgecroft to see Archie. I promised Mrs Handley.'

'Oh, I was so sorry to hear about him, but I'm so glad you could come.'

'I was longing to see you. You never know when… You know about Lieutenant de Moine?'

'Yes, his cousin came to tell us, but what about you?'

'I'm all right — still alive, me and Will. How, God knows, after all — I can't tell you, Jess — I haven't the words. And as for putting it into a letter, it's impossible, and anyway the officers would cross out anything too — terrible.'

'Is it terrible?' Jessie looked at his face and saw that it was. Josh looked so much older, his face lean and lined, the once-smooth skin red and pitted, his hair darker and coarser. He was thinner and his eyes reminded her again of Alexander's. And there was something about his mouth, something twisted, as if he had been in agony.

'It is, Jess. I don't think any of us will forget it if we live to be a hundred, and that's not likely. So many, Jess, so many — nearly all the Kendal lads. We've others in the Lonsdales now, lads from Lancashire, Essex even. There's a corporal who's from Canada. Enlisted in Liverpool.'

'Canada?'

'I know — that's where we should go after all this. A big new land — there's opportunities there in farming. I'll bet they need teachers. Or Australia —' he smiled for the first time, and she glimpsed the boy who had been her brother — 'I was thinking it'd be a damn sight warmer than out there than here. You'd come, wouldn't you, Jess?'

'I'd come anywhere, anywhere.'

'You all right here?'

'Yes — it's not what I wanted, but I can put up with it. I know there'll be something brighter when —'

'If our luck holds. Will says he'll come to Canada with us. He sends his best, of course. You do look pretty, Jess, in that collar with your hair all shining. Pity Will can't see you now. He always asks after you. It's funny being without him — in an odd sort of way, I want to get back and see that he's all right. It's like we're brothers, you know, like if we're together, we'll be all right.'

If, she thought, unable to answer. To hide her tears, she stood up and asked, 'Do you want tea? A sandwich?'

'Oh, that'd be grand. A good cup of tea. It always tastes of stew out there, though they give us rum in it before — well — and the cheese tastes of soap, and the bread's always frozen, and there's ice in the jam when there is any.'

Jessie put the kettle on the range. There was fresh bread and butter, ham, and cake. She didn't care if Mrs Cobb was keeping the ham for Caroline's supper. She could go without.

Josh didn't fall upon the food, but he ate carefully and with relish. She saw that some of his fingernails had a line of black near the flesh, as if he'd scrubbed and hadn't quite got the dirt out, and there was dirt ingrained in the skin of his hands. Mud, she thought, so thick you couldn't wash it off. A lump came into her throat, but she swallowed and told him about Mrs Cobb, Miss Caroline and Lady Emmeline. She couldn't bear to sit in silence and watch him eat and think about the frozen bread and the soapy cheese.

When he had eaten and finished his first cup of tea, he said, 'Lieutenant de Moine told me about his mother and his brother. It seems a rum household — no rummer than ours, I suppose. I shan't be going back to Swarthgill. Poor Ma, she had a hard life. We want something better, Jess, a new kind of life.'

'I've never heard from Pa, but he has my wages.'

'The devil he does — who arranged that?'

'I don't know. Him and Mrs Cobb?'

'Well, you tell her that it isn't fair. He has part of my pay, too. He's a — well, I won't say it, but honestly, you should do something about it. Ask your Miss Caroline. If I'd known, I could have mentioned it to Lieutenant de Moine.'

'Did you know him well?' Jessie remembered Charles saying that Josh and Alexander were friends.

'I was his runner — my job was to take messages when he was on duty. We talked a bit when things were quiet. Out there, we were friends in a way, despite him being gentry. He wasn't that different from me. He liked to talk about the land and nature — he wanted a cottage in the hills. Just wanted to walk and walk. Didn't care about his big house or money. I knew what he meant. Peace and quiet. Sometimes a shell'd explode a bit too near and then we'd have to duck, I can tell you. He was brave, you know, but it gets to you — never knowing when... You can make a mistake — forget where you are in all the smoke, the shells screaming, and artillery fire. We saw the corporal blown to bits. Lieutenant de Moine stood up — he must have thought ... I don't know. I saw him fall...' Josh trailed off, his face darkening, his eyes full of shadows. 'It was a terrible time — oh, the shelling — bits of hot metal bursting from the sky, and the noise. The dead all about us...

I'm sorry, Jess, I shouldn't be telling you. You don't need to know. It's between me and Will. Don't say anything to —'

The door opened and Mrs Cobb came in. She looked at the empty plate and the cake and at Jessie, and then she stared at Josh.

'You're Esther's boy. You're very like — your ma. Yes, I see it now.'

Jessie had never thought so. Josh was not like Pa, either. People only said Jessie was like Esther. But then Mrs Cobb had known Ma when she was young, and if she was going to be pleasant, then whatever she thought about Josh's looks was all right with Jessie.

Josh stood up. 'Yes, Jess's brother. I'm on leave briefly and going up to a pal's, but I wanted to stop and see Jess. I hope you don't mind, Mrs Cobb.'

'Well, I'm glad Jessie's fed you up. I'll leave you to your cake and tea — you'll want to be private.'

Jessie smiled when Mrs Cobb had gone. 'I thought she might be annoyed about the food. She's not so bad really, just a bit cold.'

'She looks a bit of a tartar, but it was good of her to leave us alone. Now, that cake, if you don't mind. And when you've made another one, you can send it to me.'

'I will — but you did like the book?'

'Course I did. I knew why you'd sent it — for us and those good times we had. Remember the cave?'

'Oh, I do — the crystal cave. It was like magic.'

They didn't talk about the war again, only about the fossils and the stones and flowers they used to collect — the wild daffodils, the sweet honeysuckle, and the violets in the woods — until Josh said he would have to go.

'Funny we should think of them — the violets, I mean. The gas — it smells of violets. We could smell it, and Lieutenant de Moine said they grow in a place called Hag Wood, where someone died. It preyed on his mind somehow. He didn't say who it was.'

Jessie didn't tell him. Ethel was nothing to do with Josh. To mention murder now was unthinkable. She waited.

'Violets and death. Just before he — don't mention what I said about him to anyone. No one should think he was a coward.'

'I won't. You can trust me.'

'I do, Jess. You and Will. Think about me and send that cake.'

She walked him to the front of the house just as the motor car came with Caroline, who shook Josh's hand very prettily and said how glad she was to have met Jessie's brother. And before the Singleton Hall chauffeur drove away, she asked him to take Josh to the station.

'A serving soldier, Banks, on leave from the front line. He deserves a lift.'

'Yes, Miss, I'll take him.'

'And you'll come for me on Monday, Banks, won't you? I asked Miss Morris, and she said it was all right.'

'Certainly, Miss, for the London train, is it?'

'Yes, please.'

'Right, sir, hop in the back.'

Jessie and Caroline watched as Josh climbed into the back of the Rolls-Royce. Jessie's heart turned over at his huge, delighted grin and the comical salute from the back window as the car rolled away. *Oh, Josh, be safe. Come back to me.*

19

It was the wettest and stormiest summer Jessie had ever known. The house felt damp, the fires wouldn't light, and Jessie had to bite her lip at Nurse's tutting when the smoke billowed out because the coal was damp — silent Mr Turner had replenished the coal in the yard. Mrs Cobb had made no comment on that. She took the produce he brought, but Jessie saw through the kitchen window that there was no conversation.

Caroline returned from what was an overnight stay in London. She was uncharacteristically reticent about her trip, only saying that she'd been invited to a party by one of Alice Herd's friends. Jessie wondered if it had not been a success — if Caroline had been disappointed in some way. When she asked if Caroline would be going again, she only said that she might.

'Everything's so uncertain. I do wish people would make up their minds. And this ghastly weather. It's enough to drive one mad.'

Thereafter, she was like a restless spirit, forever complaining that she was bored to death and why didn't someone invite her to something? She always asked if there were any letters and if not, was plunged into gloom. Jessie found it hard to keep up her soothing compliments, but she did because Caroline had asked Mrs Cobb about Jessie's wages and said that she was sure Jessie was entitled to them. Mrs Cobb didn't look so sure, but when Caroline got an idea in her head, she would pursue it, and she liked to best Mrs Cobb from time to time. Mrs Cobb eventually said she would see to it, which made her rather more irritable than her summer cold. She complained that Jessie was never where she should be.

'What does Miss Caroline want you for again? She's not going anywhere — she can't want her hair doing.'

'She has a new magazine which shows some new styles. She's asked me to try them.'

Jessie didn't dare tell Mrs Cobb about Caroline's new fad — telling fortunes. She'd found a dog-eared book in the library, *The Ladies' Oracle*. The idea was that you placed your pencil on a sign and chose a question to which you wanted to know the answer. Then there was the number of the page which would give you an answer. Caroline wanted to know what kind of lover she would meet and marry. The answer was, of course, that he would be handsome, gallant, amorous, rich — anything she wanted, really. Jessie disliked being made to choose a question and resented Caroline's giggles when the answer was that Jessie Sedgwick was destined for an old man with no teeth. 'It might be a rich old man, though,' Caroline would splutter, 'who'll leave you all his money.'

Jessie hated the cards even more. Caroline fancied herself as a fortune teller. Clubs portended happiness. Hearts foretold triumph — Caroline loved the Queen of Hearts. Spades were ominous, signifying sickness and grief to come. Caroline laughed them off. The joker was the worst, a winking, cross-legged figure in black, the image of which Jessie found hard to banish when she lay in bed, listening to the wind flinging gusts of rain at the window and moaning in the chimney and the house creaking and sighing as it settled down for the night — the joker seemed to know a secret and was laughing at her. She couldn't shake off a feeling of dread.

A few letters came from Josh, always assuring her that he was well enough. The battalion had moved into Belgium and was behind the lines, in training near the sea. They had bathed there, and what a relief it had been to plunge into the clean water and wash off all the mud and grime. They'd go to the seaside when he came home, he said, and walk on the sands, and she'd be able to go into the sea, too. And a letter came near the end of the month to tell her that the battalion would be going up the line in July. He'd write when he could. Caroline had a couple of letters from Charles, but she didn't tell Jessie anything about him, except that he was well, and that he was pleased to hear that she was contributing to the war effort.

Caroline had come back from a tea at Singleton Hall, all smiles for once. Usually she declared such occasions "frightfully dull" — she only went in case she might be able to ask for the use of the chauffeur again. 'So proper, so out of date,' she told Jessie. The guests at the tea parties were the vicar, his sister, an elderly lady companion of Mrs Morris, who owned the hall, and Mrs Morris's spinster daughter, Sara, who was very much occupied with good works and had hoped that Miss Mason would lend a hand. Caroline had recruited Jessie to do her knitting for her. Now the National Egg Collection appealed. Caroline had heard from Miss Morris that someone she knew had received a letter from a soldier who had been given one of her eggs. The lady, a farmer's wife at Tossbeck, had written her name and address on her eggs. The extraordinary thing was that the private had been a labourer at that very farm at the time he had enlisted.

'Imagine, Jessie, Charles might get an egg with my name on it — wouldn't he see that as a sign?'

Even Mrs Cobb cracked a smile at this. Caroline was paying a rare visit to the kitchen. 'Sounds like a fairy tale to me, Miss Caroline. I mean, what are the chances?'

'Fate, Mrs Cobb — we don't know. Strange things happen all the time. Anyway, it was in the newspaper. Sara Morris told me. So, shall we do it — contribute to the National Egg Collection? I'll take them to Singleton Hall.'

Naturally, it was Jessie's task to go out in the rain and collect what eggs were there, and to brave the tower if one of the hens was missing. It was usually the same one, a skinny, bedraggled brown hen that rarely laid. Too nervous, Jessie knew. She called her Miss Skittish and felt sorry for her. She was an outsider. The other hens pecked at her and chased her away. Sick, maybe, Jessie thought. She remembered the hens on the farm. They could be bullies if one of their number was sick. They had no pity. There were twelve hens in the yard at Moonlyght, so usually about a dozen eggs a day, but not so many in this wild weather. Hens liked sunshine, and there was precious little of that.

However, it was a rare dry morning when Caroline decided she would like to collect the eggs with Jessie. 'I want to tell Sara Morris that I've collected them. She always looks down that long nose of hers at me as if she doesn't believe I'm capable of anything. She looked at the socks — and at me — very suspiciously. I told her you'd helped, you see. I know I should have told her you'd done the knitting, Jessie, but she makes me feel so small, and I might need to ask for the chauffeur again.'

Jessie instantly regretted her casual remark about the missing hen which would probably be in the tower, for Caroline immediately wanted to go and look for it. 'I've not been in there for ages.'

'I'll get a lamp. It's dark in there.'

The tower was as damp and dank as Jessie remembered, but the shadows shrank back into the corners when Jessie shone the lamplight round the floor. She couldn't help remembering poor Ethel, of whom no one ever spoke. She often thought of her and the unknown man who had killed her in Hag Wood, and what message she had wanted to give Charles.

Even Caroline stopped talking as they peered into the corners. Jessie wondered if she was affected by the suffocating atmosphere and the high walls surrounding them. A young man had died here. Had he slipped, or had he come back from the Front so damaged that he had jumped to his death? And Alexander up on those steps — would he have done the same if Jessie had not been there? Josh had said Alexander was not to be thought a coward. Perhaps Josh knew that Alexander had stood up to face the shelling on purpose.

Caroline looked up the stairs. 'Dare I go up there, I wonder? I'll bet Sara Morris wouldn't dare. She thinks I'm just —'

'Don't!' Jessie cried, swinging the lantern away. There was something on the stairs, something white, caught for a moment in the wavering light. It looked like paper. Had Ethel left a note for her all that time ago, and had it blown there in the wind?

'Why ever not? What's the matter with you? You look scared to death.'

'Don't, Miss, please. It's where I saw —'

'What? What did you see? You're scaring me now.'

'Just the stairs — they're dangerous. They look broken — you might fall...' Jessie trailed off.

Caroline paled suddenly. 'I didn't think — I'm sorry.' She stared up to the high ledge. 'I remember — it was — I don't want to think about it. I wish I'd never come.'

They turned to the door, and Caroline suddenly said, 'Wasn't it queer about Ethel Widdop?'

'What made you think of her?'

'Oh, nothing really, just this place. I saw her a few times coming out. She looked furtive. I wonder if she was meeting that fellow — the one who —'

'You never said, Miss, when —'

'I didn't want to. I mean, it wouldn't have helped Ethel, would it? I didn't see the fellow, and saying somebody looked furtive is hardly evidence, is it? I told Charles afterwards, and he said the same. She might have been in the tower to get coal or look for a hen. He said to leave the speculation about her private life to Mrs Cobb. No one knew —' she looked back into the shadowy space — 'no one ever found out.'

'You never saw anyone else in the tower?'

'Only Alexander sometimes... He found Jonathan, you know, and I think he couldn't keep away until Charles told him it wasn't good for him. Oh, I don't want to talk about it. Now, the eggs — how many will there be?'

A dozen eggs were marked with Caroline's name and the address of Moonlyght, and Caroline went off in the Morrises' Rolls-Royce with a neat little basket and a triumphant smile. It was Mrs Cobb who told Jessie that the eggs were sent to wounded soldiers in the hospitals in England. When Caroline came back looking a little deflated, Jessie hadn't the heart to ask about the eggs. The enterprise seemed to be over. There were no more teas at Singleton Hall.

However, a letter came from Alice, inviting Caroline to come to London for a week in September, and that cheered her up.

'Fate, Jessie — just when I'm down in the dumps, something lucky happens. Charles says he might get leave, so I'm writing to say I'll be in London. He might come to see me there, and I'll make sure I cheer him up this time. I have my ways, and I told you it was on the cards. The Queen of Hearts — I told you.'

20

September was drier but windy, with squally showers, and there was little news from the Front. Josh wrote that it was difficult to send letters. He had been in heavy fighting and constant shelling from the enemy. Such an awful swish they made as they came down. They all dreaded that noise. The cake was a treat, though, because there didn't seem to be any cake in Belgium — a queer flat country, it was. It made him long for the moors and the hills, but they'd been in the sea again and that had been good. The rain was dreadful and the mud thick in the trenches. The Lonsdales had been relieved by the Lancashires, but they'd be going up the line again soon.

The house was quiet without Caroline, and Jessie was very much by herself with her thoughts of Josh and Will Beswick and the action to come. She carried on with her knitting and baked another fruit cake to send, but she felt restless and uneasy. It was worrying about Josh, of course, but she couldn't help thinking of Ethel and how Caroline had seen her coming from the tower, and how only Alexander ever went in there. She remembered how Alexander had spoken of Ethel's golden eyes, and how he had said he was sorry about her death. He had said her name in the tower. She wondered if Ethel had met Alexander there. It was so odd that he should remember a servant's eyes, but then she thought of how distinctive Ethel's eyes had been, and Ethel had liked Alexander — he was kind, she had said. He was, Jessie thought, remembering his smile. Josh had said he was brave and that they were friends. She couldn't believe that Alexander had anything to do with Ethel's death. And then there was Ethel pushing herself forward at

Charles, Charles who had advised Caroline not to mention she had seen Ethel at the tower and had told Jessie to put Ethel out of her mind. Yet, he had shaken her hand and apologised for his drunken state in the kitchen. It was a jigsaw in which the pieces didn't fit.

She almost wished Caroline would come back — at least her chatter and doing her hair and mending her clothes filled the days and took her mind off the dark things, the sense she had that something dreadful would happen, as if the silent house was waiting, too, whispering secrets in the night. And the tower always brooding over them.

Jessie had found blood and feathers outside the door of the coop. A fox, she assumed. Poor Miss Skittish. Another death. She knew it wasn't important, but it upset her. A killer come in the night to snatch her away and no one cared. The other hens hadn't noticed. Nothing left but those few feathers tossed about on the wind. And she brooded on that paper she had seen on the tower stairs. There was nothing to stop her going to see if it was still there. She hadn't told Mrs Cobb about the hen — she'd just cleared up the feathers and locked the coop carefully at twilight. She could have gone any early evening or when Mrs Cobb was in her room, but she dreaded the place. She'd have to go up the stairs to retrieve whatever it was. Suppose it was a note from Ethel? What might Ethel have written? Jessie didn't want to know. There were too many secrets at Moonlyght already.

But on another rainy and wind-swept afternoon, the thought of that paper on the stairs nearly drove her mad. What if Caroline had some idea of going in the tower and found it — a note addressed to Jessie Sedgwick, who was not supposed to have known Ethel Widdop, a note giving the name of the man who was her lover? She felt sick at the thought that Caroline would realise that she had lied, think that she had talked of it to Ethel, that Jessie Sedgwick had believed that someone at Moonlyght was responsible for Ethel's murder.

She made up her mind and ran across the yard through the pelting rain to stand peering up the stairs. *Alexander*, she thought. Had he dropped something when she had seen him huddled there, looking up as if he had seen something at the top of the tower? Or somebody? Jessie climbed up on her hands and knees, feeling along each step. Small, loosened stones and grit fell behind her and a shower of grit fell from above, as though someone moved up there. The wind, surely. The wind that breathed its icy breath on her neck. She dared not look up. Then she saw it. Not a letter, thank God, but a very thin book with a white cover, all stained now with rain and dust. She slipped it into her pocket and inched her way back down the stairs, the stones crunching under her feet as she went.

She ran back to the house, thinking how daft she had been to believe that a note from Ethel would have stayed on the stairs all these months.

It was Alexander's book, a book that would have fitted in his pocket, a book of poems called *A Shropshire Lad*. Jessie read it in bed by the light of her candle when the wind blew, and lightning cut jagged scars into the sky. She never seemed to be able to sleep at night. She felt she was always listening, ready to start up at any moment. She imagined the doorbell ringing through the house in the middle of the night and someone unknown bringing bad news.

Alexander's name was on the inside cover, and there were pencil marks under some of the lines. At first, she couldn't understand the poems. They seemed to be about some long-ago period when Victoria was Queen. There had been a plate in the parlour at Swarthgill where Grandad Albert sat. It showed a severe, plump old lady with a veil and crown on her head. It commemorated her Diamond Jubilee back in 1897 and there were pictures of castles, and captions proclaiming that she was Queen of England and Empress of India — not that she had known what that meant. Josh had shown it to her, and they had marvelled at the idea of her being crowned sixty years before. She had been eighty-two when she died. It seemed impossible that someone should live so long.

Pa had smashed the plate in one of his drunken rages after Josh had gone to war. "Bloody Queen, bloody King and Country. Bloody General. Bloody bastard. They owe me —" and worse, he had cursed and cursed.

What puzzled her as she read the poems again and again was that they seemed at the same time to be about this war and the young men who were dying. Had the poet, Mr Housman, foreseen the future? How could that be? Alexander's underlinings brought tears to her eyes and frightened her, too. One poem seemed to be about a young man who had shot himself, and suggested that it was better he had, for *After long disgrace and scorn / You shot dead the household traitor...* She couldn't help thinking of Ethel — was she the household traitor, or was it the young man himself, *the soul that should not have been born?* It must be him, for there was another underlining in the next poem: *Stand up and end you...* That was what Alexander had done. *When your sickness is your soul...*

She found herself weeping. Alexander had known he was sick. Shell shock, Charles had said, but maybe it was because he had killed Ethel. She still couldn't believe that. She could more easily believe that it was because of Lady Emmeline. Alexander felt that he should not have been born.

Such suffering shook her to the very core. The other poems were about parting, loss and death and the grave, lads that lay underground or on the bed of earth, men marching away, never to return. Lads that died in glory, lovely lads, dead and rotten…

Jessie started as the wind slapped at the window, and she heard thunder, deep and rumbling. Was that what the faraway guns sounded like? She wept again for all those lads, and her heart trembled for Josh when she read the lines, *The saviours come not home tonight / Themselves they could not save.*

And that was how Charles found her in her bed, with the open book on her knee, weeping as if her heart would break.

He had come that day, but she hadn't seen much of him. He had sat with Lady Emmeline for a while. And with Nurse. Poor Lady Emmeline looked more like a ghost than ever, and Nurse seemed frail, too, but would not let anyone come near her mistress. Mrs Cobb had served Charles's supper in the dining room, ever careful of the new regime. She had said that Charles was sitting over his port. That was enough to send Jessie up to her bed immediately after she had washed up.

She heard the hall clock strike ten as her door opened. Mrs Cobb, she thought, her heart lurching. What had happened? She smelt tobacco and something scented, sharp and lemony. A man's shape in the doorway, out of the circle of candlelight. It was Charles stepping over the threshold.

'Don't be scared, Jessie,' he whispered. 'I'm not drunk. I heard you weeping. What is it? You sounded heartbroken — have you had news?'

'No, sir,' she said through her tears. 'I was just —'

'Thinking again, little Jessie? I told you not to.'

She heard the smile in his voice. 'I'm all right, sir. You don't need — no, please, don't come in. Mrs Cobb might hear.'

He shut the door. 'Don't worry, I only want to talk to you. It's very lonely down there, and up here, I think. We're pals, remember? Tell me what you're reading.'

'I found it, sir, in the tower. Mr Alexander must have dropped it.'

'What were you doing in the tower?'

'I was with Miss Caroline. There was a hen lost. The eggs, you see —'

She heard him chuckle. 'Oh, yes, the great egg collection — how's that going?'

'We only did it once, sir. Miss Caroline thought that the eggs were being sent to the Front. She thought you might get one with her name on it.'

'Just like her — no sense. But the book?'

'Poems, sir, *A Shropshire Lad.*'

'Ah, Housman, we all read him out there. Prophet, he is. Let's have a look.'

Jessie handed Charles the book and he sat down on the chair by the bed. He was too close, and she was conscious of her hair tied back with string and her patched nightgown. He'd said she was shabby, and he hadn't seen her in her new dress. What would he think now? He shouldn't be here.

But he was looking down at the page she'd been reading. The candlelight showed his carved profile and his fine hands holding the book. He didn't say anything, but she heard his breath, rather shaky, as if he was moved, too.

'*After long disgrace and scorn…* Poor Alexander, poor, poor Alexander —'

'Do you think he…?' She didn't really know what she was going to ask.

'I don't know, little Jessie. I only know it doesn't matter. He took the bullet in his brain — or wherever. He paid. He's gone into the dark and he'll never be found. *A dead man out of mind…*'

Jessie had read that line in the last poem of the book. 'They shouldn't be forgotten, sir.'

'No, but I wonder…' He turned the pages. 'You've read this?' He read the words to her, his voice low and mournful:

'*Long for me the rick will wait*
And long will wait the fold
And long will stand the empty plate
And dinner will be cold.'

The silence was weighted with sorrow. Jessie thought of Ma alone at the kitchen table after she had gone, and the ruined farmhouse of her dream came back to her. She couldn't speak.

'You were thinking of your brother.'

'I couldn't help —' And she wept again.

'There, there,' he whispered, and he blew out the candle.

21

It hadn't been violent. It had been tender. 'Hush, hush,' Charles had said, and Jessie had found herself turning to him, blindly reaching for his comforting arms. Afterwards he had wept in her arms. They had wept together, then they had lain quiet for a long time until he told her he must go. No one must know that he had been with her. He had kissed her gently and crept out quietly.

She remembered everything about the morning after; had known that she must behave as though nothing had happened. She had risen early and gone down to put coal in the range, filled the kettle and set about cutting bread and making tea. She had to take up the coal at about eight o'clock. Nurse and Lady Emmeline would need their fires making up, as it was very cold in the mornings for September. As for Charles — he was leaving early, he had told her, to see the solicitor, and then he'd be off to London. He didn't say he would write to her, and she hadn't asked. She hadn't asked anything.

She had gone out to set the table in the dining room for his breakfast, which Mrs Cobb would serve. She was in the screens passage when she heard someone coming down the stairs. It could only be Charles. She stood and listened, wondering if she should take in the tray, wondering what he might say to her, and feeling the rush of terror at what they had done.

Then she heard him undo the bolts on the front door — one always made a screeching sound because it was stiff. She heard the door open and then close.

She darted into the dining room and looked out of the window. She saw him walking away, carrying his suitcase, his figure dissolving into the rain and mist. He didn't look back. And terror became shame.

It was nearly the end of September when Caroline came back. Her face was stony. She had no smile for Jessie, who was terrified that Caroline knew something. However, her rage had nothing to do with Jessie.

The garnet bracelet was on the floor, its clasp broken. It looked as though it had been stamped on. Jessie picked it up and all the other things that had been swept off the dressing table. The room looked as if a whirlwind had passed through it.

Caroline was lying on the bed smoking — something Jessie had never seen her do before. Nor had she ever seen Caroline in such a temper. She was unpredictable, selfish, easily bored, but she'd always been kind in her fashion. Now, Jessie didn't know what to say in the face of such black-browed sullenness. Something had happened in London, but she didn't dare ask.

'Throw it out — that bracelet. I don't want it. She said it was hers. She's a liar.'

'Who?'

'Alice Herd, the traitor —' Caroline's laughter pealed out. 'Oh, Lord, Jessie, I've just thought, Herd — she looks as fat as a cow. Well, if that's what he wants, he's welcome to her.'

'You mean Mr Mountjoy?'

'The deskman, yes — him — thinks himself so grand. But what is he, after all? A clerk, a pen-pusher, while the real heroes are out there. Engaged! They announced it at the party. After he'd — he'd said it was me he wanted, and I — I've been a fool. I never guessed. Anyway, he's not a patch on Charles. I saw him, you know — just briefly. He called at the hotel and said he'd been up here to see the solicitor. He took me to tea at Claridge's. Told me I looked as beautiful as ever —'

Jessie bent down to pick up some stockings and to hide the sudden tears that sprang to her eyes. She fumbled about the carpet.

'What are you doing, Jessie? I'm telling you about Charles.'

'A pin, Miss, I thought —'

'You can tidy up in a minute. Do you think — I mean — do you think I should marry Charles?'

'I don't know, Miss. Has he asked you?'

'Not yet, but it makes sense, doesn't it?'

'I don't know.'

'Oh, Jessie, you are dull today — what is the matter with you?'

'Nothing, Miss — I just worry about my brother. I haven't heard from him for a while.'

'Try not to think about it. I don't want to think about Charles at the Front, either. It's all rather misery-making. It was bad enough finding out about Alice. Do you know, she said she'd given the bracelet to me — it was one of hers, and she thought garnets would suit me better than they suited her. I don't believe that for a minute. Harry Mountjoy gave it to me. He's marrying her for the money, you know. The Herds are stinking rich, and they want a title for their daughter. She'll be Lady Mountjoy one day... Imagine the moo cow stumping about in a tiara.'

'Is Mr Mountjoy poor?'

'I don't know. But people always want more. Now, Charles isn't rich like they are, but I love him for himself, of course, and he loves me for myself. I've only got the allowance that the General left me — unless Lady Emmeline leaves me something. Imagine me — mistress of Moonlyght! Charles and I could restore the house, blow all the cobwebs away, have parties as they did in the old days...'

Jessie couldn't stop herself. 'The war will have to end first.'

Caroline didn't miss the unaccustomed bitterness. 'I know, I know. I'm not stupid, but one has to look ahead. One has to have plans — otherwise everything's so dull.'

Plans, Jessie thought to herself, when she had escaped from Caroline, her arms full of laundry. Josh had plans for her and Will Beswick to go to Canada after the war. Will, who asked after her. The enormity of what had happened flooded her so that she felt as if she couldn't breathe. She had no right to think of Will now. She couldn't go to Canada. Josh had meant — she knew what Josh had meant. He had thought it a pity that Will hadn't seen her in her new dress. Josh and Will were like brothers. How could she go with them? Will would expect — she had thrown away her future. She wanted to run away, to simply disappear. Then Will and Josh could go to Canada. But Josh wouldn't go. He'd search for her. He would be devastated, thinking she might be dead, wondering why she had left him. It would be too cruel. She would have to bear it.

Jessie stood on the back stairs, flooded with shame and the realisation of what she had done. She heard Mrs Cobb calling from upstairs, and she flew up to find her on the landing outside Lady Emmeline's room. Nurse was lying on the floor, her face the colour of clay. Her eyes were closed but she was whimpering.

'She's had a fall — knocked out, I think, but she's coming round now. It's her leg — I don't know if it's broken. You'll have to help me get her to bed. Miss Caroline will have to go across to Mr Turner and ask him to fetch Doctor Kennedy.'

They managed to get Nurse into bed and then Jessie went to Caroline's room. Caroline was writing a letter when Jessie went in. She frowned when Jessie told her.

'Oh, Lord, why me? Couldn't you go?'

'Mrs Cobb needs me.'

'Oh, I can't walk all that way. How far is it, anyway?'

'Turn right at the end of the drive down the hill towards Mossgarth. Fiddler's Hill Farm is on your right — about half a mile. Mrs Cobb says Mr Turner will take you to Kirkby Lonsdale for the doctor.'

'Oh, I needn't go, need I? In the farmer's cart, all that way.'

'Well, no, only Mrs Cobb thought —'

'The doctor doesn't need me to tell him about a sprained ankle.'

'It might be worse than that.'

'And it might not. She's tough, old Nurse — she'll live until she's a hundred.'

Jessie wasn't sure, having seen that clay-coloured face and heard the laboured breathing. Whatever it was, Nurse was in great pain.

Caroline went, albeit reluctantly, and Jessie began to put the brushes and silver-lidded pots back on the dressing table and to rescue the garnet bracelet. The room smelt of smoke and that curiously musky perfume that Caroline used. She remembered Caroline telling her that Alice Herd had given the bracelet to her on behalf of Harry Mountjoy because it wasn't done for a young man to give an expensive gift to a single woman. Now, she wondered how much Caroline had imagined about Mr Mountjoy's feelings for her. Certainly, she had spent time alone with him, but those seemed to be somewhat secret meetings. Caroline said she'd been a fool — did that mean that she had done with Harry Mountjoy what she, Jessie, had done with Charles Bennett? What did Charles feel for Caroline? Was it true that he loved her and that they would marry? Or was Caroline imagining that?

What did Charles feel for her? He had been gentle and tender with her. He had asked her to comfort him, and she had hardly realised what he was doing, but she had not resisted. She had wanted comfort, too. Her cheeks burned again. Charles might marry Caroline, but he wouldn't marry her. He was a gentleman. The owner of Moonlyght would not marry his kitchen maid.

As she was about to leave the room, Jessie picked up some scattered papers which had fallen from Caroline's desk. She remembered the first time she had seen that desk and the silver inkwells, how she'd imagined sitting there and dipping her pen into the ink. A year ago, a whole year. How changed everything was, and how changed she was. She felt her throat close and the tears begin, but she brushed her eyes with her hand and took a deep breath. "No use cryin' over spilt milk." That's what Ma would have said.

Jessie put back the papers and saw the letter that Caroline had been writing when she'd interrupted her. She couldn't help herself when she saw the words, "Dearest Alice" and the sentence which followed. Caroline was writing to tell Alice that she would be thrilled to be one of her bridesmaids in October. Moments before, Caroline had been ripping her friend to pieces. But that was Caroline. She wouldn't be able to resist another trip to London and another chance to flirt with Harry Mountjoy, even if he was going to marry Alice Herd.

Caroline went for Mr Turner, and Mrs Cobb stayed with Nurse while Jessie checked on Lady Emmeline, who didn't stir. Jessie looked at the thin face, so pale that it might have been carved from marble. Jessie wondered what thoughts lay behind that mask — did Lady Emmeline think only of Jonathan for whom she waited, suspended in her dream world? Jonathan, who would never come.

Nurse's ankle had been badly sprained. She wouldn't be up and about for several weeks. Doctor Kennedy took out his stethoscope, listened to her chest and shook his head.

In the corridor outside the bedroom, he had told Mrs Cobb that Nurse's heart wasn't strong — she'd need care. Looking after Lady Emmeline was probably too much for her now. It was time to get more help in the house. Perhaps Mrs Cobb could take on the nursing of Lady Emmeline?

'Miss Caroline'll have to shape herself,' Mrs Cobb told Jessie irritably after the doctor had gone. 'She'll have to take her turn with Lady Emmeline. More help, indeed. From where? No one in the village'll want to come here when there's war work in the munitions factories an' good pay for lasses these days. In any case, we can't have folk gossipin'. We'll have to do what we can for Nurse, an' she's not easy. When's that weddin' Miss Caroline's supposed to be goin' to? She only thinks of herself, that one.'

'In a week — she's going on Monday.'

'Well, she can do summat before she ups an' goes. I'll have a word.'

Caroline was not at all pleased to be recruited to the sick room, though she preferred Lady Emmeline's silent presence to Nurse's peevish temper. It was Jessie who had to put up with that. Not that she minded. The constant rushing up and down the stairs, the emptying of chamber pots, the trays and teas, the fires, the coal, the hens, and the hundred other tasks all stopped her from thinking too much.

She could hear Caroline's chatter when she went in with coals or a tray. Caroline helped prop Lady Emmeline up onto the pillows, or helped her to her chair, and gave her tea or a little bit of food. Lady Emmeline looked at her as if she were a stranger, but once, as she was going out, Jessie heard her ask

Caroline about Jonathan, and she froze. Caroline didn't answer, but Jessie heard her say, 'Tea, Lady Emmeline, darling, do try some.'

'It's ghastly,' Caroline said to Jessie later. 'She thinks Jonathan is still alive. What is one supposed to say?'

'I don't think she'd understand even if she was told.'

'It might shake her up a bit — you know, shock her out of this trance she's in. I mean, what use is she, lying there? And the rest of us having to dance attendance.'

'She gets up sometimes, when Nurse helps her.' Jessie didn't mention the times when she had heard footsteps in the room above her own and that terrible weeping.

'There you are then. There's nothing wrong with her. I'll bet she could come down if she had to. Anyway, you'll have to manage. I'm going to that wedding. I hope the bridesmaid's dress isn't too hideous. I rather wish I wasn't to be a bridesmaid. I could have worn black — that'd show them…'

'What colour has Miss Herd chosen for you?'

'Pink — terribly obvious, don't you think? She's wearing white — well, she would, of course. I shan't wear white for my wedding. Lots of girls wear furs and suits — the war, you see. More tasteful to wear a day suit. But Moo Cow's pa wouldn't think of that. Too busy making his millions. Mountjoy'll wear his uniform — not that he's seen any fighting. Won't Charles look divine, though, when we … and I in my furs — mink, I think, and a mink hat — more suitable for a winter wedding, of course.'

As it came about, there was no winter wedding for Miss Alice Herd and Mr Harry Mountjoy. On the Friday before Caroline was to travel down to London, a German Zeppelin dropped a bomb in Piccadilly, on the premises of Swan and Edgar, the department store, killing four people, two of whom were Alice and Harry, who had been dining in a nearby restaurant.

The telegram came on Saturday. Jessie was in the hall when the doorbell rang. Her heart turned over as she took the telegram from the solemn-faced boy in his pill-box hat and smart uniform. She hardly dared look at the envelope, but a glance showed that it was for Miss Caroline Mason. Charles, she thought. It could only be.

Mrs Cobb came, asking who had rung the bell. She stopped as she saw Jessie's face. 'What? What is it?'

'A telegram for Miss Caroline — it must be —'

Mrs Cobb turned white. 'Oh, my God, no — I'll have to — no, you'd better — no, both of us.'

They went upstairs and stood outside Caroline's room for a few moments, listening to the music she was playing on the gramophone. "If You Were the Only Girl in the World" — the song she'd sung after she'd met Harry Mountjoy, whom she had insisted was in love with her. Jessie knocked and they went in. Caroline was at her dressing-table mirror. Jessie could see her three faces, smiling out of the glass. A cigarette was burning in a glass dish and there was the smell of smoke, perfume and powder.

She saw their faces in the mirror. 'What on earth — what's the matter?'

Jessie never forgot Caroline's face as she tore open the flimsy envelope. She was white with terror, and then she laughed.

'It's not — it's not Charles. It's Alice and Mountjoy — killed in an air raid.' And the laughter started again as she spluttered, 'Isn't it priceless — both of them dead.'

'It's shock. Get the brandy,' Mrs Cobb ordered, as she went over to take Caroline by the shoulders and shake her.

By the time Jessie flew back with the brandy glass, Caroline was calm, but she didn't cry.

'Lord, what a shock you gave me. Why didn't you open it downstairs, Mrs Cobb?'

'It was addressed to you, Miss Caroline. It wasn't my place.'

'Oh, well, I suppose you're right, and thank goodness it wasn't bad news — well, the worst news, I mean. Of course, it's dreadful about Alice and Harry, but, oh, the relief. I could do with some tea, and more brandy if you'll get some, Jessie.'

When Jessie stood outside the door with the brandy, she heard the laughter again. It stopped abruptly as she turned the handle.

Caroline was smoking her cigarette, her eyes narrowed and glittering in the smoke. 'I'll be wearing black. I said I would. I didn't know it would be for a funeral and not a wedding. Harry Mountjoy's brother says he'll write about the funeral.'

22

The funeral was in London. Caroline went off in her fur coat and her black skirt and jacket, with her smart black dress carefully packed in tissue paper by Jessie. At least she looked the part. Jessie thought how pale she looked, as if she really was the grieving friend. She hadn't laughed again, but there were no tears, either. Jessie didn't believe that Caroline felt the grief she professed in the letters she wrote to Mr and Mrs Herd, and to Harry Mountjoy's brother, Arthur, whom she said was a charming man who had returned on leave for the wedding.

'Ghastly for him,' she said. 'I think he was rather a devoted younger brother. He'll be the heir now, Sir Arthur Mountjoy, one day. Lucky for him.'

Nurse was still in pain and her breathing wasn't good, but she did get up to sit with her mistress on some afternoons. When she went to rest, Jessie had the duty of keeping an eye on Lady Emmeline.

'You're Lavender,' she said one afternoon, smiling at Jessie, who had helped her to her chair. 'I remember you now. Caroline was here, I think. Where is she?'

'She's away with friends, my lady.'

'Everyone goes away. Will you stay?'

'Oh, yes, my lady.'

'Lavender is a pretty name.'

Jessie didn't correct her. At least she was speaking, even smiling. 'Yes, my lady. Could you manage more tea, or a sandwich, perhaps?'

'Cucumber, we used to have. I don't know why. Is this egg? Eggs for breakfast — Jonathan never — who fell?'

Jessie froze. The two faded blue eyes stared at her, wide with puzzlement and fear. Was she remembering? Jessie thought for a second, then she said quickly, 'Nurse, my lady. Nurse sprained her ankle, but it's better now.'

'Caroline said — she said — Jonathan —' and two tears rolled down the sunken cheeks.

'No, no, my lady, Nurse fell. I promise you she is better.'

'Oh, of course. Nurse fell, and she came in earlier.'

'Yes, she is resting now.'

'Good, it's good to rest. I'm tired — so tired… The tower…'

Jessie settled her in bed and waited until she was asleep, but she was shaken. She remembered Caroline saying that Lady Emmeline needed to be shocked out of her trance. Surely Caroline hadn't told her about Jonathan? She couldn't have been so cruel. Jessie thought about that laughter and the glitter in Caroline's eyes when she'd said she'd be going to the funeral. She could be cruel.

Jessie never knew the truth. Of course, she never asked if Caroline had mentioned Jonathan or the tower to Lady Emmeline. She didn't tell Mrs Cobb or Nurse that the last words she had heard Lady Emmeline whisper were "the tower".

Nurse had shouted for Mrs Cobb from the top of the stairs.

'What the devil's wrong now?' Mrs Cobb said as she hurried into the screens passage, followed by Jessie. Lady Emmeline was not in her bed.

They searched all the rooms, including Jonathan's. Jessie was sent up to the attics and back down to the kitchen and into the hall. Mrs Cobb took the library, dining and drawing rooms while Nurse sat at the top of the stairs whimpering between her wheezing breaths.

'She couldn't have got out, surely,' Mrs Cobb whispered, hustling Jessie back to the kitchen. 'She couldn't manage those bolts on the front door.'

'The back door, though,' Jessie said. 'It's not difficult — I oil the bolts and hinges regularly.'

'What'd she want to go out for? She only walks at —' Jessie was opening the back door — 'All right, have a look round the yard — oh, Lord, the gate's open. An' we don't know when she went. Dear God, what a to-do.'

'You don't think — the tower?'

Mrs Cobb turned pale. 'You've not said anything to her?'

'No, but she does talk about Mr Jonathan sometimes.'

'She doesn't say what happened in the tower?'

'No, and honestly, Mrs Cobb, I haven't — I wouldn't.'

Jessie was looking across the yard. 'I'd better have a look.'

The sight of Lady Emmeline's body did not surprise her, even though she shook with horror. She looked so small in her rumpled nightgown, which Jessie pulled down to cover the stick-thin legs with their blue veins. It wasn't fitting for anyone to see that. Lady Emmeline lay face-down on the stone floor, her head at a horrible angle, one arm crushed underneath and the other stretched out. She looked like an ungainly bird, fallen from the sky. Jessie looked up at the old arch from where Jonathan de Moine had fallen, at the staircase where she had seen Alexander looking up and from where he had asked if there was anyone else there, and where she had felt the shower of stones fall on her and the wind's cold touch at her neck. Only the wind.

23

Caroline came back, summoned by another telegram sent by Doctor Kennedy, for whom Jessie had been sent across by ferry to Kirkby Lonsdale. On the journey back in his motor car, Jessie told him what had happened. In the closed car, he had not looked at her, nor had he asked any questions, merely nodding from time to time.

It was only when the car stopped at the front door that he spoke to her. His voice was kind. 'Not a word about this, Jessie, to anyone. Poor Lady Emmeline is dead — of pneumonia. I expected it. That is what I will state on the death certificate. I have looked after her for a very long time. She has had much suffering in her life, and it is not to be thought of that the family's history should yet again be exposed to the gaze of the prurient world. Do I have your word?'

Jessie didn't know what prurient meant, but she knew what the newspaper had said about Ethel Widdop. She nodded and said, 'I promise I won't say anything.'

'Thank you. Then I will make all the necessary arrangements with the undertaker for the funeral.'

He opened the car door for her and they went into the hall, where Mrs Cobb was waiting. Nothing was said at all about the fall or the tower.

The hearse came and Doctor Kennedy followed in his car with Mr Manvers, the solicitor from Kendal, and Caroline in deepest black with a thick veil over her face. Both men waited in the hall as Jessie followed her down the stairs. She felt almost like a bridesmaid following the bride to her waiting groom, so stately and slow was Caroline's descent. Mr Manvers helped Caroline into the car as carefully as if she had been a piece of porcelain. Mrs Cobb, Nurse and Jessie followed in another car to the little church beyond Crossgill, where the General and Jonathan were buried.

'United front,' Caroline had said to Jessie, who had asked if she really was meant to go. 'Oh, yes, the grieving household. Just in case anyone's watching, and we'll be too upset to talk to anyone, of course. Doctor Kennedy has sorted it all out.'

Jessie understood that Caroline knew very well how Lady Emmeline had really died, but Caroline didn't speak of it to her.

Mr Manvers spent time with Caroline in the library. Mrs Cobb mentioned Lady Emmeline's will with a sniff and a curl of her lip, and it was the next day that Jessie found Caroline in her room and some jewellery spread out on her desk.

'These are what Lady Emmeline has left me — pearls. They look very well with black — valuable, too, and this is her engagement ring. A diamond, and there's an emerald bracelet and necklace, a ruby ring and earrings, too. It must be years since they were worn. Poor Lady Emmeline — I'll miss her, you know. But she was very frail. I don't suppose she was long for this world... I have some money, too, Jessie, so I can go to London whenever I please.'

She began to put the jewels back in their velvet pouches and into the box.

'Won't you wear the pearls, Miss?'

'Oh, no, it wouldn't be right. I mean, I ought to wait until Charles comes home. He inherits everything, you know. Mr Manvers has written to him. I suppose it was too difficult for him to come for the funeral. He'll write, I'm sure. And when he comes, I'll let him put the diamond ring on this finger.'

Caroline slipped it onto the third finger of her left hand. Jessie was dazzled for a moment as the diamond caught the light and Caroline's face was in shadow.

Charles didn't come home. Doctor Kennedy came to see Nurse, who sat in her room poring over photograph albums and weeping for her mistress. Jessie took up the trays, but Nurse didn't speak to her. Sometimes she asked for Caroline, who went in to sit with her for a short while. Otherwise, Caroline smoked, listened to her music, tried out her lipsticks, and wrote her letters. She put Lady Emmeline's jewels back in the dead woman's room and waited for Charles to write back. Mr Manvers came to get the bills from Mrs Cobb and to give her what money she needed. Mrs Cobb took to her room for longer in the afternoons. Jessie made sandwiches and cut cake for Caroline's tea, but she rarely ate any of it.

November seemed to go on forever with its monotonous grey days and lashing rain, and it was cold, too. A week seemed like a month and there was little news. Charles didn't write, nor did Josh, and there was no newspaper to tell them what was happening. Jessie fretted for Josh in the agony of waiting. Caroline was bad-tempered and unpredictable, and very pale in the mornings when Jessie took her tea, which she waved away. Jessie suggested Doctor Kennedy, but was rebuffed, and there was no invitation for Christmas. Caroline had had hopes of London and Harry Mountjoy's brother, but he was away at the Front, too. Only a hero when his absence wasn't inconvenient.

'I want to get away from here,' she moaned, lying in bed still, wrapped in her red kimono. 'I can't bear it.'

When Jessie heard the sounds of retching in the bathroom and went in to find Caroline lying on the floor, clammy and cold to the touch and seemingly having fainted, she went for Mrs Cobb and between them they half-carried her back to bed. Jessie was sent for a glass of brandy. On the way downstairs, she wondered if the household had caught some bug or infection. Nurse had said she felt sick all the time, too, and Jessie felt nauseous in the mornings and so very tired. Only Mrs Cobb seemed immune to it.

Caroline was lying with her eyes closed, beads of sweat on her upper lip. She looked very pale, and Jessie could see that her eyes were swollen. Mrs Cobb gave her a little brandy and her eyes opened. She looked at Mrs Cobb. 'What will I do?'

Mrs Cobb's face was grim. 'Nowt you can do. It's gone too far.'

'How long?'

'Four — five months, mebbe. Does that make sense to you?'

Caroline didn't answer and Jessie just looked down at her feet. She realised what was meant. A lot of things fell into place. Caroline had always been dressed when Jessie went into the bedroom in the early morning, or if she was in bed, she would tell Jessie that she was going to have a bath and Jessie could come back later. Sometimes, Caroline would stay in bed, telling her that she didn't feel well enough to get up. *Five months*, she thought. It was five months ago when Caroline had gone to London overnight for a party, but she hadn't said who she had seen.

'Didn't you realise?' Mrs Cobb asked Caroline.

'I didn't — well, I wondered, but I thought —' she burst into tears — 'it couldn't be true. I thought it would go away. Can't you do anything, Mrs Cobb? People do — I've heard about it—'

'Too late for that, Miss. We'll have to fetch Doctor Kennedy. He'll advise us.'

'No, no,' Caroline wailed. 'I can't — no one must —'

Mrs Cobb was not to be gainsaid. 'Doctor Kennedy's been the doctor here for years. You need a doctor and he's the best bet. It's not going to go away, Miss Caroline. Jessie'll have to go for him — I'll write a note.'

They went downstairs in silence. Mrs Cobb wrote her note and gave her two pennies for the ferry.

'You don't know what's the matter with Miss Caroline.'

24

Doctor Kennedy was as silent as he had been the first time he had driven Jessie back to Moonlyght. He had looked at Mrs Cobb's note, his lips tightening, but he had only murmured, 'Hmm,' and gestured for Jessie to get into the car.

Jessie would have liked to be driven anywhere but back to Moonlyght. The question of Caroline's baby's father tormented her, and there was a worse fear which made her think of something coiled tightly within, so tense was she, something so terrifying that she felt the familiar sickness rise to her throat and the sweat trickling down her back. She gazed out of the window, not seeing the hills with their purple shadows or the bare trees.

The car came to a halt and Doctor Kennedy waited while she fumbled her way out. She led him up the stairs to the bedroom. Caroline was sitting up in bed, the red kimono replaced by a pretty, pink silk bed jacket with a bow at the neck, her hair neatly tied with another pink ribbon. The room smelt of lavender and a fresh breeze came through the open window. It was as if nothing had happened.

Caroline looked pale, but she managed a rueful smile at the doctor. 'Oh, Doctor Kennedy, I'm so sorry to have troubled you, but I'm afraid things have become a little complicated. I feel rather ashamed, though, of course —'

She raised her hand and Jessie saw that she was wearing Lady Emmeline's diamond ring on the third finger of her left hand.

'Thank you, Jessie. We'll have some tea — in half an hour,' Mrs Cobb's voice cut in like a blade.

As she closed the door, Jessie heard Doctor Kennedy say, 'These things happen, my dear, in time of war, but all will be well. I'm sure Charles will...'

Jessie fled to the kitchen. She didn't want to hear. All would be well for Caroline Mason. Of course it would. Charles would have to marry her once he knew about the baby. Perhaps he'd come home on leave and there would be a wedding, and Caroline would go away to have her baby. No one would say anything — not about the grand people at Moonlyght. And if they did, what would it matter to Caroline, the wife of the master of Moonlyght? It might not be Charles's child, but dead Harry Mountjoy could tell no tales.

Five months, Jessie thought, as she set the tray. Why hadn't she realised? Jessie tried to think when Caroline's monthly courses had stopped. It was hard to tell. Caroline gave her the towelettes wrapped in paper and Jessie burnt them in the range. It was just something she did, as mechanical as emptying the wastepaper basket. Jessie herself was not always regular. There was only the sickness, but Nurse had been sick, too. Could it be that she had caught something from Nurse? That must be it — the other possibility was unthinkable. She'd be sent away, but where could she go, and what would she tell Josh? Would she be able to tell Charles? But he would be marrying Caroline — there couldn't be two —

A saucer smashed on the stone flags as the door opened. Mrs Cobb come for the tray.

'What's to do with you? You look as if you've seen a ghost, you're that whey-faced. Don't you be thinkin' about what's goin' on up there — Miss Caroline'll be goin' to a nursin' home. A car'll come tomorrow, an' that's all you need to know. Clear up that mess. I'll take the tea up.'

Jessie couldn't stop shaking. She would have to leave Moonlyght — just take her money and go. She had five pounds and ten shillings — it was enough. She'd go to a city, she thought. There were lodgings, and there were hospitals. She'd write to Josh, tell him that now that Lady Emmeline was dead and Miss Caroline was living elsewhere, she wasn't needed. And when he came home… He wouldn't desert her…

Mrs Cobb came back with the tray. 'She wants you to help her pack.'

Caroline was lying back on her pillows, her eyes closed, her hands resting loosely on the counterpane. The diamond glittered in the sunlight that shone palely through the window.

'Miss Caroline?'

'Oh, it's you, Jessie. Fetch me a cigarette. The box on the table.'

Caroline took a deep drag of the cigarette and blew out the smoke with a long sigh. 'Thank the Lord that's over. Dear Doctor Kennedy told me not to smoke or drink. I must look after myself for the — I don't want it, Jessie, but they won't… Mrs Cobb says it can be adopted. Maybe I'll miscarry — they say that if you drink gin or jump down the stairs… Oh, God, I can't bear it —'

'But what about Mr Charles?'

'Jessie, I can't tell him. He's out there fighting for his country. Do you think I want him to come running back to marry me because he has to?'

'But you said he loved you.'

'He does, of course he does, but it doesn't work that way. It would come between us — I can't imagine it. No, I don't want it. He must never know about this. Promise you won't breathe a word to anyone.'

'Of course I won't.'

'Don't leave me, Jessie. I'll need you when I come back.'

Caroline went away the next day. To a seaside place, she told Jessie, where she'd be looked after until it was over. Jessie watched the car roll away and thought of Josh. He'd sent a field postcard — a card which had sentences printed on the reverse side. The soldier was not allowed to write anything, only to cross out the sentences that did not apply, so Josh was well; he had received her last letter; and he would write at the first opportunity. What should she write now? she wondered, trailing back into the house after Mrs Cobb.

No letters came to be sent on to Miss Caroline at the seaside. Jessie didn't know if Caroline had written to tell Charles that she was not at home. She supposed that some story would be cooked up to account for her absence, if Charles came on leave. But he didn't come, and he didn't write to Mrs Cobb. It was as if he had vanished from their lives. The house was still and silent. Jessie sat in the kitchen and sometimes took a tray up to Nurse and set a tray for Mrs Cobb, who preferred to eat her supper in her room.

Such endless days and impossible, exhausting nights when Jessie lay awake, feeling her stomach, wondering if there was something that moved there. Someone. She was like Caroline, she thought. She couldn't imagine it.

And then one night, when Jessie was in the bathroom, there was blood, so much blood and pain that she cried out.

Mrs Cobb found her, put her in the bath, wrapped her in towels, and took her back to bed.

'Don't move. I'll fetch something for you.'

She came back with a glass of cloudy water. 'Just drink it — it's for the pain. Laudanum. It'll help you sleep. I'll clear everything up. Don't tell me anything. I don't want to know.'

Jessie couldn't remember how long she lay in bed in a blur of pain and confusion, but she remembered Mrs Cobb, who looked after her, washing her down, bathing her burning face, changing the sheets, changing her nightgown, giving her the medicine for the pain, medicine which brought, too, a thankful oblivion in sleep. Mrs Cobb was surprisingly tender. Jessie heard her voice sometimes, telling her, 'Hush, hush, no need to talk.'

When she emerged from her fever, Mrs Cobb gave her some of Miss Caroline's towelettes and made her eat the soup she brought up, and drink the black beer which she said was a tonic for purging the blood.

At last, Jessie was able to dress herself and make her tentative way downstairs. Mrs Cobb was in the kitchen, making tea, and Jessie could smell toast.

Mrs Cobb looked surprised to see her, but she only said, 'You're looking more like it. Good.'

'Thank you, Mrs Cobb,' Jessie blurted out. 'Thank you for looking after me. I'm sorry —'

'I did my duty. Nowt to be sorry for. You've been lucky. Pity it didn't happen to Miss Caroline as well.'

At first, Jessie sat by the range for most of the day. She watched the snow falling, changing the yard and the trees beyond into a dream world. Nothing seemed real. She knew now that there had been a baby. She didn't know what to feel about that. Just empty. She imagined herself going out into that falling snow and simply vanishing — as if she had never existed. Forgotten, like Lady Emmeline and Alexander, gone into the dark earth. To die was to sleep forever, to know nothing and to remember nothing.

She came back to herself eventually, but she knew she had changed. Something had moved into place. She'd grown up.

That's what she thought. It was time to stop letting things happen to her.

On a day when the snow had stopped falling and the gate and the trees emerged from their silver sheaths, she looked up from slicing some bread as Mrs Cobb came into the kitchen and realised that she wasn't afraid of her. Words could do no harm.

'Why didn't you send me away?'

Mrs Cobb stood quite still in the doorway, staring at Jessie. She came in, sat down at her place, took up the butter knife and put it down again.

'You said things in your fever. I knew anyway. Best forgotten, Jessie. Nowt to be done — least said —' She sighed. 'Grand folks — they're different. Different rules, Jessie. You'll stay and when your brother comes, mebbe there'll be a chance. But don't be tellin' — some things are to be borne on your own. It's a hard lesson, but a true one.'

And with that, Mrs Cobb left the kitchen and her bread and butter.

25

It was in December that Jessie learnt the full truth of Mrs Cobb's hard lesson. On an afternoon when the snow began again, Jessie sat in her accustomed place by the range with Josh's last letter in her lap, which had come at the end of November, though she had been too ill to read it then. Mrs Cobb had given it to her when she was at last able to sit up. The battalion was in training in what was called a road camp — still in Belgium, he told her. They expected to be in the line at the end of the month. Will Beswick sent his best regards, and they both hoped that she was well.

She had replied, of course, and had had to lie. That was a hard lesson. She had lied to Charles about Ethel Widdop, but he had found her out because her face had given her away. She was involved in lies about Lady Emmeline and Miss Caroline, and in secrets about Alexander. Lying to her own brother was most difficult of all. Josh had never lied to her. Could the words on the page give her away? She didn't know. She had told Josh that she had been ill — just a bad cold, nothing serious. She had found it hard to write those words and to carry on with news about the weather, and how sorry she was that she had nothing to tell him, but that there were holly berries on the trees outside the yard gate, and that she'd watched an owl one night through her window, and that she longed for him to come on leave again. And to write her greetings to Will Beswick was almost beyond her capacity. She meant them, but she hated the thought that he might read something in them that she should not mean.

She was thinking about Josh and that the battalion must be in the line still, and that that surely meant in the thick of battle for there had not even been a postcard, when the doorbell pealed its deep note. She waited. Mrs Cobb was in her room. Perhaps she was dozing by the fire. The bell rang again, so she went to answer the door.

It was Will Beswick, and she knew. It was in his face. She had seen anguish in Alexander's face, and in Josh's, as they remembered what they had endured, but this was agony. His eyes seemed to burn with it, as though he were being eaten from within by fire, his face falling as he struggled to speak, the bruises under his eyes livid against his pale skin. He just stared at her as though at a vision.

'Will, oh Will, I know, I know.'

And then he was inside, shaking the snow from his coat, and she was taking his cap and muffler, leading him to the kitchen and the warmth, and feeling only for him and that torment in his face. She found the brandy, not caring what Mrs Cobb might think, just watching the colour come back into his cheeks as though he was a dead man brought back to life.

'I'm sorry,' he said. 'There'll be an official letter, but I thought it might go to your Pa, and I wanted to tell you. I didn't want you to be on your own.'

'You've been wounded,' she said, noting the bandage at his neck, not wanting to speak of what he had come for.

'It's nothing — nothing — a graze. I have to tell you.'

'He's dead, I know. What else is there?' She didn't want to know.

'Not found, Jessie, not found. I saw him fall...' The agony returned to his face. 'After all this time. Brothers. All those Westmorland men in two days...'

Jessie let him talk. It was not time to think of herself or to ask for anything. Not for pity. It was the last thing she could do for Josh and for his brother-in-arms, for the man she might have loved, might have married and gone to Canada with.

'All the Cumberland and Westmorland men, the Kendal men — none left. Cobbley from Ambleside — we called him Uncle Tom — our sergeant. When I think — when we joined — all gone. Men from Lancashire, Northumberland — men of the north, and the south — a hundred men in two days —'

What Mr Alexander had said about that July day. What she had suffered was nothing compared to this. What she was going to suffer was nothing to what all these men had suffered, these men who were Josh's brothers.

'Men from Essex. Ebenezer Cokes — we called him Scrooge, Captain Benson, Captain Sanders, Lieutenant Macduff and Second Lieutenant Duff — Plum — just Plum. And Josh —'

She would have to hear it because he had to tell it. Who else was he to tell? No one knew Josh as she did. 'Tell me, Will. I can bear it.'

'He was shot. I saw him fall and I managed to drag him to a shell hole, but it was full of water and mud. I had to go on. I shouldn't have left him, but it was an order — they said we had to go forward. I don't know where he is.'

'When?' she managed.

'A week ago. The second of December.'

And she hadn't known. The last things she had written to him were lies. She dared not look at Will Beswick in case her face betrayed her, but she took his rough, cold hands and rubbed them until some warmth came back. When she looked up, she saw that he was weeping, the silent tears running down his gaunt face.

'Jessie, Jessie — he talked of you so much, how we would all go to Canada or Australia, how we would — we, you and me, Jessie — he thought, and I didn't forget, so —'

She steeled herself. 'It's too soon, Will. I can't —'

'But you can leave here — you shouldn't be a servant. Josh said. You should be a teacher. Come back to Gressthwaite with me. There's the bicycle shop. My mother will put you up, and when I come back…'

How tempting it was. A future. But she faltered. She couldn't. 'When you come back, Will, we'll decide then.'

'I'm sorry, I shouldn't have — not when — but write to me, and then I'll know, I'll have hope. I ought to go — the train—'

They went into the hall. When he had put on his cap and coat, he turned to her and placed his hands on her shoulders. She almost stepped forward, but she drew back. 'I can't.'

He dropped his hands. 'I only wanted — I didn't mean —'

Mrs Cobb saved her. She heard the door upstairs open and close. 'The housekeeper — you'd better —'

He looked so pained and confused that she wanted to hug him now, but he turned away and went out, his shoulders hunched against the cold. Jessie watched him go down the drive. Will turned before the bend and waved. She waved back and waited until he had gone.

Then she went back into the hall where the shadows lingered in the corners, the suit of armour stood silent, and the crescent moons gleamed greenly in the snowlight.

Back in the kitchen she took up the burden of her life again. She would have to bear it alone.

Westroosebeck. That was where Josh had been killed on 2nd December, 1917. He had never been found. The attack had been in the dark during a deafening barrage, across a shattered, treeless landscape of torn wire where dead men hung like scarecrows — the dead piled up on the dead. As Will had told her, the Lonsdales had lost over a hundred men, Kendal men, Carlisle men, Penrith men, Ambleside men, men from up in Workington, and Whitehaven by the sea, places she'd never been, but Cumberland and Westmorland men, from the hills and the lakes, the farms and the great houses, from little shops and offices, farmers' boys, fishermen, grooms, stable hands, servants, miners, cobblers, carpenters, clerks, fathers, sons — and brothers.

I died in Hell — they called it Passchendaele, Jessie had read later in a newspaper. Whoever had written it had seen what Josh had seen: the gas, the flooded trenches, and how two hundred and fifty thousand men had disappeared into shell holes and drowned in the freezing mud.

Will Beswick had survived. But Josh had not. He'd died in Hell. And Jessie had looked upon Caroline Mason with a harder eye when she had come back without her child.

PART THREE: 1918

26

Jessie felt only a tremor when the telegram boy came again in January. The worst had happened. Even if Charles was the subject of that flimsy bit of paper, she could bear it. The memory of Charles had receded, as had the events of those days and nights of pain. It was as if all that had happened with Charles was a long time ago, so long ago that it might have happened to someone else, to someone younger and innocent. Another girl altogether.

The telegram was addressed to Mrs Cobb. It might be about Caroline. She didn't care about that. Caroline would not be dead in childbirth, or in a motor accident on the way home in the thick snow that had fallen. Caroline Mason was a survivor — made of steel.

Mrs Cobb opened the envelope. 'Oh, dear Lord, Mr Charles is wounded — he's in hospital.'

'Where?'

'Kirkby Lonsdale — a place called Lunefield House. Convalescent home for officers. You'll have to go.'

'Me? I can't —'

'Well, I can't leave here.'

'Why not?'

'I can't be trampin' in all this snow. You've young legs. You'll go and be said.'

'But —'

'He'll be comin' here when he's well enough. I told you, you've to forget all that.'

'What will I say about Miss Caroline?'

Mrs Cobb looked nonplussed for a moment or two. 'Nothing. She'll have written to him — whatever she's told him is nowt to do with us.'

Jessie had no choice but to take the train to Kirkby Lonsdale station and ask for directions to the town. A kindly carrier gave her a lift and showed her how to get to Lunefield House. She was astonished by the people in the street. It was as if she had landed from another planet, so cut off had she been at Moonlyght. She was tempted for a moment to walk down the street to look at the shop windows, to mingle with the passers-by. To be free. There were people chatting, carts, carriages, a motor car, a man on horseback, another on a bicycle. It reminded her of Gressthwaite, and that gave her a pang — so long ago. Another life. A lost life.

She turned away and went through the pillars of Lunefield House onto the tree-lined carriage drive from where the park stretched away into the distance. There were well-kept gardens eventually, a fountain, and then the house on a slope, a great mansion, a confusion of elaborate chimneys, towers, pointed arches, enormous windows, some festooned with ivy, porches with pillars, and one high tower — not a ruin like the tower at Moonlyght. Whoever owned it cared for it, Jessie thought. It was like a fairy-tale castle, but not one with terrible secrets.

In the hall Jessie could hear voices, though there was no one to speak to. She went to an open door from where she could see a room filled with light from huge windows and an ornate mirror over a white marble fireplace where a fire blazed. There were cane chairs and armchairs in groups, and young men were sitting smoking and chatting or reading a newspaper. Some had arms in slings or bandages round their heads; there was one man in a wheelchair with a tartan rug over his knees, and another wearing dark glasses. She was surprised by the sense of lightness. It wasn't just the light streaming in but the chatter and laughter.

A young woman in a white cap and a blue dress over which there was a white apron with a red cross on the bib caught sight of her and came over to ask whom she wanted to see. She sounded like Caroline, but her face was kinder; she had freckles scattered over her nose and lively blue eyes. Her uniform gave her a different air of confidence.

'Captain Bennett?' the young woman repeated in her clipped upper-class tone.

'Yes, I've come from his house. We had a telegram from him.'

'Come with me. He's in bed.'

That frightened Jessie. Why wasn't Charles with the others, laughing and smoking?

'Is he badly injured?' she asked as her companion led the way up the wide staircase with its oak carvings.

'No, he's recovering well. Just resting. We're taking very good care of him. He was shot in the arm, but it's healed well. He's raring to go back, brave soul. Here we are. First bed on the right.'

Jessie went into the room. One of the beds was unoccupied and Charles lay asleep in the other, his face drawn and pale. There was a bruise on his forehead, purplish green against his white skin. She noted the sling on his arm and the tenderness she had felt that night returned. He looked vulnerable somehow, as people often did in sleep when the mask worn by day fell away and the child in them returned.

His eyes opened. 'Jessie,' he said, and she was herself again.

'Yes, sir, Mrs Cobb sent me to ask if you wanted anything — if you're all right. She — we — were worried.'

'Good of you to come. Thought I'd better let you all know — I'm on the mend. Back in business soon.'

'Good. Will you come to Moonlyght?'

His face darkened for a moment. 'I think not — can't face the place just now — I need to get back. I don't want to think about Moonlyght and —'

He closed his eyes again. She wondered what the "and" meant. Did he think about her, or was it Caroline he thought about? Or Alexander? She didn't ask. The silence lengthened, but she had no idea how to break it. She just wanted to go, and he didn't want to come back.

'I can only think of out there, Jessie. Moonlyght's a dream; this place is only a dream. Only out there is real. When it's over, maybe I'll come back —'

Jessie stood up straighter. He was a stranger now. 'If there's nothing else, sir —'

He looked at her face in that old considering way. 'No, nothing. Nothing at all. I'm sorry, Jessie, for what happened. I hope you — can forgive me. I didn't mean to hurt you.'

'I'm all right, sir. I should go.'

But he reached out and took her hand. 'Look after Caroline until I get back, and then I'll sort —'

Jessie was stung into bitterness. 'You're going to marry her.' She snatched her hand away.

He looked astonished. 'No, no, I only meant — I feel responsible for her. She's so reckless — you never know —'

'She says she's going to marry you — she says you love her. She has it all planned.'

'Oh, God — I should never —'

She couldn't stop herself now. She looked down at him and anger rose like a tide. Oh, he regretted Caroline now, just as he was sorry for her. He'd used them both. 'No, you shouldn't have. It's too late now. She's having a child.'

She'd shocked him. He seemed to shrink back on his pillow. 'She can't be — after Alexander, Caroline wanted — needed, but not that — I didn't —'

Anger felt like power to the powerless. 'Well, someone did. She's away at the seaside. There'll be no child when she comes back. Doctor Kennedy arranged it all. He thinks you're the father, though. I saw the diamond ring on her finger, and so did Doctor Kennedy, and Mrs Cobb.'

'You mean she's having —'

'It was too late for that as well. I just know she won't come back with a child — whose ever it was.'

'Good God, Jessie — what a mess she's got herself into — and me, but I swear, I cannot be the father of her child. I cannot marry her.'

'Best forgotten then — like Ethel Widdop.'

'What? You don't think —'

'Ethel wanted to get a message to you. Mrs Cobb said she pushed herself at you. You told me to forget about her. I haven't.'

Charles sat up. He was angry, too. 'I did not seduce Ethel Widdop. What do you think I am?'

She didn't answer, because suddenly she was thinking of golden eyes and Alexander asking if Ethel was there in the tower. 'But you know who did, and you used me to try to find out if I knew anything because it had to be kept secret. I mean, a de Moine and a servant girl — what would people think?'

'You know?'

'He thought I was her when I was in the tower. He said she had golden eyes. You quarrelled with him.'

'He thought he loved her.'

'Perhaps he did. Why shouldn't he? She was kind to me.' She flung his words back at him: 'She wasn't just a *bloody servant girl*.'

Charles flinched at the reminder. 'I was trying to shock him out of — well, you saw what he was like — he wasn't fit — it was madness. We're all mad when we come back. Sometimes you can't — she was dead —'

'Oh, I see.' Jessie flared. It was as if something had burst inside her. 'She was not as important as a de Moine. Her father loved her. And you paid him off. Thirty pieces of silver, was it?'

He paled at that. 'Oh, Jessie, it wasn't like that. I felt sorry for the man — he told me he couldn't stay in that cottage… It was all too late. We had to go back — I had a choice to make. She was dead. There was Lady Emmeline and Caroline. And Jonathan's death. Imagine if Alexander had been accused of murder? I don't know if he did it, Jessie, I honestly don't.'

'But you were together — you arrived at Moonlyght together that day.'

'I didn't come with him. I'd been home to see my father in Keswick, but I wanted to see Alexander. I knew he was under immense strain, but I was on a different train. He was there before me. I found him in the wood with the… He was there. She was dead — he didn't know if he had done it. I only tried to protect him —' His shoulders slumped, and his voice changed. 'It was better as it was, even if — himself he could not save —'

That poem she'd read on the night he'd come to her room. 'Don't — don't ever repeat those words —'

'Sorry, sorry. It wasn't — you did matter to me, and Alexander. I only meant that Alexander couldn't help —'

She knew that he thought what Josh had thought. That Alexander had stood up on purpose. And at the thought of

Josh, her anger drained away. None of this mattered. She remembered what she had felt when she had seen Will Beswick's face. What had happened between her and Charles didn't matter. Caroline didn't matter. Even Ethel didn't matter now. Perhaps Alexander had killed her, but he was dead, too. There was nothing to be done. All too late, Charles had said. He was right.

She was saved from saying anything by the entrance of the nurse, who looked from one to the other with concern. 'Is everything all right? I thought I heard —'

Charles raised his hand wearily. 'It's fine, Nurse Mary. Miss Sedgwick was annoyed by something I said.' He looked at Jessie. 'We're friends again, aren't we?'

'Of course, sir.'

'Well, I think my patient should rest now. He looks very tired.'

Jessie walked back down the carriageway. That moment of power had passed, leaving her empty. She had spoken her mind for once, had challenged Charles Bennett, showed that she was not just a "bloody servant", that she had thoughts and feelings of her own, but what had all that passion achieved? She was still Jessie Sedgwick, with her raw red hands and her clumsy boots — who belonged nowhere.

She looked up at the distant glitter of the hills covered in January snow. Josh buried in snow fathoms deep in Flanders — never to be found again. Josh, who had stood and fought and taken a bullet in his brain.

She turned into the still busy street full of strangers. No one knew her. She might just as well have been invisible. And there was only Moonlyght to go back to.

27

Jessie reported on Charles to Mrs Cobb, whom she thought was probably glad not to have another invalid to look after. Nurse was still in her room, looking at her photograph albums, reading her Bible, forgetting sometimes that Lady Emmeline was dead, accusing Jessie of poisoning her when she felt sick — she ate too much sweet stuff and seemed to have an unlimited appetite.

'She'll eat us out of house an' home, that one,' Mrs Cobb complained. But it was Jessie who had to look after Nurse, to change the sheets, empty the chamber pot, and clear up the vomit.

Not that she cared. She welcomed the drudgery of her days. It stopped her thinking during the day and sent her to bed exhausted by night, though sometimes she lay awake, staring at the moon, thinking about the money in her drawer. Jessie had her wages now — she'd had a whole five pounds at Martinmas in November, and Will Beswick had sent her a pound note which he said Josh had wanted to send to her. She had his pocketbook and watch, too, and the book of flowers — those were carefully stored in her chest of drawers with Alexander's poetry book, which she could not bear to read now, though she could not bear to throw it away, either. And she had the garnet bracelet which Caroline had told her to throw out. Caroline had never asked about it.

Ethel Widdop's words came back to her. "It ain't a prison." She could go. There were jobs in munitions factories. Mrs Cobb had said so. There were cities where a girl could lose herself. There was Manchester, where Caroline had been. But it seemed impossible, and she was helpless. She couldn't imagine a city or the people, or a factory. She couldn't imagine herself anywhere except here in this room, looking at the moon and the empty sky.

Near the end of February, Caroline came home. Nothing was said about her child. *Best forgotten*, Jessie thought wryly, looking at the carefully powdered face, the lightly carmined lips, the full shining hair. That familiar perfume, too. Only now Caroline looked somehow harder and older. Well, that made two of them. Jessie felt some sort of life return to her as she listened to the empty words.

'I'm sorry about your brother, Jessie. Mrs Cobb wrote. I thought you might have sent me a line or two.'

'I couldn't. I hadn't the words.'

Caroline frowned a little. 'I understand,' she said. 'It's very hard, I know. Losing Alexander was shattering, and when Mrs Cobb told me about Charles being wounded, I was devastated. She said you saw him.'

'Mrs Cobb sent me. He was all right.'

'Is that all? Did he send a message for me?'

'No, he didn't mention you.'

Caroline was nonplussed by that, but she rallied as Jessie knew she would. She opened her mouth to speak, but Jessie got in first. 'It was a lovely place, the hospital. The nurses were all so young and capable. Mr Charles's nurse —'

'His nurse?'

'Yes, they are all ladies, you see — volunteers, I found out. They're called VADs and wear lovely blue dresses and have a red cross on their aprons, and they look after the officers at Lunefield. It's a mansion for convalescent officers. They seemed to be having a good time. They deserve it.'

'Well, of course they do. And Charles was up and about?'

'Oh, yes. The nurse showed me to his room. I didn't stay long because the nurse came back and said he looked tired. He needed his wound dressing.'

'Was it serious?'

'The nurse said it was healing well and that Mr Charles was very eager to get back to the Front.'

'He hasn't replied to my letters. You haven't heard, have you?'

'Mr Charles wouldn't write to me. What would he have to say to the kitchen maid?'

'No, I suppose not. Mrs Cobb hasn't heard?'

'I don't know. He'll have enough to do out there.'

Caroline looked at her narrowly, but she only said, 'I'll write again.'

A couple of field postcards arrived in February, saying that Charles was back in France, but no letters came. Caroline was restless and uneasy. Jessie kept her tone neutral. She'd had her moment of triumph. It was the reference to Josh and Caroline pretending she had been shattered by Alexander's death that had stung Jessie into spite.

It was Caroline who suggested a walk in the woods on a cold but dry April morning. Something had shifted in their relationship. Jessie caught Caroline looking at her sometimes with a puzzled frown, as if she couldn't make her out. Caroline worried about the fact that Charles didn't answer her letters. She had only Jessie to talk to about it. It was as if she suspected that Jessie knew something she wasn't telling. It was that visit to the hospital that disturbed her, Jessie thought. She had quizzed Jessie about the nurse. Jessie had kept the best until last. Caroline wanted to know if the nurse had a name.

'Oh, Mr Charles called her Mary.'

'Were they friends, do you think?'

'I don't know. She seemed to like him, but surely a nurse must like her patient. She said she was taking good care of him.'

'Did he like her?'

'I don't know, Miss. I wasn't there very long.'

The walk would be an excuse to ask more questions. There had been no letters that morning, and Jessie had seen how Caroline's face had fallen and how she had toyed miserably with her breakfast.

They went through the gate into Hag Wood. The trees were budding a tender green now, and Jessie heard a cuckoo and a woodpecker somewhere. *Spring*, she thought. There'd be violets soon, the violets that Alexander had said to remember him by. He had been remembering Ethel, perhaps, who had died in Hag Wood, perhaps at the hands of a man who had not known what he was doing, or perhaps someone else. She glanced at Caroline.

Shattered, she'd said. Caroline Mason had no idea what loss meant. She feared she might have lost Charles to the nurse at Lunefield, but it was the loss of something she wanted that caused the turned-down mouth and the sulky restlessness. Jessie watched the slender figure in the neat-fitting coat and hat walking ahead of her along the narrow path and thought she despised her.

They walked in silence for a while, until Caroline suddenly stopped and stood staring into the trees. Jessie wondered what she was looking at. There were only shadows and the sound of the wind rustling the leaves.

'Ethel Widdop died in there.'

'I know. I don't like to think of it.'

'Do you think she suffered?'

'I don't know — it depends. I mean, if it was quick, or maybe she didn't see and — oh, I don't know, Miss. Please, let's go on.'

'You didn't know her.'

'No.'

'She was cheeky, you know; Mrs Cobb said she was batting her eyelashes at Charles. Impertinence — as if —' She turned to Jessie. 'You didn't tell him about me, did you?'

Jessie was glad of the shawl which covered most of her face. 'Why would I tell him about that? It's not my business.'

'No, it isn't. I'm not Ethel Widdop —'

'What has Ethel to do with it?'

'Nothing, of course, nothing. Ethel got herself into trouble with a railwayman or some rough type. Charles and I are different — we are in love. We're engaged.'

'Perhaps Ethel thought someone was in love with her.'

Caroline laughed the brittle laugh that came when she wasn't amused at all. 'Charles? Don't be ridiculous. It wasn't Charles, it was — some rough type, I told you.'

Jessie was puzzled. Where had the idea about Charles and Ethel Widdop come from? She knew where the idea of the engagement had come from — Caroline's imagination, but why did she connect Charles with Ethel? Only Jessie and Charles knew about the message Ethel had wanted to give to Charles. Only they knew about Alexander and Ethel. Unless Caroline had seen Ethel coming from the tower more often than she had said and suspected Charles of having some relationship with Ethel.

'I don't know anything about Mr Charles and Ethel Widdop.'

Jessie noted the feverish glitter in Caroline's eyes when she said, 'I've told you. She's nothing to do with Charles. A girl like that. A servant. She deserved —'

'To be murdered?' Jessie flashed back.

'I didn't say that. I'm not interested in Ethel Widdop, and you — you're getting too uppish. You forget sometimes that you're just a servant. And Cobb thinks she can say what she likes, always harping on about Lady Emmeline and the tower. It wasn't my fault. I'm mistress here. You'll see when Charles—'

Caroline flung herself away down the path, but not before Jessie saw the tears on her cheeks. Tears of anger, she thought, and frustration. Caroline wasn't getting her own way. It made her spiteful but, Jessie reflected, she was spiteful, too. She had told Charles about Caroline, and she shouldn't have. There would be no engagement, for Charles Bennett didn't love Caroline. And he might never come back to Moonlyght. She wondered what Caroline would do then.

28

There were no more walks and no more questions. Jessie and Caroline hardly spoke. Caroline kept to herself and when Jessie collected her laundry, made the bed, or tidied the room, she would either not be there or simply go out without looking at Jessie. Jessie would see her walking alone through the gate and into the wood, and then one rainy day she was surprised to see Caroline making her way to the tower. What on earth could she want in there? Mrs Cobb must have talked about Lady Emmeline's death again. Jessie thought that sometimes Mrs Cobb goaded Caroline about Lady Emmeline. Perhaps Caroline did feel guilty, even though she insisted that it wasn't her fault. Curious, she took her shawl and followed.

Caroline was standing and smoking, looking up the stairs at the ruined arch, but she turned round when she heard the scrape of the door.

'What do you want?'

'We need more coal.'

'Oh.'

They stood staring at each other. It was Caroline who broke the silence. 'I'm sorry, Jessie. I've been a pig, I know, but it was all so horrible. I didn't mean for Lady Emmeline to die. I was fed up — I did care about her. She took me in when nobody wanted me. She didn't have to. It's just that I thought she ought to face the truth about Jonathan. I didn't think she'd —'

No, Jessie thought, *you wouldn't think*, but she only nodded, and Caroline went on talking.

'Everything's gone wrong — I can't tell you — and the baby was taken away. I never saw it, and now I feel — I don't know

'— empty, I suppose. There's only Charles, and he — he's not written — and that nurse —'

'She was only a nurse, Miss Caroline, and Mr Charles has gone back to fight. Don't you think he has enough to do out there? I mean, he can't be thinking of —'

'Me. I know, but I'm afraid. What if he marries someone else? What happens to me? I belong here. Moonlyght should be mine — and Charles's.'

She won't change, Jessie thought, but she did feel a flicker of pity.

Caroline was looking up the stairs again. 'You've never done something dreadful, have you, Jessie?'

'What do you mean?'

'Something that can't be changed. Something you didn't mean —' Caroline looked up the stairs again, murmuring half to herself. 'Poor boy — I made a mistake — I only wanted —'

Jessie didn't know what to say. Did Caroline have something to do with Jonathan's death? But she'd hardly been more than a child then.

Caroline turned to look at Jessie. 'It doesn't matter now. The past can't be changed. Only the future matters.'

Jessie counted the twelve strokes of the hall clock. Midnight and she was still wide awake in the silent house. She couldn't stand it anymore. It was unbearable to be at Moonlyght. Caroline was so unpredictable — sometimes all sweetness and light to Jessie, at other times peevish and bad-tempered, finding fault, spitefully putting Jessie in her place. Then she'd wheedle, begging Jessie to play at fortune-telling or to do her hair; but she'd become morose again when there were still no letters. Charles was still alive and that was all they knew.

Night after sleepless night, her thoughts whirled about, confused, nightmarish thoughts. She imagined she heard weeping or footsteps above and thought that Alexander or Lady Emmeline had returned to haunt that empty room above. And if she slept, she'd dream of the tower, its walls closing in on her, shadows on the stairs, Alexander's eyes looking down, or were they Josh's eyes? Caroline at the top of the tower stairs with Charles and a figure flying down like a great crow swooping on her. And then she'd wake, her heart thumping and her breath coming in little gasps. It was Caroline's fault. Jessie couldn't help going over her words that day in the tower. Caroline had been the indirect cause of Lady Emmeline's death, but worse was the idea that she had been involved in Jonathan's death. She said she had done something dreadful, but Jessie hadn't dared ask and Caroline had walked past her out of the tower, and she never mentioned the conversation again.

Today had been worse than anything. Caroline had been to Kirkby Lonsdale to visit Lunefield House. When she came back she seemed in a better mood, for she smiled at Jessie as she threw herself onto her bed and lit a cigarette.

'Guess where I've been.'

'I've no idea.'

'The convalescent home to see that nurse — to thank her for looking after my fiancée. She's no beauty, is she?'

'I can't really remember her,' Jessie lied.

'She was a lady, you said.'

'I thought she was.'

'Oh, yes, very good family and all that. Some great house in the Lune Valley, though she looks like a farmer's wife. Those silly freckles. Very dutiful, I'm sure, but a bit of a bore. Reminded me of Sara Morris, the do-gooder. Holier than thou,

I thought. Charles wouldn't look twice at her. Just as he wouldn't have looked at Ethel Widdop, or — any servant.'

'Only to give orders.'

'My, my, very tart, and why shouldn't he give orders? He owns this place, and Mrs Cobb and you, for that matter.'

And you in a way, Jessie thought, but she only said placatingly, 'Things will be better when he comes back.'

'Yes, they will, of course they will, and we'll get more servants. We can pension off Mrs Cobb, and you —'

'What about me?'

'Yes, indeed, what about little Jessie of whom Charles is so fond?'

Jessie felt the blood rush to her face. Tears sprang to her eyes.

'Oh, yes, I've seen you turning those blue eyes on him, and that nurse, Mary, she said you said you were a friend of Charles's — a friend. How dare you? Giving her the impression that you were his —'

'Mr Charles said we were friends because —'

'Because you had a lovers' tiff. That's what the nurse thought. She heard raised voices. Now, why was that? I saw you blush when I asked. You little liar. You told him about me, didn't you? Because you want him. And he didn't believe the kitchen maid. Of course, he didn't. He told you to know your place, I'll bet. Oh, and crying now, you poisonous little traitor—'

And before Jessie could move or speak, she felt the sting of Caroline's palm on her cheek. She stepped back in horror, the tears spilling down her cheeks. Caroline stepped back, too, as if she had not really understood what she had done.

Jessie walked out.

Now she sat on her bed, her hand on her burning cheek. It had hurt, but the hurt now was the humiliation she had felt, as if the shame of it was branded on her face. It was true — she had betrayed Caroline. But Caroline's assumption that Charles had not believed her because she was just a kitchen maid, and that it was she who had made eyes at Charles, was unjust. Yet Caroline, who had betrayed her friend, Alice Herd, who had got pregnant by Harry Mountjoy, or someone else, who had pretended to Doctor Kennedy that she was engaged to Charles, and who had driven Lady Emmeline to her death, had dared to heap scorn on her and slap her.

She couldn't stay — not even for Whit Saturday, when she would get her next five pounds. It was two weeks away. Even to face Caroline tomorrow was impossible, more impossible than to contemplate taking the train to an unknown future. She trembled at the thought of going now in the dark through Hag Wood. There wouldn't be a train until the morning. It wouldn't matter where the train was going. She would simply get on the first train which came.

She took off her cotton dress and put on the woollen one she had worn when Josh had come. She took out the old carpet bag and packed it with her two nightdresses, the two linen shifts, camisoles and drawers, stockings, her Bible, the flower book with Josh's letters tucked inside, and Alexander's poetry book. She had her purse with Ma's ten shillings, Josh's pound note, and the five one-pound notes that had been her wages. She wouldn't starve. She left the damaged garnet bracelet on the chest of drawers. Caroline Mason should not say Jessie Sedgwick was a thief. And she left the lace collar.

She waited motionless on her bed, watching the moon fade, and the first grey hint of dawn stealing in at the window.

29

Jessie waited impatiently on the platform in the early morning chill. No one had seen her leave Moonlyght. Mrs Cobb and Caroline were still in bed, but she wanted to be on her way before they missed her. She didn't think they'd follow. Caroline would be glad to see the back of her, and Mrs Cobb — she'd be disgruntled, but she and Nurse would have to lump it until Charles came back, of course.

Jessie had passed through Hag Wood just as it was getting light, but she hadn't looked into the trees, only straight ahead, where the path led to freedom from Moonlyght, from Caroline and from Charles Bennett. She'd hurried through a quiet Mossgarth, hoping that the ferryman would be there to take any passenger who wanted the early train. She'd had to knock at the door of Cowpot Cottage, where Joe Widdop had lived with Ethel. She wondered where he had gone as she waited for someone to answer the door. A young man came out.

'Early bird, eh? Goin' for the milk train?'

'Yes, I'm going to —' She nearly said Carlisle, then thought that no one must know. 'Gressthwaite. My family is there.'

The milk train was going north. She knew it stopped at Gressthwaite, but she wouldn't get off there. She'd continue to a station at Lowgill, where she could change for Carlisle — Carlisle would do. Mrs Cobb had mentioned jobs in munitions factories. Perhaps there would be a job there for her. Not that she could imagine factory work. And shells — Josh had said how dreadful the shelling had been, how Alexander had died. She pictured for a moment the smoke and the fire and the deafening explosions. No, she couldn't make shells to kill people. But there might be something else. There was a biscuit factory. Carr's biscuits — she'd served water biscuits often enough. They were harmless.

Jessie saw the smoke and steam clouds first, and then came the chug and rattle of the train. She watched it coming round the bend, its whistle sounding and steam pluming from its chimney. She gripped the handles of her carpet bag and felt the flutter of her heart as the brakes squealed and the train slowed and drew level with the platform. It was time to go.

She kept her head down, waiting for a door to open. Someone stepped down onto the platform.

'Jessie?' She looked up to see Charles gazing at her. 'How did you know I was coming?'

'I didn't — I'm going —'

'Where?' He looked at the bag in her hand. 'Home?'

She couldn't answer, and she couldn't get past him. She heard the thud of a door closing and looked down the platform to where the guard was waiting with his flag and his whistle. It was nearly too late. She looked up at Charles's anxious face.

'I can't stay. I must get on the train.'

'But where are you going?'

'I don't know — anywhere away from Moonlyght.'

The guard came towards them. 'Sir,' he called out, 'that door needs closing.'

Charles shoved the door and pulled her away. The whistle blew, another door was shut with a decisive clunk, and she heard the hoarse puffing of the engine as it readied itself to go. Steam billowed round them in a sulphurous, smoky cloud. Charles was momentarily unreal, a ghost come to haunt her, and then she heard the engine quicken and the wheels of the carriage rattle and the chugging speed up as if the engine was breathing faster. There was the farewell whistle and Charles was still there, flesh and blood now, still holding her arm. And Jessie wasn't on the train.

They looked at each other. 'I can get another train,' Jessie said.

'Not until you tell me what it's all about.'

He picked up her bag and Jessie followed him out of the station. It was then that she saw he was limping. She didn't comment, and they went into the trees at the edge of the lane which led to the ferry, where she told him everything. There was nothing to lose, and there was a chance that he would let her go.

'Caroline thinks I told you about her baby. She even thinks we are — she says the nurse at Lunefield overheard a lovers' tiff and that I want — she wants rid of me and Mrs Cobb — when you're married.'

Charles sighed heavily. 'Jessie, Caroline has always lived in a world of her own devising. Even when she was a child, she made up stories about herself. She is the General's daughter — illegitimate, of course. I don't know who her mother was — or even if she's still alive. Caroline doesn't know. Lady Emmeline told her that her parents were cousins of the de Moine family, killed in an accident. The General indulged her, and that's where she got her ideas about marrying Jonathan or Alexander — oh, she was sure that she'd be mistress of Moonlyght one day. They should have told her, but he — the General — thought he could control everything: his sons must be soldiers, his wife must take in his daughter, he would choose a husband for her — neither Jonathan nor Alexander, of course, but some young man who needed the money. And now she's determined to marry me.'

'You gave her a reason.'

'I was stupid — and she was so — it was madness, I know, but I stopped in time.'

'A pity you didn't stop when —'

'It wasn't the same, Jessie, believe me. Caroline hasn't a clue about the war. No idea about loss, or the madness of it all out there, but you know, and I know. We were missing someone, both of us — it happened because we were drawn together…'

She knew he was right. He hadn't forced her, and she hadn't thrown herself at him. He wasn't to blame, and neither was she. It was the war, and sorrow, and loss, and he had gone away that morning because there was no other choice. There was no point in telling him about her miscarriage.

'I know, I know,' she said, 'but I can't stay. You must deal with Caroline. It's time you told her the truth. She'll have to think about a future without Moonlyght — like me.'

'But she's not like you. She can't work; she can't support herself.'

Jessie felt a hundred years older than both of them. 'Then marry her. It's nothing to do with me.'

'I can never do that. But when the war's over … the war might decide. Come back with me. I'll find a place for you. There's a captain I know whose father has a business in Manchester. You could work in an office. I could arrange lodgings for you — let me help, Jessie. I can't let you go without anything to go to. We're friends. We always will be. And now I'm here, Caroline won't dare — she'll pretend everything's all right. Just a few days, Jessie, while I write some letters.'

'You're limping.'

'They keep trying to kill me. Shrapnel — it's a bit of a mess, but it will heal. I'll be back in a few weeks, and the Germans can have another go.'

They took the ferry and thankfully the young man didn't comment on Jessie's return, and then they were walking up the hill to Moonlyght. Jessie couldn't speak, not knowing if she was relieved or just defeated.

She left Charles in Hag Wood and made her way to the little door behind the tower where Ethel Widdop had used to get in — to meet Alexander, perhaps. Both dead and she, Jessie, returned like a thief in the night, slipping in to leave her bag and her coat so that if Mrs Cobb was in the kitchen, she wouldn't see that Jessie had been intending to go away. She stood for a few moments, listening to the stones rattling on the stairs and the wind whispering through the windows, and sensing its breath on her neck. They were here, she thought, Jonathan, Alexander, and Lady Emmeline — Ethel too, perhaps. They were all prisoners in the tower. She shuddered at that thought and walked swiftly across the yard to the kitchen door.

Mrs Cobb came in just as Jessie was arranging Nurse's tray. She had forgotten all about Nurse.

'You'd best take Miss Caroline's tea up now. She's not wantin' breakfast. She tells me Wiggins is comin' to take her to the station. Did she tell you she was goin' somewhere?'

'No, I don't know where she's going,' Jessie said, thinking about Charles on his way to Moonlyght.

'Well, find out if she's coming back today.'

Just then, the front doorbell pealed.

'Oh, Lord, that'll be Wiggins. He'll have to wait. You take up that tray while I speak to him.'

Jessie didn't move. Caroline would be coming downstairs to meet Mr Wiggins and there would be Charles. She wouldn't be going anywhere today.

30

Charles left her notes in the kitchen inside the big brown teapot that no one ever used. He knew Jessie was always the first up. In any case, there was no danger of Caroline coming down in the night to make a cup of tea, nor Mrs Cobb. And if by some chance either did come down, they'd use the china teapot which Jessie always left by the range on a tray, with the sugar bowl and some milk — just in case. She read the latest note and threw it into the fire. Time to set the trays.

They had been careful not to arouse Caroline's suspicions. She had been sweetly polite to Jessie, especially when she was serving lunch or supper. Of course, Caroline had changed her plans when Charles had appeared in the hall, though she had not flung herself at him. Something made her wary of him, Jessie observed. In fact, she was subdued in his presence. Jessie caught her watching him with a little frown. No doubt she watched Jessie at the same time — on the alert for something between them. Caroline was waiting for him to make a move, but he stayed in the library for most of the day or went out walking. One day, when Jessie went in to set the dining room table before lunch, Caroline turned from the window from which she had been watching Charles limp away from the house. Jessie noted the careful make-up and hair; Caroline had obviously been hoping for an intimate lunch.

'What's the matter with him?'

'His leg, I should think.'

'Doctor Kennedy says it's healing. Why doesn't he —' Caroline broke off and turned back to the window. 'Are you sure he's not said anything to you?'

Jessie was conscious of the words of the note which asked her to meet him in the tower after supper. Charles would say he was going out to smoke a cigar. *Risky*, she thought. Caroline watched their every move, but even she knew when he wanted to be on his own.

'No, Miss —' safer to remember her place — 'I've hardly seen him.'

'I'm going out for a walk. I need some air.'

Jessie watched her from the window, staring in the direction in which Charles had gone. Caroline took a step forward then changed her mind and went to sit down on the front steps. She took out her cigarettes. Jessie saw the smoke curling upwards in the bright air and wished she had taken that train. There was too much tension in the house. Jessie wanted air, too, but she went back to the kitchen.

Even Mrs Cobb was puzzled enough to make a comment. 'What's the matter with them?' she asked Jessie when she came in. 'They're hardly speakin' an' she's like a cat on hot bricks.'

'I don't know. Perhaps he's in pain.'

'Aye, mebbe. I saw the wound when Doctor Kennedy dressed it. I wonder if he will be able to go back — what were you doin' with that teapot?'

Careless, Jessie thought. She'd left it by the sink. 'Oh, I washed it out. It looked dusty.'

'Throw it out then — no one uses it.'

'It's not cracked or anything,' Jessie said, putting it back.

'I'll tell you what *is* dusty. That hall. You could give it a good brushing out today.'

Jessie was brushing the stairs when Charles came back. His face looked grey, and his leg dragged as he limped in.

'Oh, sir, you look ill. Let me help.'

She left the brush and helped him to a chair. His breathing was laboured and she saw the sweat on his brow.

'It's nothing — I just jarred — getting — over —' He closed his eyes.

'Shall I go for Doctor Kennedy?'

'No, just let me rest — oh, God, Jessie — I'll never go back. They won't want a crock —'

'You've done enough, sir, surely —'

He put his hand on hers. 'Never enough, Jessie — but later, I'll tell you —'

'What on earth's going on?'

Caroline was standing in the doorway.

'Nothing — don't make a fuss,' Charles said. 'Just jarred my leg, getting over the stile. I'll be all right in a minute.'

Caroline was all concern, but Jessie saw the familiar glitter in her eyes. She'd heard, and she was staking her claim. 'Oh, darling, shall Jessie go for Doctor Kennedy?'

'No, I just need to rest it.'

'Jessie, be a dear and get some brandy.' As Jessie went into the dining room, she heard Caroline say, 'Oh, Charles, you look positively grey. Jessie can get Mrs Cobb, and we can help you upstairs.'

While Caroline gave him sips of brandy, her arm round his shoulders, Jessie went for Mrs Cobb. When she came, Jessie watched as she and Caroline helped Charles to limp upstairs.

Charles didn't come down for supper. Caroline insisted on taking up a tray. 'I'll sit with him for a while, and I'll bring the tray down later.'

Jessie was on pins as she washed up. Charles wouldn't be able to get to the tower and she certainly wouldn't be allowed to go up to his room to get any trays. Caroline had him fast now. Jessie had been sent out for Doctor Kennedy, who had brought her back in his car. Caroline had come down and summoned her and Mrs Cobb to the drawing room.

'Bed rest and quiet — that's the prescription, and I shall be looking after him. You two have enough to do. Jessie had better take over Nurse's care entirely. She needs much more attention than you are giving now, and Mrs Cobb —' smiling sweetly — 'I rely on you to see that Jessie does her duty. There's no need for her to bother Mr Charles.'

And so it went on. There were no more notes for the next few days. Charles Bennett was out of bounds. Jessie looked after querulous Nurse, Mrs Cobb took the trays up to Charles and Caroline and brought them down again. Caroline took up the letters. Jessie saw her examining the envelopes carefully. She hoped there was one from Charles's friend in Manchester. She couldn't stand the strain of waiting for much longer.

'This'll have to stop,' Mrs Cobb said irritably. 'I can't be up and down them stairs all day with my legs. Mind, he says he's getting up today. I think he's fed up of all this cosseting.'

Jessie went up to see to Nurse and to collect any laundry from Caroline's room, where she found her sitting at her writing table reading a letter. Her heart jumped — Caroline wouldn't open Charles's letters, surely. She carried on reading while Jessie waited. The diamond ring she wore when she brought down the trays winked on her finger.

'A letter from London — from Arthur Mountjoy. An invitation. Naturally, I can't go — not now. I must be here for Charles. He needs me.'

'Mrs Cobb says he's getting up today. He must be feeling better.'

'Not well enough to be here without me — Mrs Cobb can't manage, and I don't think you ought to be looking after a gentleman.'

Jessie, picking up the discarded clothes and underwear, only said meekly, 'No, Miss.'

'As long as you know your place.'

Oh, I do, Jessie thought, *and it's not here.*

Charles and Caroline were waiting for lunch the next time she saw them. Caroline was not wearing the ring.

31

The morning after Caroline had put Jessie firmly in her place, Charles came into the kitchen early to tell her that he had news from his friend in Manchester, whose father was prepared to offer Jessie a position in the office of his insurance company.

'It's a chance, Jessie. You'll be paid every week. You can't stay here. I'm going back, leg or no leg. I don't care about me, but I care about what happens to you.'

'An office? I mean, what if I'm not suitable?'

'I've told them you are. You were going to be a teacher. There are lodgings, too, for ladies only.'

'But I'm not a lady —'

'You are to me — more of a lady than some I could mention.' He laughed and took her hands. 'Do it for me, Jessie. I need to know you'll be safe.'

Jessie had no time to reply, for the door burst open and Caroline was shouting — words, dreadful words about Jessie. Everything happened so quickly. Caroline flew at Charles, shrieking at him that she was the lady. Charles was grappling with her. Cups, plates, knives, the butter dish crashed to the floor. Caroline was screaming. Something caught the light, flashing dangerously. And then there was blood on her face and Charles was on the floor. Caroline coming for Jessie and Jessie stumbling and slipping on something wet, her head crashing against the table, falling to her knees, her hands out to save herself, the knife cutting into one hand.

Mrs Cobb's shocked face was suddenly at the door. Mr Turner's face was at the kitchen window, his mouth open in silent horror. And Caroline was sitting with Charles's head on her lap, crying out, 'She's killed him!' And Jessie knelt with blood on her hands, holding the knife.

A locked room, the old buttery, dark and damp, her hands tied with rope. And blood on her apron, crimson against the white. Thick blood, like the blood that had come before. Mr Charles's blood, her blood, the baby's blood, all mingled together. She sat there, not knowing, not understanding where all that blood had come from.

Constable Birks arrived with another policeman. They untied the rope, twisted on the metal handcuffs, and took her out behind the screens passage into the hall. A tall stranger looked her up and down and next to him was Doctor Kennedy, his face grim. An ambulance was outside, but not for her. Then there was a black van with doors. Constable Birks pushed her up the steps. Jessie turned round to see Mr Turner watching, his face all twisted, raising his hand and then dropping it. And inside the black van there was something like a box in which she was to sit. And then they were taking her away.

To a cell in the police station in Kendal. A man who said he was a doctor examined her hands and commented on the bruise on her forehead. A woman dressed as a nurse appeared — Jessie couldn't believe that any of them were real. She had recognised Constable Birks, but he had vanished, and these others had strange faces and asked questions. The tall stranger looked down at her and asked the same questions. She understood the words, but not their meaning. That had happened before, but she couldn't remember when. She couldn't remember anything. They called her Jessie. She didn't know who Jessie was. She didn't know who Captain Bennett was or Miss Mason. She didn't know what had happened.

There was a grey-faced woman with hard eyes like stones who wore a uniform and had keys at her waist which rattled. The woman gave her a tin cup with water in it and told her to drink, but she couldn't, so the woman held her head and the cup to her lips. She felt the water run down her chin and she was choking. They offered her food when they left her in her cell, some bread and hard cheese, but when she put it into her mouth, it was as if she had forgotten what to do with it.

There was a hard plank bed and a thin blanket. She lay awake all night, her eyes open in the dark that pressed down on her, but her mind was blank. The next morning, she was taken in the black van again to Walton Gaol in Liverpool. And when the trial was over, she was returned to the same place to serve her sentence.

PART FOUR: 1919

32

'*It ain't a prison, Jessie.*' It was now and for a very long time. Impossible to imagine. It was like nothing else in the world. There was a cell — a different one from the one she'd inhabited as a remand prisoner. This was a cell for a convict prisoner, an immoral, deceitful servant girl who had killed her master, a gallant hero of the war, and who had deprived a beautiful young woman of her devoted fiancé.

It was right that such a one was received into the prison, stripped of her woollen dress and her possessions — such as they were — taken away; her hair cut off; her body washed and examined for disease. She had had illicit sexual relations and who knew with how many men. The male doctor found she had no disease, but it was as well to be certain. So many of these women from the lower classes who came into prison were already riddled with gonorrhoea or syphilis.

They took away her name; they labelled her with a number; they weighed and measured her; and dressed her in a brown serge dress, an apron with an arrow, a cap with an arrow, a flannel petticoat, an undervest, but no drawers. They gave her a chamber pot, a tin platter, a tin mug, a wooden spoon, a slate, a metal slop bucket, a sheet and a thin blanket, and a woman in a long black dress with keys on a chain at her waist escorted her to her cell. Every noise grated; every noise reverberated with the sound of metal on metal. Keys clinked; boots scraped on the steps of iron staircases which clanged as they climbed; doors slammed along the shuddering iron galleries; the key rattled in the metal lock of the iron door and the convict prisoner looked in at her living tomb with its cold, stone walls, a dirty, iron-barred window high up which showed a patch of iron-grey sky, and an iron door to keep her in, with a spy hole so that she could be watched — though the doctor had thought she was of sound mind. Shock, he had diagnosed. It was often the case when the prisoner realised fully the gravity of what they had done. She'd come round. They usually did. And if not, there was the asylum.

A place of iron, of iron rule and iron faces. The iron door was closed; the iron key turned in the lock; and the iron spy hole slammed shut. Silence was the rule, but Prisoner 22472 didn't care. She had nothing to say. She did not care what became of her. She sat on her hard plank bed and stared at the stone walls. She would be in solitary confinement for her first month.

She got used to the smell eventually, but it was always present. It was the smell of damp — a pall of damp which clung to the skin as if misery had become a palpable thing. The air was foul; the whole place smelt of fear and suspicion, of shame and despair. And madness. That broke the silence sometimes at night when she was woken by the sound of howling, so desolate and inhuman that it sounded like an animal had got in and was crying for its freedom. The gallery rang with the clamour of running feet, of doors clanging and crashing, and the hideous drumbeat of tin plates and cups on doors, walls, and tables, and of manic laughter and jeering. And the next day, there would be an empty space in the chapel. Everyone knew that whoever the tormented, howling creature was, she would be in a straitjacket by now — in the punishment cell, that underground dungeon in which prisoners were left until they went mad and were taken to the asylum, or until they became quiet and docile — until the next time.

Chapel came after breakfast, the coarse brown bread and tea passed through an aperture in the door. She ate alone in her cell after rolling up her sacking mattress and emptying the chamber pot into the slop bucket. Then she turned on the single tap for the water with which she scrubbed out her cell and cleaned and polished the tin cup and plate. She stood at her cell door when it was time for chapel. The order came to 'Pass on' and the line of silent women trudged along the corridor to hear the sermon under the eyes of the wardresses who faced them.

When she had completed her solitary confinement, she was allowed to join the other prisoners in associated labour which came after chapel. Silence was the rule. Prisoner 22472 was found to be a competent needlewoman and was put to sewing prison clothes, hemming towels and handkerchiefs. When they were alone in their cells, they sewed mailbags for the Post Office. Dinner was taken in the cells, usually bread and potatoes. Meat was served on two days a week, or suet which looked like putty. Nothing tasted of anything unless it was of the metal plate.

The prisoners put on their bonnets and capes for exercise in the stone-flagged yard. For one hour each day they walked round and round in single file without speaking. Sometimes Prisoner 22472 wondered that the sky was still there, above the looming, ugly walls. Then it was time for work again until suppertime cocoa, which was the colour of dirty water, and more brown bread was taken in the cells. They were locked at five o'clock and the prisoner was alone again for the next thirteen hours. The prisoner could read — if she were literate — until half-past eight, or she could knit, or she could stare at the walls.

Prisoner 22472 could read. The prisoners were given a Bible, a prayer book, and a hymn book which they took to chapel every day. She read the Bible sometimes, wondering if it could be true that the meek would inherit the earth. She couldn't work out how that could be. If this cell was the earth she had inherited, then there was no comfort in it, and as far as mercy to the merciful… Perhaps she did not deserve mercy. "Blessed are those that mourn for they shall be comforted." That made her think of Josh. She couldn't remember what had happened to her and why she was here, but she remembered her brother, and that she had loved him, and that he was dead.

In the dark she repeated the words of the sermon. The sound of the word "Blessed" soothed her heart, which shuddered at night when the silence was rent with shrieks of madness.

And she learned to speak again — not that the prisoner was required to engage in conversation. She learned to say "Yes, Miss," or "No, Miss," or "Thank you, Miss," or "Yes, sir," to the Governor on his daily rounds. He had a kindly face. She did not want to talk to him, but she made sure to say that she had no complaints and that she was feeling well. She said the same to the doctor. She didn't like him. He was impatient and had a cruel mouth. She remembered the examination when she had come in and she had heard what he had said about her. Perhaps it was true.

She sewed in silence, though some of the bolder women whispered occasionally when they thought no one was watching. Prisoner 22472 sometimes smiled at the other women. She didn't mean it, but it made her one of the harmless, unnoticed ones, one of the feeble-minded, perhaps, who were no trouble to anyone in the midst of the illiterate, the drunks, the sick, the thieves, the tramping women, the prostitutes, the procuresses, the abortionists, the child-killers, the self-harmers, the attempted suicides, the disowned, the silent, the hard-faced, the raging ones, the insolent ones, the guilty ones, the innocent ones.

No one wanted to be noticed by prisoner number 19784, Maria Raferty, whose temper would suddenly flare against some other woman. A stream of invective would pour out, her big face contorted in rage, her huge fists flashing out, the wardresses rushing to control her. Next day she would be meek as a lamb.

Though she didn't speak, Prisoner 22472 listened to the low voices. The young woman with the tattooed ring on her finger whispered about her beloved Jimmy who had been killed in the war. The ring meant they were married, and she'd never forget him. Her tattooed friend, Mary, had shown herself at fairgrounds; her lover had paid for the tattoos that encircled her neck, wound about her wrists and ended in a snake's head on both hands. There was the thief whose voice was an echo of someone she had once known, someone whose voice could be sweet and musical to the ear, but cruel and contemptuous as well. The thief boasted that she was a lady and that her gentleman, a man of business, would soon come to take her away. It happened sometimes that a man would come to the prison and pay a prisoner's fine, but only because he needed to put her to work on the streets again.

There was the girl who cut her throat with a shard of mirror — you could be given a tiny square of looking glass as a reward for good behaviour. Prisoner 22472 did not want to see herself. The good girl who had cut her throat had seen herself. There were those who smashed windows or tore their sheets because they couldn't stand the monotony. They wanted a bit of excitement, so the whisper went.

33

Prisoner 22472 was obedient and meek. She had no idea of inheriting the earth, but she worked hard at whatever task she was given. Her sewing and knitting were very good. She made no complaint when she was transferred to the laundry for a while or when she was appointed to the kitchens, where the work was gruelling. There were the heavy food cans to wash, tables to scrub, hundreds of knives to polish, and sacks of potatoes to wash and peel, but it didn't matter to the prisoner. She was used to hard labour.

The chaplain, an elderly, well-meaning man, spoke kindly, though he rather regretted that she wouldn't talk to him about her crime. He thought that if she could accept what she had done, she would be better prepared for the world outside when she was released. He was puzzled by her blank look when he asked her if she would talk about it.

There were lady visitors, too, who came to listen to the prisoners' stories or to their complaints, to sympathise, and to advise on how to bear their sentence, what to say to the doctor, what readings from the Bible might comfort them, what prayers might soothe a troubled soul. Some prisoners laughed at them; some lied to them; but many found solace in telling their histories to a sympathetic ear. Prisoner 22472 dreaded these encounters. She could barely speak, except to say she was all right. She had no complaints. No, there was no one to write to. She was an orphan. Yes, she'd had a brother, but he had died in the war. Yes, she missed him. No, she was sorry, but she couldn't remember why she was here, but she would try, Miss, she would try very hard, and she would continue to read her Bible. She repeated these things time and again to all the kind faces, and they thought that in time, this poor simple girl would tell her tale. Something would be found for her on her release. Some undemanding factory work, perhaps. She might be able to learn that, or there were still jobs in service for kitchen maids.

The chaplain had charge of the prison library and was surprised to find that Prisoner 22472 could read perfectly well, and he encouraged her to take books when they were distributed to the prisoners. They made a change from the Bible and the hymn books, but some were too harrowing. She pitied Oliver Twist, recoiled from Bill Sikes, and shuddered at the account of Fagin in Newgate Prison. There was a happy ending, at least, but it seemed too much like a fairy tale for the prisoner. The chaplain recommended Jane Austen and she enjoyed reading about the remote world of Mrs Bennett and her five daughters, a world so different from the one she inhabited. It was sometimes a shock to wake from a ball or an assembly in a place called Bath, or from a grand house to find herself still in her cell and to listen to shouts and running feet and the iron clang of doors slamming, and to see the slop bucket in the corner. The lights would go out at eight-thirty and plunge her into that awful waking darkness where sleep would not always come, and she would think about why she was there and remember fragments of that life before, but she could never remember what had happened.

The chaplain had asked her to talk about her crime, but she couldn't tell him because she could not recall it. He asked her to tell him about her family. She said she remembered the farm, and Ma and her brother. He asked her to tell him about the house in which she had been employed and the people who had lived there. She said she couldn't remember, but afterwards her nights were haunted by images that came in the dark. Broken and disjointed pictures that were to do with the place to which Ma had sent her.

There was the moon. She was lying in a bed and watching the moon, and then there was a dark tower where she felt cold breath at her neck. She was waiting for someone — she could never tell if she was dreaming or remembering, because nothing made sense. Suddenly she was in a hall with a fireplace over which three moons and knights in their helmets were carved into a huge mantlepiece. There was a young woman with red hair. She remembered a lady with grey hair and a sad face in a bed. Somehow, she knew that lady was dead. She'd died in that tower where a young man had stood on the stairs, a young man who might have been a ghost. A kitchen came into her head, and a woman sitting at a table with a letter.

And then a letter came — a real letter, the only letter she ever received. It was signed by someone called Will Beswick. It was a letter full of compassion. He said he had read about her case in the newspapers. He didn't believe that she could have killed Captain Bennett. He was sure it must have been an accident. He would come to see her, and she could tell him what had really happened and perhaps he could help. It might be possible to get her a solicitor. He didn't expect anything from her, but for Josh's sake, he would do whatever he could to get her out of prison.

She stared at the page, astonished at the words. She, Prisoner 22472, was Jessie Sedgwick. She was in prison because she had killed a man called Charles Bennett. A young man's face came to her, a face full of pain and confusion, and she saw him walking away down a long drive, and then she knew who Will Beswick was because he wore a uniform. He was a soldier who had been Josh's friend, who had come to tell her that Josh was dead, and she had him sent away because…

She thought her heart would break because she remembered why. She remembered the blood and the pain — there was going to be a baby, and Mrs Cobb had known. She was the woman in the kitchen who had been kind to her then. But in the court — she remembered that now — Mrs Cobb had said she was a liar. Perhaps she was. Perhaps she had done that dreadful thing and that was why she was here.

She couldn't answer the letter. She couldn't imagine Will Beswick coming to see her. She couldn't imagine anyone coming to see her if she had done what the letter told her. She must have done it, because she was in prison. How could it be a mistake? But who was Charles Bennett? Was he the young man on the stairs in the tower who had seemed like a ghost?

She tore up the letter into tiny pieces and put it in the slop bucket. There was nothing to be done. She couldn't ask anyone about her case. She didn't want to know. She was safe in here. Perhaps they would keep her forever.

And it seemed to her that they did. She had no sense of time. The bells continued to ring, summoning her to chapel, or to labour, or to bed, or to breakfast, or to dinner, but they were only commands which she obeyed unthinkingly. Days, weeks, months and years accumulated like layers and layers of dirt and ashes and dust under which she was buried. She had been told that the war had ended, but it meant nothing to her, only that Josh had been killed and that she would never see him again. And grief came in the night and filled the dark, and passed again, until something reminded her of him, of a time and a place which seemed so long ago.

Only the seasons changed. She knew when it was winter because sometimes there was snow in the yard where they took their hour's exercise, and the mornings were as dark as night when the bell rang at half-past five. The prisoners felt the cold more intensely. They came back from their exercise with wet boots and stockings, but there were no dry things to change into. There was no hot water from the tap in the cells. Sometimes the cold water froze in their tin mugs and wash bowls. Many became sick. You could hear the hacking coughs and the smell was worse than ever because everyone had diarrhoea. There was one water closet for twenty-three cells. You could use it only twice a day. You had a bath once a week and you got used to it because you didn't think about it. Prisoner 22472 didn't think about anything, even when the wardresses were bad-tempered during the sickness and the infirmary was full. Prisoner 22472 didn't get sick — only in her soul. The wardresses weren't interested in souls, only in the nuisance of moaning bodies and all the extra work they entailed.

In the spring there was a little warmth in the sun, and once she saw a flower growing up through a crack in the stones. She knew it was a cowslip and a memory of Josh came to her, the two of them in the fields searching for flowers. Josh had known the names of all the flowers, the ragged robin, the Star-of-Bethlehem in the hedgerows and the wild honeysuckle, the blue bird's eye, and the purple violet hiding in the woods. Violets. Something about violets that she couldn't remember. And then the tears spilled from her eyes because she remembered a book with pictures of flowers. She didn't know what had happened to that book which Josh had given her, and she thought she was glad that Josh didn't know she was in here and that she had killed someone.

The seasons continued to turn. She could smell smoke in the autumn and there was a huge moon looking down into her cell. There was rain and the wind rattled through the metal corridors. She heard the wind at night and remembered another moon and the slippery touch of a counterpane. And the sound of weeping somewhere. Who had wept, she wondered, and where? Even in summer when the prisoners wore cotton skirts and blouses, it was always cold inside. The cold lodged deep in their bones. The walls of the cell were cold and damp, but occasionally through the dirty window high up she saw a patch of blue, though the sky was mostly grey whatever the season. In the exercise yard, a bird chirruped on the wall, and she watched it rise on its song and vanish into the grey.

The faces changed, too. The young woman with the tattooed ring on her finger went one day. The woman with the snakes on her hands vanished, too. Prisoner 17898, a young woman who had killed her own child, attacked a wardress, and was put in a straitjacket. Jessie heard her howling. Then she was gone, and the whispered words were, "the asylum". The lady thief's gentleman came to take her away. New faces came and old ones came back. Tramping women with weather-worn faces and hard hands came back for three meals a day and a bed and then they went again. A baby was born in a cell to a young woman on remand who hadn't known she was pregnant. The baby was sent to the workhouse.

Some died of bronchitis or pneumonia in whatever bitter winter came round, and worst of all, in the winter of 1921, Prisoner 33456 hanged herself in her cell. No one mentioned her again. There was a terrible silence two years later when a prisoner on the men's side was hanged for the murder of a wealthy widow. In the silence, the women put down their sewing, for they could hear the tolling of the bell at eight o'clock in the morning which told them that the dreadful thing had happened. The wardresses glanced uneasily at each other and at the pale, still faces of the prisoners, but no one spoke, and when the sound of the bell faded and was gone, they took up their work.

Maria Raferty, who had plenty of grim tales to tell about hangings when the opportunity arose, whispered in ghoulish chapters for days afterwards. 'Ten-foot gallows out there. They puts a white 'ood on yer an' ol' Billy Billinton pulls his lever an' down yer goes.' There was a nurse she had known in Oldham who had been hanged for the murder of her own daughter. 'Lizzie Berry,' she told her avid listeners. 'I knew 'er. She done it, even though she said not. Done 'er ma in as well, but they couldn't prove that.' Jessie heard her growling chuckle. 'Funny thing, though, man called Berry was the 'angman in them days. Mighta bin Lizzie Berry's brother. What a lark, eh? An' years ago, that Mrs Maybrick what poisoned 'er 'usband — reprieved she was, but then she was a lah-di-dah type. Served fifteen years an' served 'er right. There's them as is in 'ere what's killed an' got away with —' She was cut off suddenly by a voice which ordered her to hold her tongue if she didn't want to end up in punishment. Maria shut up, but not without a hideous grimace behind the wardress's back. 'Do fer you one day,' she muttered and was hauled away to the punishment cell. Prisoner 22472 shuddered at the idea that Maria might have meant her, but no one looked her way. They were too busy watching Maria and her meaty fists trying to pummel the wardress.

Time trudged relentlessly on. Even Maria Raferty got her release, though the whisper was that she'd be back — again. The hands of Prisoner 22472 became redder and coarser, the joints swollen and hard. She lost her back teeth. Her hair began to fall out and her face was gaunt and yellow, and her deep blue eyes seemed to fade, but that was the usual thing with convict prisoners who were in for years.

She carried on with her appointed tasks. She answered if anyone spoke to her. She ate the food that was given to her and thanked the wardress. No one noticed that there was anything wrong with model Prisoner 22472. And when the cell door was shut, she took up her sewing. She couldn't read. The words danced on the pages. At night she lay with her eyes open, not knowing if she was asleep or awake, her head filled with dreams, or were they memories? A beautiful young woman in a pink blouse shouted at her and pointed her finger, but the prisoner couldn't tell what she was saying, only that she was angry. She was at a railway station and a man got off the train, but she couldn't see his face because he was shrouded in smoke and steam. She was in that tower looking down at something, and then she was falling, falling ... and she would cry out in the dark and feel the rough stone wall next to her and wonder if she were still in the tower, and once she heard a voice she knew telling her, 'It ain't a prison, Jessie.' It was the voice of the red-haired girl, but the red-haired girl was wrong.

It was a new chaplain who eventually brought about the change. Time passed. The images faded; even Josh became a dream, and Prisoner 22472 sank into a kind of torpor, as if her mind had shut down and she was hardly there. The chaplain noticed that she did not read her Bible, nor would she take any library books, yet he'd been told she could read and had taken books before. He asked her why she had stopped reading. She couldn't answer because she didn't know.

He was a compassionate young man who cared about what happened to the prisoners. He cared about their souls. He believed that if Prisoner 22472 could be encouraged to read again, her mind would be improved and she would wake from her blankness into the light. He knew not to insist on the Bible but he spoke of compassion and forgiveness in his sermons, of a God who loved them and would gather the repentant sinners into His arms. He thought that reading might be beneficial to this prisoner in whose face he saw the vacancy he had seen in the faces of so many others. He had seen how intelligence could wither away so that the prisoner was reduced to a machine and would become unfit for any life beyond the prison after a long sentence. She would be released soon, so he determined to try again.

'Did you find the books too hard to read?'

She shook her head. 'No, sir, I don't think so.'

'You don't care for the stories?'

'I don't know.' She looked at his earnest young face. He looked innocent and he meant to be kind. There was still in Prisoner 22472 a tiny flame of that old desire to please, to return kindness for kindness. 'I'll try again, sir,' she said.

'What about poetry? Perhaps I can find some short poems for you to enjoy. You lived in the country, I think. Let me see—'

He came back from the shelves with two volumes for her. 'There, now, take these and do try, my dear. You can tell me about them next time.'

The prisoner went back to her cell and put the books on her stool. She didn't want to read, and she didn't want to talk to the chaplain again. She was afraid that he might ask again about her crime, and now she knew what she had done, she could not bear to see how his innocent face might change when he knew, too. The chaplain had talked about repentance. She was sure she was sorry, but she had killed someone and that was unforgiveable. The dead could not come back to forgive you. The Bible didn't say that murderers were blessed like the meek and the merciful. She was damned, she knew that, and she would never see Josh again because he was in Heaven.

She looked at the mailbags piled up in the corner. She need not think when she concentrated on the thick needle threading in and out of the coarse cloth. You got into the rhythm of it, even though your hands hurt, and it was soothing because you were used to it and when a bag was finished, you could pick up another and another. But she didn't move. Her heart was beating too fast, and her hands were shaking. She was afraid. The chaplain had used the word "release". She thought of the young woman with the tattooed ring on her finger. She had been released. Where had she gone? Into that world beyond the high walls of the exercise yard from where she had once seen a bird fly away, the world she could no longer imagine. The thief had gone with her gentleman, but there was no one waiting for Prisoner 22472.

She thought of the woman who had killed herself in her cell. She had torn strips from her sheet and woven them into a rope, then she had moved her bed, placed the stool on it, and climbed onto the stool to hang herself from a window bar. And she had gone out, too — out of the world.

34

Prisoner 22472 contemplated her stool and the window bars. She lifted the books from the stool to place them on the bed. One was a slim volume with a white paper jacket, rather grubby from the fingers which had touched it.

The words on the cover danced at first but became still as she stared. She knew those words and she knew the name of the poet, A. E. Housman.

She read the final verse of one of the poems:

Long for me the rick will wait
And long will wait the fold
And long will stand the empty plate
And dinner will be cold.

She remembered weeping over those words because Josh was far away in an unimaginable place and Ma was dead, Ma who had waited for Josh, not knowing that he would never return. She remembered Will Beswick coming to tell her — oh, his agonised face. She remembered Moonlyght, the place where she had gone as a kitchen maid. She remembered that the red-haired girl was Ethel Widdop and knew she was dead; she remembered Alexander on the stairs in the tower; and Charles telling her to put Ethel's death out of her mind. Charles Bennett — she remembered him reading the poem and how she had wept for Ma and for Josh and how he had held her, and the baby which had died before it was born. And she remembered Caroline, who had wanted to marry Charles, and who had slapped her, and she remembered the train. She was running away from Moonlyght and Charles stopped her. He was going to find her a job in an office…

He had been laughing and he had taken her hands. That was when it had happened. Caroline in her fury, the blood and the knife in her own hand, and Mr Turner's face at the window all twisted. She remembered that in court they said she had been shouting at Charles, but she only remembered the laughter.

She had fallen. She remembered the pain as her hand came down on the knife, but then there had been Caroline with Charles's head on her lap, shouting to Mrs Cobb that Jessie had killed him.

She sat for a long time, looking down at her coarse, swollen hands which never looked clean. She saw the blood there and felt the knife in her hand. Did that mean she had done it? But why? If Charles was laughing, why had she attacked him, and why was Caroline in such a rage? She understood then. Miss Caroline thought that she and Charles wanted to be together. Had Miss Caroline killed Mr Charles? Or had she? She couldn't remember.

She took up her sewing again. The needle went in and out and she thought of nothing.

The prisoner was escorted to a reception room where one of the lady visitors waited for her. She kept her eyes down. She had no desire to be questioned or advised. She just wanted to be in her cell, doing her work, not thinking, not feeling, not remembering.

'Sit down, please, Jessie.'

Jessie looked up, startled to hear her name. This lady had the same warm, brown eyes as Mrs Roberts from the school, and there was something in her low, musical voice that sounded like Mrs Roberts's voice. She stared at the lady. She wasn't Mrs Roberts.

'Please, Jessie, there is no need to be frightened. Please sit down.'

'Yes, Miss.' Jessie sat and looked down at her hands.

'You know that you will be going out soon, Jessie, and I want to talk to you about what you will do when you are free. Have you thought about it?'

Jessie looked up at the lady, who must have seen the terror in her eyes. 'Have you any family to whom you can go, who would look after you?'

'No, Miss.' Perhaps they'd let her stay here if she had nowhere to go.

'I see. However, you are eligible for release on licence if you agree to come into a refuge for at least a year. You will be looked after and trained for useful work.'

'Refuge?'

'Yes, where you will be safe. I am from the Lancashire Female Refuge, which is here in Liverpool at Mount Vernon Green. Our job is to look after young women and girls like you who have come out of prison and have no other help. We help those who want to be helped and I know that you have worked hard in here, so I am sure that you will do very well in the refuge. It will prepare you for your life after. There is hope, Jessie. You did something wrong, something that I am sure you didn't mean to do, and now you have paid for it. It is time to think about your future.'

Future. It was a word that she had not thought about in years. The death of each day brought just another day, and another, and another. She had lost count of days a long time ago. The word 'future' had no meaning, and it hadn't a meaning now.

'Yes, Miss,' she said. It was her habit to be obedient.

'You'll come to the refuge?'
'Yes, Miss.'

Jessie left prison as quietly as she had gone in. Miss Elvina Smythe — the lady from the refuge — brought her some clothes. She took off the apron with the broad arrow, the brown serge dress, the flannel petticoat, and the undervest, and she put on the soft cotton drawers and camisole, the lisle stockings held up with garters, and the white cotton blouse, buttoned up to the neck, the dark grey skirt which reached her calves. There was a pair of stout shoes with laces, and a dark grey coat which was warm to the touch. There was a soft felt hat, too, which she pulled down low over her forehead. Somehow it felt safer.

Jessie had no idea what she looked like, but she felt different, not like Jessie Sedgwick who had lived on the farm and had been top of the class; not like the kitchen maid at Moonlyght; not like Prisoner 22472. Who was she now, this young woman in the clothes of a stranger?

The cell door was partly open, but there was no stern wardress to slam it shut. Jessie looked at the place which had been her home for six years. How had she survived? she wondered now. Yet, she felt herself trembling at the thought of leaving, for what would she find at Mount Vernon Green? She had thought about the words and how peaceful they sounded. The word "Mount" made her think of the Sermon on the Mount, which had been her comfort in those early months, and "green" made her think of the moors and fields at Swarthgill, where she had roamed with Josh, where they had been happy. Until the war came. The war which had turned her world upside down. Josh had told her about the dragon's teeth frozen in time and how the dragon would wake. So it had, and she and millions of others had been seared by the flames, some consumed entirely. And here she was, Jessie Sedgwick, who had killed a man, and who was to be restored to a new world, whether she wanted it or not. She would have to bear it. Who had said that to her long ago?

'Jessie?' Miss Smythe opened the door. 'Are you ready?'

'Yes, Miss.'

'Good. It's time to go. Don't look back, Jessie. It's time to look forward now.'

The cell door closed behind her. She followed Miss Smythe along the gallery and down the staircase, the sound of their feet reverberating along the steps.

There was the great door of the prison, where the porter opened a smaller door. She followed Miss Smythe into the street. The key turned in the lock. There was the wide street, the cars, and above, the blue expanse of the sky and white clouds sailing across towards far distant hills. Jessie started at the shriek of a train whistle.

Miss Smythe turned to her. 'I know. It's overwhelming. My car is over there.'

Jessie stared out of the car window; she had no recollection of the journey she had taken to the prison all those years ago and was surprised at the fields and the farms, and the trees. How extraordinary to see all that so near to the prison. But very soon she saw the louring pall of smoke and the narrow streets on each side of the wide road. Trams rattled along, and there were more cars than she had ever seen, buses full of people, more narrow streets with rows and rows of terraced houses all huddled together, women sitting on steps and children playing in the gutter. There were tall buildings with flying flags, a huge church with a spire, shops with enormous glass windows and people everywhere. When the car stopped in a queue, she looked out at a woman on a bicycle — a woman wearing trousers. She grinned at Jessie and then pushed off, her scarf flying like a flag behind her. Jessie would have liked to be wheeling off into the distance. There was a bent old man pushing a handcart, and there were still plenty of horses and carts trundling ahead of them.

The faces looked pinched in the cold. There were women with shawls over their heads and still wearing ankle-length skirts, but there were much shorter skirts, too, and bowler hats and flat caps. To the former prisoner, it looked like a terrifying new world of noise and crowds, of smoking chimneys and soot-blackened streets.

'You'll find it quiet and restful,' Miss Smythe said as the car turned away from the main road. 'We're not far from Waverley Park and the Botanic Gardens — lovely green spaces with lots of fresh air.'

'I can go out?' Jessie asked.

'Not on your own for a while, but we do go to the park and the picture house for a treat, and the Pavilion Theatre occasionally — if there is something suitable.'

Jessie couldn't imagine the Botanic Gardens or the park, even less the picture house, but a memory came to her suddenly. Caroline had been to a picture house in London. She had wanted to marry a man called Harry Mountjoy. Another name came. Alice Herd had been killed by a bomb, along with Mr Mountjoy. They'd been engaged and Caroline had been furious.

The memory dissolved as the car slowed and Jessie saw that Mount Vernon Green was as green as she had imagined. It was tranquil, too, with a circle of grand houses in the centre of the triangular green space, hidden away from the surrounding narrow streets of terraced housing and the factory and timber yard just over Mount Vernon Green.

The house was large and imposing. Jessie couldn't believe that she would be allowed to go up those steps, under the porch with its stone pillars, and into the house with its smartly painted green front door, but Miss Smythe hurried her out of the car and into the large hall with its black-and-white-tiled floor. Everything seemed bright and light. She was taken upstairs to a large bedroom in which there were six beds with curtain rails round them. The coverlet was a deep shade of pink; there was a locker by the bed upon which was a Bible, and there was a mirror on a little chest of drawers which stood against the wall. Jessie didn't look. She was shown the bathroom and lavatory and given fresh, clean towels, a cake of creamy soap, a toothbrush, and a tin of tooth powder.

'There's another skirt and blouse, a nightdress and some underthings in the drawers, Jessie. I'll leave you to have a look. Come down for lunch in a few minutes, please.'

Miss Smythe left her, and Jessie sat down on the bed and ran her hand up and down the soft coverlet and then up and down the smooth, clean sheets underneath it.

PART FIVE: 1924

35

Jessie didn't mind the work. The young women worked in the laundry, cooked, knitted, sewed, and made their own clothes, and shirts to be sold to bring more income to the refuge, which was supported by charitable donations and run by the Church of England Temperance Society. There were lessons in reading, writing and arithmetic for those who had not been in prison long enough to be educated there or those who had simply given up hope of ever having a better life. Some were on probation for petty crimes such as drunkenness, fighting or stealing. The refuge gave them a chance to start again.

There was no rule of silence in the sewing room, or the laundry, or the kitchen. The livelier girls chattered and giggled and sometimes talked about prison and the wardresses, as if it had been some kind of hated school and the wardresses particularly stern teachers. The Governor was a gent, all right, but, blimey, what did he know about women? The doctor was a brute, and the chaplain meant well, but was a bit of a wet weekend. As for the lady visitors, they were all right. Made a change to get a visit. They went on too much, though, about 'ow there was chances to better yerself. They ought to try livin' in a back street with twelve other kids.

It was similar to prison, of course. There were rules and the days were regimented. Time for breakfast, for dinner, for a light supper, and for lights out. There were punishments, but no straitjackets and no banishment to the cellar, only marks deducted for bad conduct, and marks, of course, for good behaviour.

The matron, Mrs Moffatt, was a practical, good-humoured, patient woman; there was an air of quiet authority and competence about her, and the women were inclined to obey. They didn't want to lose their place. Most of them knew it was their only chance, and they even listened to the chaplain, who came to give them religious instruction. No hardened criminals were admitted, nor what were deemed women of bad character, though very occasionally there was an escapee — Louisa Riley had climbed out of a bedroom window and was found by Mrs Moffatt in the neighbouring public house, the Mount Vernon Arms, having a glass of beer with her brother. It turned out he wasn't her brother, but a sailor she had talked to in the park. She was transferred to the Magdalen Asylum for fallen women in nearby Edge Lane when her pregnancy was discovered. Jessie had frozen when she'd heard that.

'Silly cow, gettin' caught like that. Didn't know when she was well off.' This was Nellie Donovan, who had recognised Jessie immediately and greeted her like a long-lost friend. Jessie knew her by the tattooed ring on her finger. 'Them nuns at the Magdalen, they'll give it 'er.'

Nellie might have still been in mourning for her Jimmy, but there was a spark in her green eyes and a crackle in the springing red curls released from the ugly prison bonnet, and Jessie was startled into a memory of Ethel Widdop whom she had talked to in the tower at Moonlyght — and who was dead.

Nellie had no time for the nuns and there were plenty about. Jessie felt rather intimidated by the high walls and towers of another of their neighbours, the Mount Vernon Convent, and even Nellie tended to shrink away when they saw the nuns in their long black habits at the gates of the convent. 'Our Lady of Mercy, I don't think,' she whispered to Jessie on one of the walks they took — accompanied by the matron or Miss

Smythe, or one of the lady visitors. 'Brought up with 'em, I was. Lot o' cruel crows.' It seemed to Jessie that the neighbourhood was designed to remind her of her sinful past. There was the House of Mercy for out of place servants in Mount Vernon. Ought she to be in there? And like Nellie, she shrank from the gates of the Refuge for Penitents in Edge Lane.

Nellie was good-natured and cheerful and for some reason Jessie couldn't fathom, always sought her out in the sewing room. 'Remember Raferty?' she'd say, or 'God, that 'angin' day, thought she'd never shut up,' or 'Remember them times in the kitchen — blimey, that gruel. Yer could paper the walls with it,' and Jessie would smile and say she did and yes, it was awful, and yes, she was glad to be out of it, but she knew she was pretending. There was something in her that couldn't respond to overtures of friendship. That leaden feeling in her heart weighed her down all the time and she was always glad to draw the curtains of her bed cubicle in the dormitory and be alone.

She was ashamed to feel relieved when Nellie came to tell her she was going to work in Hartley's jam factory up in Fazakerley.

'Sweet, ain't it.' She twisted an imaginary ring round her tattoo. 'My Jimmy worked there before the — ah, well, ain't gonna dwell on that. Onwards an' upwards, that's me, but I won't never forget. Jimmy was an' 'ero — all of them was —'

Her eyes spilled over, but she rallied, arranged her blue beret at a jaunty angle, and was gone with a hug and an exhortation to Jessie to look after herself. 'Ain't a prison 'ere, Jessie lass — yer'll soon be on yer way.'

And that night, Jessie remembered Ethel Widdop's death in the place called Hag Wood, and Alexander, Charles, and Caroline Mason. Someone had killed Ethel Widdop, and they said she had killed Charles. The scene in the kitchen came back, but it always ended in the same way. Jessie Sedgwick, the kitchen maid with blood on her hands, holding a knife, and Caroline Mason screaming, 'She's killed him!'

36

Miss Elvina Smythe was the general administrator and court missionary. It was she who attended court to rescue those who were put on probation and had no home to go to. She and Mrs Moffatt worked tirelessly to prepare the women for the next stage. The refuge was meant to be a home, and it was for those who had endured the privations of prison, and the horrors of abusive homes.

Miss Smythe's father was a member of the Liverpool Botanic Society and Miss Smythe was very knowledgeable. She had a passion for education and singled Jessie out, telling her that learning was never wasted. She thought Jessie could do better than factory work. 'You read well, Jessie, and your arithmetic is very good. Shopwork might suit you.'

Jessie felt her kindness, but she felt the distance, too, from this educated woman who talked so fluently and knew so much. She sensed Miss Smythe's puzzled eyes on her from time to time and she was always afraid that Miss Smythe would ask her about her past and what she had done. She would have liked to be left alone, not to learn but simply to be outside to look and to breathe. It was air she wanted and the trees and the wide green spaces.

Towards the end of her first year she walked with Miss Smythe round the nearby bowling greens, another quiet green space which Jessie would have enjoyed had she been alone. She sensed that Miss Smythe had something particular she wanted to say to her. They looked in silence for a while at the greens and the trees and the carpet of red and gold at their feet.

'It is time to think about how you are to earn your living when you leave, Jessie. I do think you could do better than factory work. There are opportunities in dressmaking or in millinery work. A job in an office, perhaps. Have you given it any thought?'

'Biscuits,' Jessie said. She had thought. She wanted to leave Liverpool and go to a place where no one knew her. She had remembered the railway station, the man getting off the train — the man who knew her, and stopped her. It was Charles, she remembered. She had been going to Carlisle. She had thought of the biscuit factory in Carlisle. She thought she could start again, and this time catch the train she had missed and go on to Carlisle, innocent of any crime.

'Biscuits?' Miss Smythe repeated. 'Oh, well I do know Mr Crawford of Fairfield Biscuits. It's beyond the tram depot, not too far from here, and you could come back to see us. I will speak to him. Some of our girls have positions there — if that is what you really want.'

'No,' Jessie blurted out. 'I mean, I'm not sure.' She had no wish to work in any nearby factory. She did not want to work with girls from the refuge. She did not want to be anywhere in this city which contained Walton Gaol.

Miss Smythe was patient, if puzzled. She only said that Jessie must think about her future, and they would talk again.

In November, there was an outing planned to the picture house on Tunnel Road. The choice of film was always a matter of some difficulty for Mrs Moffatt. She had to hope that there was something suitable at the Picture Drome, the nearest cinema to which they could walk or take the tram for the matinee. She didn't want to take them into the heart of the city. That was the way to lose someone. She avoided anything to do with crime, or forbidden love. The outings were rare and usually paid for by a donation from a benefactor. She decided that Colleen Moore in *Painted People*, a comedy-romance, was probably safe enough. The girls loved the pictures of Colleen Moore in the magazines; she was so pretty with her wide smile, bobbed hair, and big eyes, and some of them had seen the bright yellow poster showing a smiling Colleen Moore with her powder puff, and there was the added attraction of an orchestra and a banjoist.

Miss Smythe, however, had another engagement at the Scala Picture House. She had been invited to a showing of a film about the war called *Ypres*. It was a grand charity occasion to be attended by the Lord Mayor, who would inspect the Guard of Honour mounted in Lime Street. Miss Smythe, who had observed Jessie's reluctance over the proposed trip to the Picture Drome, thought that Jessie would prefer to accompany her.

In the car going back, Jessie's throat ached and her whole body was rigid. Miss Smythe looked pale, her lips pursed in an unfamiliar way. Her back was very straight, too, and she gripped the steering wheel tightly. Jessie felt wretched. Miss Smythe was angry with her, she was sure. She hadn't spoken at all at the picture house; she hadn't responded when introduced to Miss Smythe's father, Reverend Smythe; she hadn't thanked Miss Smythe for her kindness in taking her, but, oh, it had been dreadful.

How she sat through it, she never knew. Only by gripping the arms of the seat, only by knowing that Miss Smythe was sitting beside her, her face intent and serious, only by closing her eyes from time to time to banish the terrible scenes, but she couldn't banish the memory of them repeating themselves in her mind. There was a gentleman on the other side of her, so that she was trapped. There was silence in the cinema, and that was dreadful, too, and worse when she heard the sound of a sob. She could have wept, but she dared not. In the car, she could not banish the images from her mind. It was as if she was seeing the film again: smoke, guns, a blasted landscape, great explosions, men lying dead, the king, a little dog at his heels, the horses, vans with red crosses, soldiers marching down long, dusty roads, a man on a horse galloping into the smoky distance.

Neither spoke until they were inside the house and Miss Smythe ushered Jessie into the office. 'Tea,' she said briskly. 'Stay here.'

Miss Smythe came back with two cups of tea on a plate and some biscuits. She sat down on a chair opposite Jessie. 'Drink first and eat a biscuit. I need a cup of tea, too.'

Her voice was very gentle. Jessie drank, but she couldn't manage the biscuit. 'I'm sorry, Miss.'

'It was too much. I'm the one who should be sorry and I am. I shouldn't have taken you. I should have asked. You lost someone, didn't you?'

'My brother.' And Jessie wept.

Miss Smythe took the cup from her, passed her a handkerchief, and waited for the sobs to subside.

'I do understand, Jessie. I wanted to see it. I thought it would help me to know, to understand, to reconcile myself to what happened. I was engaged once before the war. My fiancé was a cavalry officer. He was killed at the Battle of Ypres in November 1914, eleven years ago to the day. There has never been anyone else. Seeing all that didn't help. It seems such a waste. It wasn't glorious. I lost my brother, too, in 1918 at Passchendaele.'

Jessie looked up. 'That's where my brother was killed. He was never found. His friend came to tell me that he saw him fall into a shell hole, but he —'

'I know, I know — so many. All those lives lost. Nothing can make up for that. We shall never recover, but we do have a duty to them to do the best we can in this world, which is why—'

'Why you want me to think about my future. It's too hard.'

'And you have had a dreadful time in the prison. It might help if you talked about what happened. How you came to —'

'Kill someone?' There, she had said it. 'I don't know. I can't remember. I remember that Charles was dead, and that Miss Caroline was screaming that I had killed him, but I don't know why.'

'In court they said that you had a miscarriage and that you blamed Captain Bennett.'

'It was true — I can't explain how it happened between us — you'll think I was —'

'I won't. These things happened in the war. It's not possible to judge — at that time, so many things were different. Life was so — precarious; one never knew what the next day would bring, the next hour. You might be in the garden or taking tea, and the knock on the door would bring a telegram, and all was lost, and you never knew. But I knew, Jessie, and I'm not ashamed. I loved my fiancé — it happened when he came home on leave. How could I say no? I didn't have a miscarriage. Or a child — I wish I had, but I know very well what would have happened. I'd have been sent away to have the child and brought back —'

A memory awoke in Jessie. She interrupted, 'Without the baby…'

'Yes. I'm a respectable middle-class lady, you see —' She gave a half-smile. 'My father is a vicar, so —'

'The same thing happened to Miss Caroline. She wanted to marry Mr Charles.'

'Did you love him?'

'I don't know. It was after my brother died. I was reading the poems of Mr Housman — he said, "Himself he could not save" and I was crying because of Josh out there who might die, and then Mr Charles came in. He knew the poems and he was grieving for his cousin, Mr Alexander, who was killed, too. It was a comfort, I think, just two people…'

'Did Miss Caroline know about you and Mr Charles?'

'She said I was pushing myself at him. It wasn't true — he was going to find me employment. I wanted to get away from that place. She came into the kitchen. She was shouting — that's all I remember…'

'It's no use, Jessie. Suppose it was an accident and Mr Charles was killed by mistake, you can't do anything about that now. You must accept what has happened. You have to look forward. I do think you can do better than a factory. I have friends — a lady's companion, perhaps?'

'No, no, I couldn't be a servant again.'

'You wouldn't be a servant — you'd care for a lady, read to her, deal with her letters —'

The thought horrified Jessie. 'No, Miss Smythe, I never want to live in someone else's house again. I'd rather live in lodgings.' She looked at Miss Smythe and knew she mustn't say that she wanted to be alone. It was time to put up a fight. She'd done it before. 'I want to be independent, and I don't want to stay in Liverpool — or anywhere near that prison.'

'I understand, I do, so let me have a think about my contacts.'

Jessie crept into the bedroom and pulled her curtains closed round the bed. When she closed her eyes, she saw a burning city with skeleton trees, hurricanes of shells, cavalry men charging through woods, the contorted faces of men as they fell. Refugees fleeing — a woman with a pram, a child's bewildered face, a man on a bicycle with a mattress on his back, a bent old woman with her possessions in a check cloth. It was Belgium. Belgium where Josh had bathed in the sea — they were to go to the seaside when he came back…

The film played on: a man with haunted eyes, standing with a cigarette in his mouth, another watching a tin can boil on a fire; then a man looking at his watch, and behind him soldiers waiting in tin hats holding their bayonets, their faces set; an officer in high leather boots, holding his pistol, his mouth opening and closing, the screen filled with smoke; and one tormented face, a man standing alone amongst the dead.

What they had seen, what they had felt, what they had done, Josh, Alexander, Charles, and Jonathan, too, perhaps. Jonathan, who had come back so damaged, so haunted that he had jumped from that ledge in the tower.

Exhausted, Jessie slept at last, and when she woke her first thought was that it was time to go, and if Miss Smythe couldn't find anything for her away from Liverpool, then she would go to Carlisle and work in the biscuit factory.

37

It was fortunate that Miss Smythe couldn't pursue her discussion of Jessie's future. She was called away to nurse her sick father, who had caught a cold after the outing to the cinema, where he had stood in the freezing weather to watch the Lord Mayor's procession. The cold had turned to bronchitis. But Miss Smythe left a letter for her. She had written to a friend in Lancaster whose father owned an oil cloth and linoleum factory. They would take her on at the factory if that was what Jessie wanted, and there were sure to be opportunities for promotion. Jessie must write to her to tell her how she was getting on. Mrs Moffatt would give Jessie money for her train tickets.

Jessie departed early in the morning before breakfast. Only Mrs Moffatt was there to bid her goodbye and wish her luck. Jessie didn't look back. She caught the tram to Lime Street Station and was on the train to Lancaster within the hour, looking at the names as the train stopped and started. Sandhills — was that near the sea? At Walton, she turned away, not daring to look at the travellers on the platform, relieved when no one got into her third-class carriage. Aintree was next and then Ormskirk and Preston, and finally, after about an hour and a half, she was in Lancaster.

An obliging porter gave her directions to White Cross Mill — she could take a bus from outside the station. And then she was bustled out into the street in the crowd of other hurrying passengers. She had no idea how much a bus would cost. She had her grant of two pounds in her purse, and some coins. She'd walk. Down the hill, the porter had told her, cross the main road, and turn right. Keep going until she reached a junction. She'd see a big hotel, The Toll House. Down the road by the hotel, she'd see the canal. Keep going until she reached the mill. Couldn't miss it.

Shops, pubs, little alleys, a street market with stalls and shouting vendors and women crowding to listen to the prices. Everything was a bargain, it seemed. There was a policeman standing at a corner, but Jessie didn't dare approach him. Eventually she turned into a narrow street where there were fewer people, but they hurried by. There was a large, old building across the road and the door was open. She looked up to see that the sign told her that it was The Grand Theatre. She'd ask there for directions to the mill. Outside, a poster advertised that the Lancaster Footlights Club was presenting *Milestones* on Monday, Tuesday, and Wednesday. She stared at the name of the author, Arnold Bennett, and she almost turned away, but her eye caught another notice which advertised for seamstresses. She went in.

A slender woman was coming down a grand staircase. She was wearing a headscarf tied up in a turban which didn't cover the razor-sharp black fringe on her pale brow. Her lips were painted deep red, and a cigarette hung there, the smoke curling upwards. She was dressed in what looked like men's overalls, a man's none-too-clean shirt, and tennis shoes with frayed laces. At the same time, she looked as though she owned the world. Perhaps she owned the theatre.

She took the cigarette from her mouth and asked, 'Can I help you?'

The voice reminded Jessie of Miss Caroline's, cut-glass and confident. The woman's cool blue-eyed gaze looking down from the stairs made Jessie hesitate. 'Chop, chop, darling, can I help?'

Jessie blushed at the word "darling", but she opened her mouth and stuttered, 'Advert. I mean — I can sew.'

'Oh, jolly good. Just the person we want. Name?'

Jessie blurted out, 'Esther Vernon.'

And that was it. She was wanted immediately. Two of their regular girls had walked out. Cash paid and no questions asked, except turbaned Miss Wilhemina Carew, known as Bill, took note of the battered carpet bag given to Jessie by Mrs Moffatt, and recommended a boarding house in a nearby street. 'Tell her Bill sent you. It'll be all right as long as you pay up in time. Ten bob she charges, bedroom, breakfast, and supper. We'll pay you fifty shillings a week. You'll be all right.'

And she was. The landlady was glad to have a quiet girl who paid on time, ate very little, and didn't bring men into her room. Some of the theatricals were too fond of a drink and little parties upstairs — parties for two, more often than not.

No one at the theatre asked any questions. The theatre's population was a transient one. The Lancaster Footlights Club put on their plays at The Grand, but there were visiting companies, too, with their directors, their lighting and props men, their musicians, singers, actors, and dressers. There were pantomimes, musical comedies, variety, serious plays — the repertoire and the people changed nearly every week.

No one was the slightest bit interested in Esther Vernon. She was there and no one stayed long enough to ask questions. Everyone called everyone 'Darling' or 'Sweetie'. It didn't mean anything. The actors and actresses were generally charming, good-humoured, gay as butterflies, and just as fleeting. They thanked you, tossed their costume at you for repair, begged you to get cigarettes or chocolates or gin for them, sometimes tipped you, gave you their dying flowers, and didn't know one seamstress from another.

The seamstresses didn't stay. The pay wasn't enough, though Jessie was satisfied — it was a thousand times better than sewing Post Office bags in a cell and even though the sewing room was draughty, the smiles were warm, and no one watched your every move, unless you were on stage, of course, an idea which filled the former prisoner with horror. The seamstresses found better opportunities in the shops or in the linoleum factory. Some went to more glamorous places like Blackpool or to Morecambe, where there were piers, fairgrounds and cafes, and the beach. Others transferred their loyalty to the picture houses, where they could earn more as chocolate girls selling sweets and cigarettes, or ice cream from a tray.

And no one treated Jessie as if she were something the cat had brought in. It was true that some of the actors thought they were royalty and were quite ready for a fling with a pretty girl — just to while away the time before they moved on to bigger things in Manchester or London. Bill could always put them right about their ambitions on the stage or in bed with a curl of her carmined lips and a narrowing of those cool blue eyes. But then Bill was royalty — or practically. Lady Wilhelmina Carew, daughter of a lord.

Even Lady Wilhelmina left eventually, though she had sworn undying loyalty to the Lancaster Footlights Club. London called and she went.

Jessie didn't mind, though she'd liked Bill, who treated everyone with the same kind of sharp good humour, mocked the actors for their vanity, laughed at most of the actresses, but never forgot her lines and received the most applause. Jessie saw her first as Kate in *The Taming of the Shrew*. She didn't understand much of the language, but she recognised that Bill was head and shoulders above the others. She was too shy to say so. In any case, Bill didn't have time for compliments, nor for relationships. She didn't care what anyone thought of her, or her overalls and trousers and her peaked cap. She was Bill and proud of it. She didn't care tuppence about his lordship, her father, though she took her allowance. Bill went away with a cheery, 'Good luck, old girl, you've been a brick. Look me up in London if you ever come my way. You'll see my name in lights.' Jessie didn't doubt the name in the lights, but she would never see it.

She was content to be Esther Vernon. Bill called her 'Pins' and Jessie didn't mind at all. She didn't mind being wheedled for a favour as "Darling," or thanked for being "such a sweetie." She could be called anything, as long as it wasn't Jessie Sedgwick. No one could know about her crime or the prison. Even her dreams faded, and she taught herself not to think about Moonlyght, or Caroline, or Charles Bennett's death. There was nothing she could do about the past. It was enough to deal with the present.

Jessie stayed at the theatre for five years. She was just reliable Pins, who would listen to your complaints or your lines, mend your torn dress and not tell the director, find your gloves or shoes, dry your tears, make you a cup of tea and a sandwich, fetch your ciggies or sweets, or run out for a bottle of gin or a new pair of stockings. All right, she never said much, but then everyone else had plenty to say. Everyone gossiped and quarrelled, swore to kill their rivals who corpsed them or stole the limelight, shrieked that they'd seen the theatre's resident ghost, or screamed blue murder at the sight of a rat or a lost button. Jessie Sedgwick was the still point in this turning carousel, and she found a measure of peace for the first time in years. She liked being needed and busy; she enjoyed the work, the bustle, the constant change, the crises, the laughter, even the tears. She liked being a spectator at the backstage show.

Until Ted Gorman cornered her in the costume store and whispered foul things to her. Of course, it wasn't Ted Gorman from Swarthgill Farm, it was a carpenter, a vile-smelling, dirty-mouthed man at whom the actresses laughed and called a creep, but he was more than that. She had noticed him watching her. He'd pause at the sewing room door and give her a long look and lick his lips. She'd be left trembling. He looked at her as if he knew something about her. But he couldn't, surely. He couldn't know about the prison. Once, hearing footsteps behind her on her way home, she had turned, and under the streetlamp, she saw him standing still, watching, his face like a goblin mask in the sickly light. She felt the peace she had gained draining slowly, very carefully, and piece by piece, she felt the new life she had constructed crumbling about her.

In the costume store, he grabbed at her, and she felt his mouth on hers, the foul breath of Ted Gorman, and his hand between her legs. She was saved by someone coming in. He had time to whisper that he'd get her one day before leaving her heaving behind a curtain rail. Nobody knew and she couldn't tell. And what if the carpenter had found out that she was Jessie Sedgwick, ex-convict? He'd tell. They'd know she was a liar — and worse.

She left a note for the theatre manager. They wouldn't miss her. The carousel would spin on.

PART SIX: 1936

38

She had thought, she had hoped that the past had been locked behind a dark door and the key thrown away. And then it leapt out in the dark in the form of a goblin-like creature, for that was how she had seen the carpenter under that lamp.

So she had fled, and that was why she was here in Preston, sitting on a threadbare sofa in a dingy room full of someone else's furniture, though Peggy Greenhalgh, her landlady was, like the one in Lancaster, glad to get her money punctually, glad that her tenant, Miss Vernon, saw to her own food, and glad that she was quiet and polite and had regular work.

Jessie had chosen Preston because that was the nearest big town. She remembered the train stopping there on the way to Lancaster. There had been plenty of people coming and going from the train. She had seen the factory chimneys and the smoke, and the little streets of red-brick houses. She could lose herself there.

Nobody looked at her in those streets; she was just one of hundreds of working women in their shawls and shabby coats and darned stockings, their ashen faces hollow against the biting wind as they came out of the shops and factories. There was even a biscuit factory, Thomas Powell and Son, not that she sought work there. Her method was to take casual work anywhere. There were always notices of vacancies at the cotton mill, the dye works, Horrocks's textile factory. They wanted packers or cleaners or canteen staff. Jessie didn't mind what she did. And there were lots of laundries who took on women for ironing, or sponging and pressing, sorting and packing.

Laundry work was hard and hot, but Jessie could cope with that, and she never stayed long enough to get to know anyone. She took her money in its brown envelope and when the temporary job finished, she moved on, hardly making a ripple in the even days of the laundry or factory.

This evening, she had come home from Mr Sing Lee's Chinese Laundry. Chinese laundries had a bad reputation. Some were rumoured to be opium dens or involved in trafficking young women, but Jessie needed a job. Mrs Greenhalgh, pleasant as she was, wouldn't brook any rent arrears. She had made that quite clear, since Jessie couldn't produce a reference from her previous landlady.

Mr Sing Lee took her on. It was hard work in the laundry at the back of the respectable-looking shop in a side street, its window notices welcoming customers, old and new, hand washing and starching to the highest standard, specialising in suits, collars, and household linen. Quick service guaranteed. She and two other young women, and sometimes Mrs Lee, plunged sheets into the big boiling coppers, navigated the huge mangles, and strung out the linen, the shirts, the nightgowns on the lines across the rooms; she ironed and starched, used the polishing machine on the collars, and sponged the suits, and Mr Lee tied the laundry up in brown paper parcels fastened with twine and labelled and shelved in the shop.

Genial, smiling Mr Lee. Fortunately, his English wasn't good enough to ask probing questions. She told him she had no family — they had all died. He looked distressed — he had his wife, and three little girls upstairs, all as pretty as dolls. Thereafter he treated her with a kind of delicate consideration, though the money wasn't very good, and the hours were long. Thirty shillings a week, but there was an endless supply of green tea, and Mrs Lee taught her to like Chinese food. There was plenty of rice at dinnertime and Mrs Lee often gave her a little, lidded bamboo box to take home.

Sometimes Jessie gave the food to an ex-soldier with one leg who used a bus shelter as a refuge from the rain or the cold, and in the hope of begging a copper or two from a boarding or alighting passenger. Jessie's heart tuned over when she saw him for the first time, wearing an old army coat with a medal pinned to it and with his crutch resting on the bench. She offered him Mrs Lee's box of rice and vegetables, which he wolfed down. He had a room, he told her, but he wasn't supposed to be in it during the day. He'd had a job in a factory, but he'd been laid off for poor timekeeping. 'Can't move so fast,' he told her bitterly, 'but them managers don't care.' He'd served in France. 'Bloody slaughter, butcher's shop out there,' he said, and she felt her nails digging into her hands, which were thrust into her pockets. She couldn't answer, but she let him go on. He had no one else to tell. He'd been engaged before the war, but his girl had let him down. 'Didn't want a crock like me,' he said. He looked out for Jessie in the shelter and even if she had no food, she'd give him a shilling. It was the least she could do. Unwashed and unwanted, after all he had endured. He might have been Josh, or Archie Handley. No, not Archie. She remembered Mrs Handley, who had not let down her wounded son.

Then one day, the soldier wasn't there. It was a bitter November. She'd heard him coughing as if his lungs would collapse. 'Gas,' he'd spluttered at her, and she'd bought some cough medicine for the next time, but he was gone, and she never knew his name.

Another ghost, she thought, crowding about her to bring back the past, which had crept up on her this night. She glanced down at the newspaper. Not a goblin thing with foul breath, but words on a page which she might never have seen, but that a stranger sat next to her on the bus. Words that brought it all back:

The death has been announced of Captain Sir Arthur Mountjoy of Moonlyght Tower near Kirkby Lonsdale. Captain Mountjoy, who was awarded the Military Cross in the last war, died from natural causes. He had been an invalid for much of the time, having suffered greatly from the effects of gas poisoning. He leaves a wife, Lady Caroline Mountjoy. There are no children. Captain Mountjoy was the second son of Sir Henry Mountjoy. His elder brother who served in the War Office was killed in a Zeppelin raid on London in 1917.

Our readers may remember that Moonlyght Tower was the scene of a tragedy in 1918. Captain Charles Bennett, M.C., who had recently inherited the house from Lady Emmeline de Moine, was killed by a servant, Jessie Sedgwick, who was imprisoned at Walton Gaol, Liverpool for seven years, the charge being manslaughter. The servant girl had believed, quite erroneously, according to witnesses, that Captain Bennett had promised marriage. She had alleged that he was the father of her miscarried child…

She closed her eyes. She was bone-weary. She slept for an hour, perhaps, and when she woke up, she thought of Bill's straight blue stare, Bill, who stood up to anyone and went her own way, and Elvina Smythe who worked for others because she said she must do her duty to the dead.

She went to the green-spotted mirror and thought about three moons and a strange green light in the hall at Moonlyght, and letters carved into a stone mantel: *The light that shines in darkness.*

She tied on a headscarf and put on her dark grey raincoat, leaving her overall on the peg. She checked that she had money in her purse, opened the door, looked back at the shabby room, at the newspaper on the worn sofa, closed the door quietly, and went downstairs and out into the cold grey morning. She made one purchase at a shop on the way to the railway station.

39

Jessie stood on the platform at Lowgill Station, looking across at the opposite platform. Doors clunked shut and the guard blew his whistle. The engine emitted a cloud of steam and smoke and heaved itself forward, and the train from Preston set off for Carlisle where young Jessie Sedgwick should have gone all those years ago. Her platform was empty, but there would be a southbound train soon which would take her to Crossgill Head, or she could go on to the terminus at Ingleton, take the Lancaster train and then go on back to Preston, or she could take the next train to Carlisle from this platform. She could go to Scotland. She could go anywhere.

She heard the sound of the whistle and the engine slowing. She took the southbound train. She didn't get off at Gressthwaite, though she saw the high moors, the bronze heather, the drystone walls, and the dots of sheep, and thought of Swarthgill Farm, of that first journey in 1916. She remembered turning round on the milk cart and seeing the empty space in the yard where Ma had been. She would never go back.

She alighted at Crossgill and went across the road into the little lane by the woods where she had stood with Charles Bennett, and he had persuaded her to go back with him to Moonlyght. If only ... on how slender a thread their fate had hung. Just a matter of timing. Suppose Mr Charles had missed his train from London... Suppose she had chosen to go the day before. How different...

No use supposing. She went down to the river and saw that the ferryman was there, waiting for any passengers from the train. It wasn't the young man who had taken her the last time. On the other side, she looked at Cowpot Cottage and thought of Joe Widdop. He had been a kind man. Where had he gone? Another casualty of Moonlyght, and Ethel, so full of hope and life. She took the path that skirted Blades Wood, where she stopped to look up into the sky where she had counted the crows all those years ago. A murder of crows, that's what they said. She hadn't thought of that then.

Murder. She knew she hadn't killed Charles Bennett. Caroline Mason had picked up the knife and flown at him, and Jessie Sedgwick wanted her to know that she knew, and she wanted Caroline Mason to feel afraid. It didn't matter what happened afterwards.

She walked on through Mossgarth where the children still shouted to each other, and the dog still barked, and then she was walking up the hill where the high hedges gave way to dry stone walls broken by five-barred gates through which she could see tracks going up to farms. She stood at the gate of Fiddler's Hill Farm — the house looked deserted. Perhaps Mr Turner had died. She heard a dog bark. Someone must be there.

Taciturn Mr Turner had been kind to her. She remembered his face on the day the policemen had taken her away from Moonlyght. At her trial Mr Turner had told the court he thought he had heard laughter before he heard the screaming, but he had not seen the actual stabbing. He had heard the screams and run to the kitchen window. He could not say if the accused had killed Captain Bennett. The kitchen window had been open while he was shovelling coal in the yard. He had heard voices and thought he had heard laughter. Yes, he supposed it might have been shouting, he answered the prosecution counsel's sharp question. Yes, it was true he was a bit deaf. No, he couldn't swear that it was laughter. But he had not imagined that the young woman would be violent. Yes, he admitted miserably, he hardly knew her.

Caroline and Mrs Cobb had sworn to tell the whole truth and nothing but the truth, but they had not. They had lied. Jessie Sedgwick meant nothing to them. Caroline Mason wanted to save herself. She had always wanted to be mistress of Moonlyght. And Mrs Cobb had betrayed her cousin's daughter to save her job. She had said that that side of the family — well, they were not respectable. The accused's mother had been pregnant when she served at Moonlyght. Jessie Sedgwick had gone the same way. She had hidden her pregnancy. Mrs Cobb had guessed who the father might be — a young soldier who had visited. She didn't know his name, nor had the accused told her. She had no idea that Jessie had harboured ridiculous ideas about Captain Bennett, who had become engaged to Miss Mason in November 1917.

The jury had looked at the grieving fiancée who had pulled down her veil to hide her tears, though a choking sob could be heard. They had seen the lace edged handkerchief in the delicate hand on which a diamond ring glittered in the dim light of the court room. They had looked at the girl in the dock, too. The girl who wouldn't speak. The girl who didn't weep. The farmers, the grocers, the ironmonger, the little men of little property, who knew about insolent servant girls grown uppity in the war, thought of their sons away at the Front, and a gallant officer done to death.

The judge had directed the jury to a verdict of manslaughter on the grounds that the accused had not actually wanted to kill the victim but had yielded to the passion of the moment. However, it was clear that the prisoner was a young woman who had conducted an illicit relationship, taking advantage of her employer's trust in her, and she had lied. What was most distressing, of course, was the death of Captain Bennett, a soldier decorated for gallantry who had served so courageously throughout the war.

Jessie opened the gate and walked towards the dilapidated farmhouse. The dog still barked, then it came hurtling towards her, its eyes wild and white, its jaws wide, and then she heard a shout. A man's voice telling the dog to shut up. It did, but it stood still and growled at her, and then a man came round the side of the house, and he too stood still and stared at her. It was Mr Turner.

'Oh, Missus, sorry about the dog. Here, Bess, heel.'

The dog trotted away and Mr Turner came nearer. 'Dost tha want someone?' he asked.

He didn't know her. She thought of going away, but she said, 'It's about the house with the tower, Moonlyght.'

He came closer, the dog at his heel. 'Just up the road, on the right — tha'll see the — do I know thee?'

'It's Jessie Sedgwick, Mr Turner.'

'Well, I'm blowed! I never expected — tha'll be wanting to see them — Miss Caroline — Lady Mountjoy, I should say, and Mrs Cobb?'

'I didn't kill Mr Charles. I want her to tell me the truth.'

He looked at her and she saw the sorrow in his eyes. 'Tha's had a hard time. Tha'd best come in, lass, before tha goes rushin' up there. I'll make us a cup of tea.'

She followed him round to the back of the house and into the kitchen, which was full of packing cases, though the kettle was on the range, and there were still a table and chairs, and some cups and plates on the table.

'You're leaving?' she asked.

'Been given notice. Lady Mountjoy doesn't want the farm no more — now that Captain Mountjoy's gone. It doesn't pay, so she says. Well, I reckon she's probably right about that. They've no money up there. The place is fallin' down. The captain wasn't as rich as Miss Caroline thought, I reckon. Anyways, I've had enough.' His eyes clouded. 'Nigh on twenty years since my lad … well, nay point in it now. Let the place rot.'

'I remember, Mr Turner, when Mrs Cobb said your boy had been killed. I am sorry. My brother, too.'

'I'm sorry for that, lass. I'm away to live with my sister. She has a greengrocer's shop in Gressthwaite — her husband died of Spanish flu in 1918. Terrible thing, that was, after all we'd been through. Lot o' them as came back died, too, and that old Nurse up at Moonlyght. Mind she was an old 'un.'

'So, there's just Miss Caroline and Mrs Cobb?'

Mr Turner brought the teapot to the table, an old brown one like the one Charles had left his notes in. She wondered if it was still there. Mr Turner sat down and poured the tea. 'That's right. Just them two.'

'Does she not have a personal maid?'

'Nay, lass. They had more staff when they first married, but folk don't want to be servants nowadays, and they don't pay like the shops or the factories. The captain was a decent enough fellow, but not up to runnin' the place. Invalid, really. Gas, see. I don't think they was a happy couple.'

'When did they marry?'

'In 1920, I think. She went away after — sorry, lass, I didn't mean to — what dost tha want with them two?'

'It's time for a reckoning. I didn't kill Mr Charles. It took me a long time to remember — anything — but I have remembered, and they lied in court. Mr Charles was laughing in the kitchen. He was joking because he was happy that he had found me a job which would take me away from Moonlyght.'

'I thought I heard laughter, but that barrister — too clever for me — caught me out, askin' me to swear on the Bible. All that stuff about me bein' a bit deaf an' not knowin' whether it were laughin' or screamin' or rowin'. It were my fault, I shouldn't have said I heard… Never felt right about it, lass, but what can tha do? I mean, they won't admit it.'

'I know, but there are other things. At the trial, Mrs Cobb lied about my ma — said she was forward and that she was expecting before she married. I want her to say she lied about that.'

Mr Turner looked uncomfortable. 'Eh, lass, let it go — water under the bridge, that tale.'

'What tale? Tell me, please.'

'I don't know what good it'll —' He saw her desperate face. 'My wife served up at the house afore we was wed an' she told me about Bert Sedgwick. He were a gardener there. Had an eye for the girls, but they was too canny to fall for him.'

'And my ma did?'

'Not exactly, lass. She married him, yes, but she hadn't much choice, see, as she were — well, expectin'. Not Sedgwick's bairn, but there were money in it. The other servants knew — my wife were that sorry for her. Sedgwick were a brute.'

'He was paid to marry her?' So much became clear suddenly. 'Oh, God, I remember — Mrs Cobb met my brother and she was about to say that he looked like someone and then she changed her mind and said he looked like Ma. But he didn't look like Ma or Pa. He wasn't Pa's son. Pa hated him and that's why, but whose —'

Jessie remembered then. Charles Bennett saying that Josh and Alexander were friends. Josh said they talked together about nature and the countryside. They thought the same things. Josh had seen him die and had kept his secret. Sometimes she had thought they were alike — the eyes — she saw one face in the other, but that had been the war, surely. It couldn't be. She looked at Mr Turner. 'Who? Please, tell me.'

'They said — the servants — that it was the General. He'd done that sort of thing before, and poor Lady Emmeline knew. He was a brute to her and his sons — damned hypocrite. Church on Sunday and seducing servant girls…'

'Josh, a de Moine? And Mrs Cobb knew?'

'Must 'ave done.'

'Poor Ma — Pa was hateful to her, to all of us. I was frightened of him. It was partly because of him that Josh went to fight. He had to get away. And he was killed.'

'The General did a lot of damage, one way and another. That lad, Jonathan — supposed to have fallen, but it were whispered he'd jumped. Felt a failure, I should think. The General were all for them boys carryin' on tradition, but out there, it were terrifyin'. Hell on earth. We know all about that now, an' who could blame a lad, any lad who couldn't take it?'

'And Ethel Widdop?' Jessie asked.

'Joe Widdop knew his daughter 'adn't been about with a railwayman. He'd 'ave known. She mighta been a bit cheeky, but she weren't a fast girl an' Joe were a clean-livin' man. But what could he do? They paid him, o' course, an' he 'ad to take it. Don't blame him. A broken man, were Joe Widdop. He couldn't stay in that cottage after what happened.'

Another memory came. Charles had said that Caroline Mason was illegitimate. 'What about Miss Caroline? Was her mother a servant?'

'So they said, but a lot o' girls came an' went. But it's all passed, lass. Nowt to be done; tha's still young, and tha can find…' His words faltered. 'Mebbe I should come with you.'

'It is kind of you, Mr Turner, but I have to see them on my own. I want them to see what they have done. I'll do it for Ma and Josh, and Ethel. And they kept everything I had — my bag that Ma gave me, Josh's things, and his letters and his photograph. I want to see him again.'

'And afterwards?'

'I don't know. I can't see beyond that.'

40

The road ahead was empty and on the next rise she saw it going straight on into the unknown distance, as it had done the first time. She thought of Ma — poor Ma who had suffered too because of the de Moines. The General might have had a title, but he was just as much a brute as Pa. Poor Josh, too, born in the wrong place. He had deserved better than Swarthgill Farm and Pa. He was clever and sensitive, and he was lost because of Moonlyght.

On the right she saw the trees which concealed Moonlyght, and there were the stone pillars wound about with ivy and topped by the familiar verdigris moons. The same rough drive to the house, all rutted and stony. The dark woods on either side. Hag Wood where Ethel had been murdered. Then the house and its ruined tower, the defender of the de Moine family against invaders. But it was they who had destroyed themselves from within that grey house with its forbidding battlements, its stone-framed windows and the huge oak door in its battlemented porch, still firmly closed. The place was silent. In the autumn twilight no birds sang.

Jessie went round the back to the kitchen door. She looked through the window as Mr Turner had on that terrible day. She saw it all now with absolute clarity. Caroline Mason had picked up that knife and she had attacked Charles Bennett. She probably hadn't meant to kill him, but that didn't matter. She had revenged herself on Jessie Sedgwick, and Mrs Cobb had known. She had known about Ma and the General — and Josh, and she had nearly given the secret away. She had known that Ma was a victim of the de Moines, but she had let Ma's daughter be destroyed, too.

She turned the door handle and went in. Everything was just the same, even the old brown teapot on the shelf. Not quite the same. It was shabbier and dirtier. Unwashed pots on the draining board, the tea towel grubby, the floor muddy, though there was a tray on the table with a tarnished silver teapot and cream jug. The silver had been polished when she had taken that tray up to Lady Emmeline with the lavender wrapped in a napkin in its silver ring. Caroline Mason had caused her death.

She went into the screens passage from where she had heard Charles Bennett leave in the early morning after that night. Then she heard voices and went into the hall, where the light still fell greenly and the knights still watched from the windows and the stone mantel, and the silent knight in armour kept vigil by the stairs.

The voices came from the drawing room, one high and querulous, the other low but sharp. Caroline Mason and Mrs Cobb quarrelling. Mrs Cobb knew too much.

She stood outside the door. A whiff of scent came to her. That sweet and musky scent. Caroline Mason's scent of deceit. She felt in her pocket for the knife which she had bought in Lancaster. She would have the truth, and she would have Josh's letters and his photograph.

She pushed open the door. It creaked and Caroline Mason turned round on the sofa. 'Who the devil are you?'

Mrs Cobb knew. 'Jessie Sedgwick.'

'How dare you come here? You — a convict…'

'Oh, I dare.' Jessie felt an exhilarating surge of power, as if all the wasted years gathered as a force in her blood. She dared say anything. She had nothing to lose.

'There's nowt for you here.'

Jessie heard Mrs Cobb's laboured breathing and saw the sweat on her brow. She was a sick woman. 'My bag, my things, my letters and the photograph of my brother, Josh, the General's son. My mother was made to marry Bert Sedgwick. You knew all about that, didn't you, Mrs Cobb? And you slandered my mother in that court.'

'What nonsense is this?' Caroline asked.

'No more nonsense than you being the General's bastard, too. Mrs Cobb knows all about it. Your mother was a servant, just like mine.'

'That's a lie. Cobb, tell her —'

Mrs Cobb didn't speak.

'My mother was a lady. The General said so. I'm a de Moine and I'm mistress here, so you can get out.'

'Not until I've finished with the pair of you. I want my things —'

'You think we kept them? A murderer's cheap things and a few trumpery letters from a farm hand —'

In a second, Jessie was behind her on the sofa, gripping her shoulder, the knife held to her neck. 'You want to know what prison does to people, how it makes them hard and fearless, and how they couldn't care less about themselves or anyone else. You said I killed Charles Bennett with a knife. How does the knife feel now? I paid the price for your lies. I want my things and I want you two to tell the truth.'

'And what will you do with the truth? Who will you tell, and who will believe you?'

'It doesn't matter. For the first time in your life, you will tell the truth. You will face what you have done.'

'Do something, Cobb.' Caroline tried to twist away, but Jessie was too strong for her and dug her fingers into the thin shoulder.

'This knife will be in your neck before she has time to move. Get my things, Mrs Cobb. I know you've got them, because they didn't matter to you. They'll be in my old room, I'll bet.'

'What are you going to do to her while I'm gone?'

'Nothing. I'm going to listen, and then I'll decide.'

'You wouldn't dare —' Caroline's protest was cut off by the sudden sharp prick of the blade at her neck. 'Get her things, Cobb.'

Mrs Cobb went. Jessie noticed how slowly she moved. She was stouter, red-faced, and wheezing. *Heart*, Jessie thought, *if she has one*. Well, it served her right. She sat down opposite Caroline, who she noticed had aged, her mouth a slash of red, her skin coarse under the coating of powder and rouge, and that lovely soft hair, short now and crimped into stiff-looking waves. She looked as brittle as some of the actresses at the theatre. Not Bill. Bill was worth ten of Caroline, but she was smiling — her teeth were still perfect. Jessie had to give her credit for her attempt at bravado.

'So, you want to know the truth. And if I won't tell you, you'll kill me. I don't think so. You'll have to kill Cobb, too, and then what, prison again?'

'No one knows I'm here. No one knows where I am. Jessie Sedgwick disappeared after she came out of prison, and she'll disappear again. It's easy.'

'I don't understand you — what does the truth matter now?'

'It matters to me. It matters for my brother, for my mother, and for Ethel Widdop.'

'What's she got to do with it?'

'Alexander de Moine killed her. Charles knew.'

'Alexander was mad. Anyone could see that. It was her own fault.'

'Because she threw herself at him, or was it Charles? Just like my mother threw herself at the General, no doubt.'

'I didn't say that, but it's what servants do — Widdop was a slut.'

'You asked me once if I had ever done something dreadful. You said that you had made a mistake. We were in the tower, and you were looking up at the ledge from where Mr Jonathan fell.'

'And I told you that the past can't be changed. Why are you going over all this?'

Jessie was implacable. 'Did you have something to do with Jonathan's death? You killed Lady Emmeline. You spoke to her about the tower. Did you kill them both?'

'I didn't — I didn't know she was going to throw herself off the tower. She could hardly walk. I only wanted —'

'You said you wanted to shock her — and you did. What about Jonathan?'

'I was a child, for God's sake. I was at school when he died. It was the General's fault. He made Jonathan join the army. He had to go to the Front even though the General was dead by then, but he couldn't stand it. He jumped because he couldn't face going back.'

'So, what did you mean?'

'I need a cigarette…'

Jessie tossed her the packet and a box of matches which were on the table beside her chair. She noted that Caroline's hand trembled as she tried to strike the match. She heard the deep intake of breath, and the smoke came out of Caroline's mouth in a perfect ring. Caroline was wearing the diamond ring. The ring she pretended that Charles had given her.

Jessie held up the knife. 'I'm waiting.' She saw Caroline glance at the door. 'Mrs Cobb will leave you to it. We won't see her again until she's sure I'm going. She doesn't care about you. She never did. You're just a servant's daughter —'

Caroline put her hands over her ears. 'Shut up! Shut up! It's not true. You know nothing about my mother.'

Jessie held up the knife. 'Now, tell me what you meant in that tower. Remember, I don't care either.'

Caroline looked at the knife. 'It was to do with Alexander.'

'I've said I know what he did, and so did Charles —'

Caroline flushed under her powder and rouge. 'Oh, Charles, is it now? It's all your fault. If you —'

'We'll come to that. You knew about Mr Alexander and Ethel Widdop. You said nobody ever found out. What was your part in it?'

'She — she was pregnant. She wrote to me asking for money. She told me it was Alexander's baby. I didn't believe her — he wouldn't — I told him about her — that she'd —'

'Been with someone else. You thought that might have been Charles, so Ethel Widdop had to pay.'

'I didn't know Alexander would kill her.'

'He loved her.'

'Love! For God's sake. She was a servant —'

'Like your mother. A kitchen maid, just like me.'

'You're a liar. You lied about everything. You thought Charles had a thing about you. He didn't. It was me he wanted. He would have — but you betrayed me.'

Jessie laughed. 'And you betrayed everyone. You'd have married Alexander if he'd wanted you. You didn't love him. Anything to be mistress of Moonlyght. And look at it. It's a wreck. The title not enough? Captain Sir Arthur Mountjoy not as rich as you thought?'

'No, he wasn't. I loathed him. He was a spineless ninny, and his brother was a gold-digger. That's why he wanted to marry

Alice. Served them right, that Zeppelin. And prison served you right. You brought it on yourself, mooning after Charles. He'd never —'

'You're right, he'd never have married me, but we were friends. He came to the kitchen to tell me that he had found me a job and I could leave Moonlyght. I was going, and you destroyed your own future as well as mine. You were here and I was in prison, but what's the difference? You made a prison for yourself.'

Caroline seemed to shrink into her chair, her eyes darting round, her face white now, the rouge standing out clown-like against the pallor. 'I saw you with him. He was laughing. He had your hands in his. I knew you and he — it wasn't fair — I was the lady. You — a kitchen maid. It was your fault, but I didn't mean —'

'But you did. Say it.'

'I killed him.' Caroline lay back, her eyes closed, and Jessie saw the tears running down her cheeks, making ugly rivulets in the thick powder.

Jessie went to the door and called out. 'You can come in now, Mrs Cobb. Your mistress needs you. Leave my bag by the front door.' She turned back to the weeping woman. 'Ask Mrs Cobb about my baby. Ask about the soldier father. Who he really was.'

She held the door open for Mrs Cobb. She handed her the knife. Mrs Cobb took it and passed her without a word, and Jessie went through the hall and out the front door. She was free.

41

The smell was the same; the damp still wound itself round her; the wind still whispered through the window slits and breathed at her neck and the moon still shone through the open roof. Grit and stones still rattled on the stairs and when Jessie looked up, she could see the shadows there waiting. Ghosts.

Ghosts in the moonlight and in the shadows. Memories of things ill-done. That man on the bus who had left his newspaper. How his smell had lingered, as if he had left the ghostly presence of his poverty and hopelessness. Her cell in the prison. They were there, the women who had been and gone, their suffering as tangible as the damp, soaked into the very walls, into the corridors, into the clothes she had worn, the towels, the sheets, the mattress. You could boil and scrub, but the smell would never come out. Like bloodstains after a murder. Ethel's blood was there in Hag Wood, its iron smell deep down in the soil.

The dead of Flanders. They said that poppies grew there now. The grass had grown and the trees had flourished again, but the blood of the fallen was a stain deep down where their bones had turned to dust and ashes.

The dead of Moonlyght, that house which had laid its icy hand on her as well as everyone else. Their suffering and sins sunk deep into the walls. Ma, Josh, Lady Emmeline, Jonathan, Alexander, Charles. The scent of lemon cologne and tobacco. The ghost of Charles Bennett. Lavender and ashes for Lady Emmeline. Violets and gas for Alexander, and for Arthur Mountjoy, too, whose wife had despised him.

Mrs Cobb would tell Caroline about the father of Jessie's lost baby, and Caroline would know that Charles Bennett had not loved her. She would remember her own child, perhaps, and the memory would be searing. Caroline Mason had thrown everything away; she had to live on and bear that knowledge. Mrs Cobb had nowhere else to go. Two prisoners here, sentenced for life, and beyond death, too, even Caroline. Her deceitful scent would linger, the ghost of what she had been in life.

Jessie took her Bible from her old carpet bag and there were Josh's letters. She put them in the inside pocket of her coat, next to her heart. She looked at the photograph and there he was on the high moor, his dark hair copper in the sunlight, his laughter coming back to her as he turned, his smile so open and loving. They were going to the crystal cave. And there was the scent of sweet wild honeysuckle.

'Josh,' she whispered.

'Jess.' He was waiting and she went up the stairs to meet him.

Mr Turner found her lying just as Jonathan de Moine had lain there, and Lady Emmeline. He turned her over carefully, and gently closed her eyes. He sat with her for a while and held her hand. She looked peaceful somehow, and so young and pretty, as she had looked when he had cleared the snow for her and fetched the coal. He remembered her lovely, deep blue eyes. Just a lass. He picked up the photograph and looked at the boy and thought of his own lost lad. He saw the book that had dropped from her bag. It had fallen open. The words there struck him to the heart:

Long for me the rick will wait,
And long will wait the fold,

And long will stand the empty plate,
And dinner will be cold.

He wept for his lost wife, his boy, and for the innocent lass. A terrible wrong had been done, on top of many, many dreadful wrongs, but there was naught he could do about it. He was too old and too weary. It was over. Let her rest. Let them all rest.

After a while, he got up and went to his cart. Time to fetch Doctor Kennedy. He'd know what to do. How to hush it up.

HISTORICAL NOTES

My interest in the Lonsdale Battalion began when I was researching the First World War for *The Legacy of Foulstone Manor*, and I came across a reference to the death of a Sedbergh soldier who was killed on 1st July 1916. This was the first day of the Battle of the Somme. On that day, 800 men and 28 officers of the Lonsdale Battalion had advanced and 100 were killed, 19 were missing, and 371 were wounded. The final notes from the commanding officer issued the night before to the battalion instructed that 'All not hit MUST push on. Must do our job.' The commanding officer, Lieutenant-Colonel P. W. Machell, was shot and killed on that first day as he climbed from the trench, preparing to lead his men.

The Lonsdale Battalion was a 'pals' battalion, meaning that local men joined together. Men who were farm servants and general labourers, shopkeepers, miners, clerks, industrial workers and shepherds all wanted to do their bit. Lord Lonsdale recruited this volunteer battalion in September 1914. His poster, asking "Are you a man or a mouse?" was displayed all over the two counties. The first recruits were based in Carlisle, where Cumbria's Museum of Military Life has exhibitions about the Lonsdale Battalion. A wonderful website, www.thelonsdalebattalion.co.uk, gave me the war diary of the battalion. British Army war diaries between 1914 and 1922 are unit-specific accounts recording a variety of daily activities. They covered the unit's entire involvement in the war, from their initial landing on foreign soil through to their departure at the end or their disbandment, whichever came sooner. The war diary allowed me to find out exactly where the characters

Alexander de Moine and Josh Sedgwick were on the dates I needed, which actions they were involved in, and when and where they might have lost their lives.

A book by Colin Bardgett, *The Lonsdale Battalion* (1993), tells the story of the battalion and is a poignant reminder that the 'pals' battalions lost many men who were brothers, neighbours, and friends. Some 490 names on the Roll of Honour belong to men who were born in Cumberland or Westmorland; there are more, born elsewhere, but who enlisted in either of the two counties. Later in the war, after the casualties had reduced the battalion, men were transferred from other battalions and regiments. On 31st July 1918 the Lonsdale Battalion was disbanded, the survivors joining the 5th Battalion Border Regiment. The Roll of Honour for the Lonsdale Battalion lists 792 names. The Border Regiments lost over thirteen thousand men.

All my research into the history of the Lonsdale Battalion informs the story of Jessie Sedgwick's time at Moonlyght, the home of the de Moine family, which at the beginning of the novel has lost one son already. Jessie suffers, too, from the absence of her only brother on the front line. The idea of the 'pals' battalion is reiterated in the story of Josh and his friends, who join up after attending a recruitment meeting in Kendal.

My research took me to Lancaster Prison, a rather forbidding place in Lancaster Castle. A somewhat gruesome description of a hanging there is to be found in Dickens's short story, *The Bride Cake*. I went there a while ago in search of Dickens and the setting of the story, but this time I went on the tour of the prison which held women only from 1877–1915. The historic part of the prison shows exactly what it was like in the nineteenth century with the narrow cells, heavy iron doors and metal stairways. The experience of being in a cell with the door closed gave me a glimpse of what Jessie's life might have been like in prison. It might have been only a few minutes, but I felt the chill, the damp, and something horribly suffocating. I can't say exactly what. My sister went in and came out looking rather pale. She felt the same. In 1915, the prisoners were transferred to Walton Gaol in Liverpool, so I placed Jessie there and based her experiences on my reading about Walton in a book from 1922, *English Prisons Today*. That made grim reading, too.

Unsurprisingly, I came across Dickens again in my research. He is quoted in a scholarly article about Susan Willis Fletcher, who was imprisoned in 1884 and experienced solitary confinement which Dickens asserted 'tampered with the brain'. In her memoir, *Twelve Months in an English Prison*, Fletcher described her experiences of being in solitary confinement: 'Each prisoner is locked in her solitary cell for twenty-three hours out of every twenty-four which is in itself a very dreadful punishment bad for the health of the body, worse for the health of the mind.' That was in 1884, but in the 1920s women were still being kept in solitary as a punishment, and even as part of the ordinary routine, they spent as many as sixteen hours alone in their cells as Jessie does, sewing mailbags. The effect on the prisoners' mental health is well-documented. It's disturbing to think of the number of women who were committed for trivial crimes, and to think of those who, like Jessie, were entirely innocent. And to think it happens today.

There is an enormous amount of material on the internet about women in prison in the early twentieth century, but two other contemporary books from the Internet Archive were invaluable. *Women and Prisons*, written in 1912 by Helen Bragg and *Penal Discipline* (1922) by Mary Gordon, who was appointed as the first female inspector of prisons in 1908. Here I found the details about the prisoners' treatment on entry, the examinations by doctors, the prison clothes and the routine. It made very grim reading, but apart from being a remarkable pioneer in the prison service, Mary Gordon was a humane and compassionate woman who set out to improve the lives of the women in prison.

The research for this book proved fascinating, and I shall not forget those hideous few minutes of confinement in Lancaster Prison. I might write about crime, but I shall make every effort not to commit one.

A NOTE TO THE READER

Dear Reader,

Names are fascinating. Dickens always had to find the names of his characters before he began. I like to trawl through the *Oxford Dictionary of English Surnames* to find my names. It is where I found the surname 'Moonlight', which is also spelt 'Monelyght'. A Robert Monelyght existed in 1442, and the name comes from Old English and possibly means someone given to roaming about at night. I don't know if the fifteenth-century Robert did so, or why if he did. Up to no good, perhaps. I liked the spelling of 'lyght' for its oddly unexpected and mysterious quality. The surname 'de Moine' dates from 1086 and seems to mean an official who had civic control over a castle or monastery. In the dictionary, the name is linked to the name 'Moon' which I linked to 'lyght'.

Naturally, I was looking for a house in some decay with a tower, and a ghost preferably. I found several in my area, plenty with ruined towers. Pele Towers are common in Cumbria. They were built in the fourteenth, fifteenth and sixteenth centuries for the protection of their owners in the times of the Scottish raids. They were strong, rectangular towers with six-foot thick walls. Many have been restored, but there are plenty of ruined ones to inspire the passing author. Kirfitt Hall, which is only just down the road from me, has a very atmospheric tower which was a ruin for most of the twentieth century, as old photographs show. It also has an interesting ghost story. Anne Boleyn, a headless ghost, of course, is supposed to haunt this house where legend has it that Henry VIII stayed when he was wooing Katherine Parr.

The old photographs of Blease Hall near Kendal, now restored, show an almost ruined house with its resident ghost, a maiden who died for love. Her funeral procession is said to be seen by night passing round the house.

My fictional Moonlyght is located at the site of Killington Hall, which is more remote than Kirfitt. In fact, it is very hard to find, as I discovered when driving over a rather deserted stretch of moorland from Kendal and missing my turning several times. However, it has a battlemented Pele Tower, which looked very forbidding in the twilight — just the place for some ghostly goings-on, but the house and tower I invented are a mixture of the old houses I went to see. Too late, I realised that my choice of location meant that Jessie Sedgwick couldn't cross the river from the railway station at what was called Middleton Head. Such are the perils of getting lost on winding country roads. However, luck was on my side because on an old map, I found the word 'ferry' just in the right place, so it was possible for Jessie to get over the river, and I brought in the ferryman, Joe Widdop, and his daughter, Ethel. The railway existed then; it was once known as the Lune Valley Railway, which carried passengers to Lowgill from where they could change for Carlisle. Dr Beeching finished it off in 1964, but it's possible to walk the line in places and to imagine the train taking Jessie Sedgwick to Moonlyght.

Lunefield House, built in 1869 in Kirkby Lonsdale, is no longer there, but it was used as a hospital for officers and staffed by VADs like Mary of whom Caroline Mason is so jealous. The initials VAD stand for Voluntary Aid Detachment; this was mainly composed of young women, very often from upper and middle-class backgrounds, who worked in hospitals, drove ambulances, and worked in canteens and as clerks. Vera Brittain is probably the most famous VAD, describing her harrowing experiences in her book, *Testament of Youth*.

Reviews are very important to writers, so it would be great if you could spare the time to post a review on **Amazon** and **Goodreads**. Readers can connect with me online, on **Facebook (JCBriggsBooks)**, **Twitter (@JeanCBriggs)**, and you can find out more about the books and Charles Dickens via my website, **jcbriggsbooks.com**, where you will find Mr Dickens's A–Z of murder — all cases of murder to which I found a Dickens connection.

Thank you!

Jean Briggs

Sapere Books is an exciting new publisher of brilliant fiction and popular history.

To find out more about our latest releases and our monthly bargain books visit our website:
saperebooks.com

Printed in Great Britain
by Amazon